A TASTE OF PERFECTION

While Thomas dozed, Tabby arose, bathed and sneaked hurriedly down to the kitchen. As she entered, she could scarcely believe the delicious odor that assailed her nostrils. Centered on the table, circled by excited servants, was the cake.

"Come, Miss Tabby, and have a bite," Molly proudly offered.

"I'm almost afraid." Tabby bravely sauntered forth. Plucking a bit of the golden concoction, she placed it in her mouth, rolling it round her tongue like a connoisseur tasting wine. Suddenly, she gripped the table. She ate a bite more, studying.

"That has to be it!" she cried. "This just *has* to be the correct taste! It is very buttery with a marvelous touch of lemon. No wonder Lord Maxfield appreciates it so! I vow it's the best pound cake I've ever eaten!"

Molly and the staff drew a collective breath of relief.

"Bring me a box, someone, and fetch a footman. We'll send a piece straightaway to the duchess, who has the final say. Oh, I do pray she will give her approval. I so want Lord Maxfield's birthday to be perfect."

—from "Lord Maxfield's Birthday Cake" by Cathleen Clare

BOOK YOUR PLACE ON OUR WEBSITE AND MAKE THE READING CONNECTION!

We've created a customized website just for our very special readers, where you can get the inside scoop on everything that's going on with Zebra, Pinnacle and Kensington books.

When you come online, you'll have the exciting opportunity to:

- View covers of upcoming books
- Read sample chapters
- Learn about our future publishing schedule (listed by publication month *and author*)
- Find out when your favorite authors will be visiting a city near you
- Search for and order backlist books from our online catalog
- Check out author bios and background information
- Send e-mail to your favorite authors
- Meet the Kensington staff online
- Join us in weekly chats with authors, readers and other guests
- Get writing guidelines
- AND MUCH MORE!

Visit our website at
http://www.zebrabooks.com

SWEET DELIGHTS

Cathleen Clare
Alana Clayton
Joy Reed

Zebra Books
Kensington Publishing Corp.
http://www.zebrabooks.com

ZEBRA BOOKS are published by

Kensington Publishing Corp.
850 Third Avenue
New York, NY 10022

First Printing: September, 1999
10 9 8 7 6 5 4 3 2 1

Printed in the United States of America

Contents

LORD MAXFIELD'S BIRTHDAY CAKE

by
Cathleen Clare

One

"Th-thank you." Sniffing the roses, Tabitha lowered her gaze to hide the worry and dismay she knew would be reflected in her eyes. She and her new husband, Thomas, Lord Maxfield, had just returned from their honeymoon in Italy the day before, and it seemed as if he intended to persist in his gift buying, even at home.

Seeming to sense her displeasure, he lifted her chin with his forefinger. "Perhaps full-blown roses are a bit garish for a lady of such delicate beauty. Rose*buds* might be preferable, or maybe orchids. Yes, that's it! Orchids would be just the thing."

"Oh, no!" exclaimed Tabby, mentally calculating the exorbitant cost of such exotic blossoms. "Roses are fine, and I do love these. They are a such a lovely, soft shade of pink. Indeed, they are my favorites."

"Why do I not believe you?" His eyes twinkled, but there was an underlying question in them. "You do love orchids, don't you, my dear?"

She was saved from answering by the reverberating clang of the front door knocker. With the marquess's faint nod of permission, the nearby butler opened it. Tabby's entire family—mother, father, sisters, and brother—stood on the brick stoop outside.

"We heard you were home!" cried her exuberant younger sister, Nell, rushing forward to throw her arms around her sibling, soundly crushing the flowers. "Oh, how happy I am to see you!"

Tabitha winked at her husband over the girl's shoulder. "One would think we'd been gone for centuries," she said dryly.

"It seems that way!" Nell stepped back and extended a hand to Thomas. "And it is very good to see you too, sir. It appears that you've taken good care of our dear Tabby May."

"I'd have spoiled her rotten if she'd have allowed it."

Nell sobered. "No, our Tabby wouldn't have allowed that. She's very self-reliant."

"Well, we'll see about that." He grinned, as the rest of the family filed in, and extended his hand to shake that of Tabby's father, the honorable Mr. Kinsdale. "It's nice to see you again, sir . . . indeed, to see you all."

"I hope that we haven't been precipitous in calling so soon." Mrs. Kinsdale embraced her daughter. "But we missed our Tabitha most dreadfully."

Thomas affectionately slipped his arm around Tabby's waist. "I can well understand. I hope I shall never be separated from her for more than a few hours at the very most."

Tabby smiled up at him, once again reveling in the fact that he was hers. Lord Maxfield just had to be the handsomest man in the realm. With his dark hair, hazel eyes, and trim, fine figure, he could eclipse any gentleman the *ton* deemed attractive. Along with his heart-stopping looks, he was also quite wonderfully thoughtful and kind. Her marquess was as marvelous within as he was without.

As if he felt her perusal, he looked down, his gaze locking with hers and his lips curving, treating her to a display of his breathtaking dimples. The present company fled from Tabby's mind. It was as if the two of them were alone together, in a private place where no other could intrude.

Nell burst into laughter, drawing them back to the here

and now. "You two are *still* smelling of April and May!" she cried. "My, but Italy must have been romantical, to have rendered you totally oblivious to your current surroundings!"

Tabby blushed thoroughly, the color staining her entire face, neck, and the exposed portion of her bosom. In London's high social circle, it was considered rather gauche to appear to be in love with one's own spouse, but suddenly she didn't care. She *was* in love with him. She outwardly adored him, and she was determined to be the most perfect wife.

"Cease your teasing, Nell," she admonished. "I only hope you will be as lucky when you marry."

"If all my children are as fortunate, I shall consider our family blessed," approved Mrs. Kinsdale, presenting her cheek for Thomas's light peck.

"If Thomas and Tabitha are as happy as we are, my love, their marriage will be more than successful." Mr. Kinsdale beamed down on his wife, and they exchanged a glance much like the one their daughter and son-in-law had shared. There were displays of affection aplenty.

Handing the roses to the hovering butler with a murmured request that he put them in water, Tabby changed the subject. "Come, let us go to the drawing room, where we may converse in comfort."

Taking her mother's arm, she turned to lead the way, abruptly realizing that she wasn't sure where the room was. Happily, a footman anticipated her and opened the door. She made a mental note to explore her new home as soon as possible. When they returned from their journey last night, she'd seen only the library and their bedroom suite. This morning, they'd dined in the breakfast room. All of those rooms had been beautifully decorated, but they didn't hold a candle to this one.

The drawing room was painted a beautiful shade of blue, with creamy woodwork accented in gold. Two brilliant crystal chandeliers glistened in the late morning sun. Exquisite paintings adorned the walls. The glowing walnut furniture had to have been made by England's finest cabinetmaker. Over it all was a magnificent painted ceiling.

Tabby audibly caught her breath. This room must have cost a king's ransom. How big a dent it must have made in the Maxfield family purse! She hoped that it had been paid for long ago by a previous generation and that it did not loom as a huge debit in Thomas's account books. The richness of Maxfield House, combined with all the money Thomas had spent on their honeymoon, made her wonder if her husband was a spendthrift.

"What a lovely room," her mother voiced in awe.

"Indeed," her father seconded. "Tell me, is that not a bronze of Pompey that I spy?"

"It is." Thomas guided him across the room to view the statue. Tabby's brother followed, leaving the women alone.

Tabby, Mrs. Kinsdale, Nell, and the youngest child, Agatha, seated themselves by the marble hearth.

Nell bounced excitedly on the sofa. "Is marriage truly just as splendid as you guessed?"

"Even more so!" Tabby enthused, her cheeks coloring again. "Thomas is a wonderful husband, Nell, except . . ." She fell silent as French, the butler, approached.

"Does my lady wish a tray of refreshment?" he whispered.

"Does Lord Maxfield wish . . ." she began, then corrected herself. She was the mistress here, as Thomas had firmly pointed out when they had arrived. "Yes, please. A tray would be most welcome."

French bowed and softly walked away.

"My," Mrs. Kinsdale observed, "he's very grand and proper. I'll wager he's the embodiment of efficiency."

"I wonder," Tabby mused, more to herself than to the others. "Of course, I haven't even scratched the surface of the household matters, but there seems to be so many servants here. Too many, really. I can scarcely move without one of them leaping to aid me! Moreover, I even have *two* personal maids! A dresser and her assistant. Gracious, they even tried to bathe me like a child! I quickly put short shrift to that. Can you imagine?"

Her two sisters collapsed in giggles, but her mother sighed dreamily. "I can hardly imagine having too many servants. Such coddling sounds heavenly to me."

"Well, it is not," Tabby stated. "It is absolute nonsense! My goodness, I am not helpless! Even when I put period to their efforts, they still stood about. I felt like a figure in a raree-show!"

The girls chortled, and Nell said, "Oh, Tabby, I can picture it all! Tell me, what did you do?"

"I sent them on their merry way." She nodded emphatically. "It is immodest enough putting up with their assisting me in my dressing, let alone having them standing there observing my unattired state. Even on the few occasions when your abigail, Mama, helped me dress, I was already clothed in my shift when she appeared. This . . ." She shrugged her shoulders and ceased speaking, as her sisters' laughter drowned any further words.

It took at least five minutes for the girls to overcome their hilarity. Even then, Nell's throat continued to tremble and her eyes still danced with mirth. "Oh, Tabby, you may complain about being looked after by *two* personal servants, but I would give my eyeteeth just to have one. I do believe that the marquess is absolutely on his way to spoiling you thoroughly."

"No, he will never do that." Tabby shook her head. "I am not of that disposition. We were not brought up to waste money."

"Ha! Lord Maxfield must be wealthy beyond all belief," Nell countered. "That's what Mama says."

Mrs. Kinsdale simply glowed with pleasure. "I am certain that Lord Maxfield has no financial worries."

"Are you really?" Nell prodded. "Tell us of the marriage settlement."

"Well, I was not privy to the details. That was the business of Lord Maxfield and your father. But just look around you. Anyone with such a marvelous house must be fabulously wealthy."

Mortified, Tabby quickly glanced across the room to the gentlemen. They were far enough away that they couldn't have heard her mother's hushed voice, but that didn't ease her discomfort. This was not a topic for speculation.

"Oh, I knew that our Tabitha would snare a fine, rich peer," Mrs. Kinsdale went on smugly. "After all, she is an heiress."

Tabby's eyes widened with shock. "What do you mean?"

Her mother smiled secretively. "You are heiress to me. I am certain your father explained that to Lord Maxfield."

"But you have no money!"

"I have jewels."

Tabby visualized the paltry real jewelry her mother had and the impressive quantity of fakes. Her mama would definitely try to fool Thomas. Surely her father had not!

Mrs. Kinsdale simpered. "Let us end this talk of finance. Just suffice it to say that Lord Maxfield is tremendously affluent."

"I've never heard rumors to that effect," Nell claimed.

Tabby was not so sure either. Having been reared in a family of small financial worth, she refused to assume that her husband was moneyed. Having wed the second son of a viscount, and a man of scholarly bent, her mother was adept at putting on a good show. She continually fooled the whole *ton* (and creditors) into thinking that the Kinsdales were well-to-do. And she had taught her daughters how to do it, too. No, Tabby would never assume that Thomas was wealthy. She would continue the strict economies she'd learned from her mother.

"Tabitha need never worry about money again, and

there's an end to it," Mrs. Kinsdale pronounced with finality.

"But . . ." Nell tried to continue.

To Tabby's great relief, French returned, putting a final period to the discussion of capital. He set down the huge silver tray laden with a tea service and the largest assortment of cakes and biscuits that she had ever seen served as a mere refreshing repast. "If there is anything else, madam, I shall procure it immediately."

"French!" Thomas called from across the room. "Please bring the gifts my lady and I have brought for her family."

"Gifts?" Nell and Agatha exchanged sparkling stares.

Once more, Tabby felt uncomfortable. Thomas had insisted upon bringing everyone gifts from Italy. Small mementos would have been one thing, but the expensive presents he purchased were quite another. While she was happy to remember their families, his spending had been outside of enough. What an effect the items must have had on her husband's purse!

"How kind of you to think of us," her mother said, as the gentlemen approached.

"You are fast becoming my favorite brother," Nell laughingly told him.

"And mine," Agatha agreed.

Tabby wished a large hole would open in the floor and swallow her entirely. The nerve of those girls! She tried to favor them with a quelling glare, but they wouldn't look at her.

Thomas chuckled. "I am only too happy to have two new charming sisters."

"I wish you had a brother," Nell bemoaned, "who was just as handsome and kind as you."

"Nell!" Tabby exclaimed, horrified. But no one paid her heed. They all were laughing too hard. Her cheeks burning, she began to pour the tea. By the time everyone was

served, French and a footman had returned with the boxes.

"I hope you enjoy these as much as Tabitha and I did when we chose them," Thomas said. "Nell, since I can tell that you scarcely can wait, you may have yours first."

Tabby's sister wriggled in anticipation as he presented her with a small velvet box. "This is so exciting. It's like birthdays or Christmas!"

"I hope you are pleased," Thomas said.

"It is definitely not a trifle," Tabby muttered.

Nell carefully opened the lid and gaped at the lovely necklace. "It is beautiful," she whispered in awe.

Her gift was a veritable work of art. The chain was of dainty ivory openwork. The pendant was oval, upon which was the portrait of a lady, executed in butterfly wings and surrounded by pearls. On the reverse was a compartment for tucking a lock of hair. It had been very costly, but Thomas had spent even more on gifts for their mothers and her father.

"I have never owned anything so wonderful," Nell vowed, reverently slipping it around her neck. "How does it look?"

"Marvelous," Mrs. Kinsdale admired.

Seeing her sister's joy, Tabby was suddenly glad that her marquess had insisted on purchasing the bauble, and all the other things, too. She would just cut a few corners on household expenses to make up for it. From what she had seen of Maxfield House, it would be easy to do and, actually, rather imperative anyway.

"My sweetest sister!" Nell leapt up to throw her arms around her. "How kind you were to think of me, even on your honeymoon!"

Tabitha hugged her in return and did not admit that the valuable necklace was all her husband's idea. "I'm so pleased that you like it."

"I shall treasure it always!" The girl flew to Thomas to

embrace him, too. "Oh, thank you, thank you! I am delighted beyond all belief!"

Happily, Tabby watched the rapture of her family as they received their gifts. Agatha also thrilled in a necklace, similar to Nell's. Mrs. Kinsdale gasped with pleasure at her Florentine jewel box with the magnificent emerald earrings inside. Her brother, Daniel, thrilled in his jeweled cravat pin. Real tears filled her intellectual papa's eyes as he gaped in awe at the precious illuminated manuscript from the Renaissance period.

"I have never in my life expected to own something like this," he breathed, reverently carrying it to a table to carefully turn the pages. "Do you realize what a treasure this is? This is the kind of thing one usually sees in museums only!"

Tabby knew that it must be costly, but she didn't know the actual price, for Thomas had gone out and purchased it before she had risen one morning.

"I . . . I . . ." Mr. Kinsdale slowly shook his head and groped for his handkerchief to wipe his eyes. "I am utterly overset."

"I am glad you are pleased, sir," Thomas said, looking very proud to have found just the thing to enthrall his new father-in-law.

Mrs. Kinsdale rose, went to her husband's side, and lovingly squeezed his hand. "You must show this marvel to all who appreciate things like this."

"Oh, I shall! A rarity such as this must be seen and appreciated by all."

Tabby exchanged an amused glance with her sisters. Their papa thought only of displaying it for the very beauty of the manuscript. Their mother saw it as a real gem in the counterfeit Kinsdale crown, something to flaunt.

Nell set aside her teacup and rose. "Come, Tabby, let us take a turn about the room."

Although dubious of her sister's motives for privacy, Tabby acquiesced.

When they were in the farthest corner from the others, Nell feigned interest in a porcelain figurine and shyly eyed her. "Are you still overwhelmingly in love with Thomas?"

Tabby gave up trying to hush her in hopes that a few answers to her questions would curb the girl's curiosity. She bent her head, pretending to discuss the item. "Even more so, but . . ."

"Yes?" her sister urged.

"At the risk of bringing up the subject of money again, I fear that Thomas spends too freely. It worries me."

"I tell you, he's wealthy! Just look around you, Tabby," she hissed. "This is not the average home; it's a veritable palace. And the way he dresses . . . Only the finest tailor could construct such apparel. Why on earth do you think him poor?"

"I do not think him poor, just . . . just average."

"Fustian! If he hadn't wealth, he would never have married a dowerless lady."

"I . . . I think Mama tricked him."

"He seems far too intelligent to fall for Mama's games."

Tabby shifted uncomfortably. Here was the subject of money again, and it was her fault that it had been revived. "I do not wish to discuss this further."

Nell ignored her. "You should ask him. Ask him how financially fit he is."

Her mouth dropping open, Tabby stared with horror at the girl. "That is ridiculous! I cannot believe you suggested it."

Her sister laughed. "You will not believe pure reason, so how will you know the depth of his pockets if you do not ask?"

"It is none of my business," Tabby said flatly. "It would garner me a sharp set down."

"I doubt it."

"No, Nell, I shan't do it. The very idea! You have grown daft in my absence." She rolled her eyes heavenward. "You are a total ninnyhammer."

Her sister shrugged. "Have it your way, but you are creating useless anxiety for yourself."

"That may or may not be, but my responsibility is to the household. I intend to manage it as economically as possible. Now there's an end to it!"

"Goose," was all Nell replied as they proceeded to finish their circle around the room.

Shortly thereafter, the Kinsdales went on their way, leaving Tabby with a profound sense of relief, though the comment about her being an heiress still distressed her. She wondered if she should mention it to Thomas, but quickly decided against doing that. What if she found he believed she had a fortune coming to her? Then what would he do? No, she would avoid the topic until she had proved what a good household manager she was. Then he'd see that she'd *saved* him a fortune, and nothing else would matter.

When they turned from the door, French presented Thomas with a newly arrived message. Her husband scanned the contents and gave a resigned chuckle. "My sister, Charlotte, wishes us to dine with her tonight. I vow we should return to Italy! Shall I never have you completely to myself again?"

Her heart filled with happiness at his statement. Perhaps their honeymoon never would end, in their minds, at least. She slipped her arm through his and squeezed.

He sighed. "Well, my darling, how shall we answer her?"

"I suppose we must admit reality. We are back in London again and fair game for all who desire our company." She laughed lightly. "We should be honored that we are so in demand."

"Very well." He grinned boyishly. "We shall accept her invitation. But until then, let us bar all others from our presence. Surely we can extend our honeymoon just a while longer."

"Surely!" she concurred and companionably strolled to the library with him.

Thomas, Lord Maxfield, glanced over the papers on his desk and passed a hand across his forehead. His plan to spend the rest of the day alone with his wife had not come to pass. Soon after luncheon, his man of business had arrived with important items for him to peruse and sign. He would have given the man short shrift, but Tabitha had insisted that he give the matter his full attention, while she would meet with the housekeeper and take a tour of her new home. Actually, he'd hoped to show her the house himself, for he was proud of its assembled treasures, but he realized that she would learn more of her domestic responsibilities from Mrs. Dobbs. Now, awaiting her return, he wished that he'd set out to join their excursion. He'd grown accustomed to his bride's presence and he missed her, even in this short span of time. He smiled, thinking of how besotted he'd been with her, from the very beginning of their acquaintance.

Tabitha Kinsdale had to have been the loveliest lady in an entire Season of beauties. From the moment he saw her—petite, blue eyed, and flaxen haired—he'd known that he'd wed no other. He was surprised when her father informed him that she had little dowry, but that didn't matter. He had more money than he knew what to do with, and finding the family was not as well-to-do as they'd seemed had only increased his desire to possess her and to shower upon her all that money could buy. But it hadn't worked out that way. Frankly, Tabitha hadn't seemed to like his largess . . . just as was illustrated that very morning.

While she was conferring about the day's menus with Mrs. Dobbs, he'd hurried out to buy the roses, but when he'd presented them to her, she had seemed disappointed, even dismayed. At first he had thought that she didn't like roses, but then she'd assured him she did. Her pleasure, however, was obviously false, and he just couldn't understand why.

The marquess had never known a lady who did not like to receive flowers. Moreover, his wife's odd turn of mind went even deeper. On their honeymoon, she seemed to shrink from each gift he had bought for her or their families. He sighed and shook his head. Her taste must certainly run counter to his own. He'd just have to try harder. The thought made his head ache. Literally. He set aside his papers, rang for French, and began to massage his temples.

"I've a megrim," he told his butler. "Please bring me some headache powders."

He took the medicine, and by the time Tabitha entered the room, he was improving, although the potion was making him sleepy.

"Is something wrong?" she immediately detected.

"Only a trifling headache." He chuckled in an attempt to make light of his condition. It wasn't very masculine to fall victim to illness in front of one's new wife, whom one wished to impress.

"It cannot be insignificant," she parried. "You look quite pale."

"It's nothing." He couldn't admit weakness to her. "Paperwork always makes me drowsy."

She looked worried. "I see."

It wasn't *precisely* a lie. The powders were doing their job and his headache was easing. He thrust the documents into his desk drawer.

"How was your tour?" he asked cheerfully.

"Just fine." She smiled with enthusiasm. "The house is so lovely."

He was pleased. He had spared no guinea in refurbishing it for her. "Remember, you are its mistress. Manage it in whatever manner you choose."

"Thank you. There are a few things I might wish to change," she murmured hesitantly, "if you do not mind."

He nodded. "Please accomplish whatever you feel necessary. I know I'll be satisfied. Just send the bills to me."

Her eyes widened to two large pools of blue. "Oh, there will be no bills! These are matters of economical efficiency."

Immediately thinking of his mama and sisters, Thomas was amused. If his new wife was frugal, she would be the first woman he'd known who possessed such a trait. Tabitha was probably unsure of the meaning of the term. He considered asking her for a detailed explanation of her economy, but he changed his mind. She would think he was teasing her, which in a sense he would be.

It was difficult to remain sober and say, "You must carry on in any way you deem proper."

"Your support means everything!" In her fervor, she candidly leaned forward. "Sometimes servants resist new ways."

"You're afraid they'll complain to me?"

She smiled ruefully. "Well . . . that had crossed my mind."

He chuckled. "Don't worry about it. I am happy to leave the running of the household to you. Any servant who grumbles to me about wielding his feather duster with more vigor will be sharply sent on his way."

"I am grateful," she laughed.

"If that is so, come here, my darling, and give me a kiss."

She readily rose and came round the desk.

He collected her on his lap and tilted her chin for a kiss.

"Thomas! In the daylight?" she cried, aghast.

"Of course 'in the daylight.' I don't believe there's a law governing such an act." Before she could protest, he brought his lips down upon hers in a deep, soul-satisfying kiss.

"Your headache . . ." she began when she could speak again.

"It has ended."

"Then perhaps you should finish your paperwork."

"The urge to do that has fled, too." Once more, he claimed her lips and Tabitha, giggling, capitulated.

Having spent the afternoon quite shockingly with her romantical husband, Tabitha feared they would be late for the dinner with his sister, but thanks to the speed of her abigail and her assistant, she was bathed, gowned, and coifed just at the precise time to depart. She did, however, have a rather unpleasant task to perform before going out. Turning on her dressing table bench, she somberly regarded her personal servants.

"Betsy," she told the junior of the two, "I am sorry to say that I must let you go."

The girl gasped. "Ma'am! If my work has not been satisfactory, please allow me another chance. I will . . ."

"Your service has been above excellent," Tabby assured her, "and I have written a glowing reference to that effect. It's just that I cannot afford to retain both of you. Never fear. I shall give you a bit of extra money, over and above what is owed for your wages. I'm certain you will find employment quite soon."

"But my lady," her elder servant protested, "I do need Betsy's assistance. There is a great deal to do."

"You will find that I require very little," Tabby answered

in rebuttal. "Indeed, I prefer to perform much of my dressing myself. You will only need care for my clothes, Evans."

The maid's mouth twitched, narrowing into a fine line of disapproval. "Very well, madam," she said tightly.

"Thank you for understanding." Rising, Tabby presented the tearful Betsy with her letter of reference and left the room. She did not fool herself into thinking that the servants understood. They didn't. Not by half! But it was a matter of necessity. After all, she had not had a personal abigail before she was married, only infrequently being served by her mother's dresser. One servant was more than enough.

Descending the stairs, she mused upon the difficulty of dismissing an employee. Jobs were not always plentiful. Yet retaining two personal servants was an unnecessary luxury. She must set aside her compassion. She would have to repeat this scene for a number of others, as well. There were just too many servants at Maxfield House. Any amount of them often stood about with nothing to do. What a waste!

Thomas was waiting for her in the downstairs hall. He bowed. "You are looking particularly lovely this evening, my dear."

She inclined her head. "And so are you."

Her marvelous Thomas looked purely wonderful in his informal evening attire. Of course, he was delectable in any garb he chose to wear. Once again, as countless times before, she could scarcely believe that he was hers.

He helped her with her wrap and presented his arm. "Shall we?"

They left the house and trod down the brick walk to the carriage. A brisk fall breeze stirred Tabby's hair. Soon it would be winter and the holiday season. She assumed they would celebrate Christmas in the country at Maxfield Hall. Hopefully, both of their families would be present. She would try her best to be a perfect hostess. She had dozens of delicious holiday recipes. Perhaps she should immediately begin setting aside household money so that she would have plenty of cash for the ingredients.

She settled herself in the luxurious Maxfield carriage. My, but it was spacious and comfortable. Again, she wondered at Thomas's opulence. It worried her.

She glanced sideways at her husband and smiled when she caught him looking at her. "This is a most comfortable carriage."

"It is new," he told her. "I bought it only last spring. Little did I know then that I would be seating a most lovely lady inside."

"A lot has happened since then."

He took her hand and kissed it. "And all of it is good."

She pushed all financial thoughts from her mind and sighed dreamily. "I pray that I don't disappoint you."

In the gaslight she could see a mischievous grin play at the corners of his mouth. "How could you when you are far above perfect?"

She laughed. "You are bamming me, sir."

"Never." He stretched his arm across the back of the seat and kneaded her neck. "Of course there are certain times when you are more perfect than others, such as this afternoon when you . . ."

"Hush!" she protested, warmth suffusing her cheeks. "If I think of those things, I shall arrive at your sister's all a-twitter!"

"Then since you are utterly charming when you are so agitated, perhaps you should constantly think of those times."

Her flush burned deeper. "I do not believe that is a good idea."

"Why not?"

"Do not tease me." She meant to speak sternly, but the words came out in a giggle. "I shall contrive to be perfect *without* such daring recollections!"

He squeezed her neck one final time, then removed his hand. "I imagine you would be most unhinged were I to remind you in front of Charlotte."

"Thomas, you wouldn't!"

"Just watch me," he said wickedly.

"That would be most scandalous. Whatever would she think?" Tabby gasped.

He chuckled. "She would merely surmise that her sister-in-law and her brother have a healthy, normal relationship."

"Do be still," Tabby begged. "I do not want to arrive at her house with my cheeks as red as fire."

"Very well, but your blush is quite becoming." He took her hand and held it until the coach drew to a halt in front of the impressive residence of the Duke and Duchess of Cottington.

As she descended to the pavement, Tabby had a sudden quiver of butterflies in her stomach. She scarcely knew Charlotte, and she was acquainted even less with her husband. What if they didn't like her? Feeling ever so much on trial, she clung to Thomas's arm as they entered the magnificent edifice.

A footman took their outerwear and a staid butler led them down a large, formidable hall.

"Darling, you look terrified," Thomas remarked, looking down at her.

"I am," she quaked.

There was no time for consolation. The servant threw open a door, and they entered the drawing room.

"Heavens above!" Charlotte cried, rising to her feet from her chair beside the crackling fire. "I know you accepted my invitation, but I refused to believe you would actually come until I saw you in the flesh! Look, Cotty, they are really here!"

His Grace smiled patiently. "Of course, my dear."

Tabby's sister-in-law strode across the room to greet

them. She bore a definite family resemblance to her brother, but she wasn't pretty as one might have expected. Charlotte was a handsome woman, but in a rather masculine way. She was very tall, thin, and large boned, and her swinging gait proclaimed the fact that she was an avid horsewoman.

First, she soundly hugged her brother; then she turned to Tabby, her hands outstretched. "I am so happy to greet you, Tabitha. I look forward to our becoming fast friends."

Tabby's fingers were crushed in Charlotte's hearty clasp. "I, too, look forward to that," she smiled.

The duke approached more quietly, shook Thomas's hand, and bowed over Tabby's. "Welcome to our home, my dear. We hope to spend many happy hours in your company."

With their effusive greetings, Tabby's nervousness fled. The duke and duchess were prepared to be friendly, and so was she. She walked with Charlotte to the fireside and seated herself.

"The fire is so warm and cheerful," she said, "and this is such a lovely room."

"I can't take credit," her new sister-in-law declared. "Cotty's mama did the decorating. I'm not so good at domestic pursuits. I'll wager you are though, aren't you, Tabitha? You have the look of it."

Thomas chuckled, overhearing. "And just what *look* is that, Charlotte?"

"Oh, feminine, I suppose," she replied. "No one's ever accused me of being that!"

"That's for certain," said her husband. "She can outride me, any day, and you should see her handle a high-perch phaeton."

"I hope that's not a complaint," rejoined his wife.

"Certainly not, darling. I have always applauded your equestrian skills."

"Thank you, love." She turned back to Tabby. "Do you ride?"

"Not well," Tabby admitted.

"I'm not surprised. Few of the belles of the *ton* take an interest in horsemanship," Charlotte pronounced.

Tabby laughed. "A belle?"

"Definitely!" She tossed her head, much like a restive colt. "Now don't pretend ignorance. You know you were the Beauty of your Season. *There's a prime 'un,* I thought when first I saw you. And I was right!"

Tabby eyed her with amazement. "You noticed me?"

"How could I help it?" Charlotte brayed. "My brother was making a cake of himself over you. Oh, my! You had him at your feet from the very first moment!"

"Charlotte, you are impossible," Thomas avowed.

"I may be that. However, I'm right, aren't I?" She grinned. "But maybe I'd best change the subject. I don't wish to mortify you, Tom!"

The duke rolled his eyes. "Sometimes I rue the day I met you, my dearest."

"Fustian! Who would you have to break your colts?" she fired back. "Now be a dear, Cotty, and bring us a sherry."

Tabby, her head swimming from Charlotte's rapid interchange, was glad of the respite the wine provided, as Thomas's sister slowed her quicksilver tongue to sip the beverage. Thomas used the opportunity to present them with their gifts from Italy. For the duke, they'd brought an ancient Etruscan figurine to add to his collection of classical statuary. For Charlotte, they'd purchased a jeweled ivory rendition of Pegasus. Both recipients were thrilled with their remembrances. Shortly thereafter, dinner was called.

At the table, Charlotte again brought up the subject of horses. "You say that you don't ride well, Tabitha?" she asked.

"Truthfully, I scarcely know which side of the horse to

mount," she confessed. "In my family, such sport was not considered to be a viable pastime for women."

"More's the pity," her sister-in-law pondered. "That must change. Male or female, all of the Maxfields ride. You aren't afraid, are you?"

Tabby shook her head. "I just never had the chance to participate."

Actually, the Kinsdales were too poor to provide animals for each family member. Her father had a horse, though he seldom rode for pleasure. Her brother had a steed, which he enjoyed to the utmost. Mrs. Kinsdale had developed a pretense of preference for the domestic skills. Therefore, the Kinsdale ladies were quite noted for their beautiful needlework.

"Have you never been involved in archery?" Charlotte demanded. "Or even croquet?"

"No," said Tabby, feeling somewhat unsophisticated.

"My wife is a *lady,"* Thomas interjected.

"Be still," his sister admonished. "Wouldn't you like to play a game of croquet with Tabitha?"

"Not particularly," he drawled.

"You're probably afraid she would win," she scoffed. "Well, my gel, I'm at least going to teach you to ride. When shall we start?"

Tabby hesitated. With the economizing of Maxfield House, she already had a great deal on her plate. But she wanted to make friends with Charlotte as well.

"Don't be afraid," her sister-in-law urged. "I won't toss it at you all at once."

"Maybe she doesn't want to learn to ride," Thomas interposed.

"Fustian," Charlotte scorned. "Everyone wants to ride. Fresh air and animals are good for people. Set the time, Tabitha."

"What day would be good for you?" she queried.

"Tomorrow is as good as any. We'll go early in the morning, so we won't have to contend with crowds in the park. Say, eleven o'clock?"

Tabby glanced at Thomas. An engagement at eleven o'clock was rather early, according to their usual schedule.

He shrugged.

The duke was also watching him. "Perhaps your brother prefers to teach his own wife to ride, Charlotte," he remarked. "They have barely ended their honeymoon."

"Fiddlesticks. All good things must come to an end," she retorted. "Tom can attend to matters of business while Tabitha is occupied."

Tabby thought that was a very good idea. "I shall be ready," she promised, "but what about a horse?"

"I have horses aplenty," Charlotte told her, "and I have just the ideal mare for you to begin with. I bought Maud in anticipation of teaching our little boy when he's just a bit older. She's a beginner's mount."

"When she is ready," said Thomas, "I'll go to Tattersall's and buy Tabitha a horse of her own."

More money spent! Tabitha hiccupped. "I'm sure it will be a long time before that is necessary."

"Have you a habit?" Charlotte asked.

"No," she demurred, a vision of flying pound notes dancing through her head.

Thomas's sister smiled beguiling at him. "Dear brother, you may take Tabitha to Cecile's tomorrow. Hopefully, she'll have a habit already made up for someone else. If you cross her palm with silver, she'll sell it to you. That will take care of our immediate problem; then you can order more."

Cecile! Tabby barely kept from gasping. That was the most expensive dressmaker in London. She was the personal designer to the very elite of the *ton*. Tabby had coveted her fashions as soon as she had seen the first ball gown made by Cecile, but owning such a dress had been only a dream. There were other adequate modistes who charged far less.

"Will you do that, Tom? I simply must fulfill an engagement I have accepted tomorrow, or I would go myself," Charlotte pressured. "Oh, what am I saying? I am treating you like a child, Tabitha. Do forgive me! I'm sure you are quite capable of going to Cecile's yourself."

Damn! Tabitha said shockingly to herself. She could hardly bear to spend more money, after the huge outlay of the honeymoon, but it seemed that it was mandatory. However, if she went by herself, she could acquire something cheaper.

"No one need accompany me," she said. "Thomas has more important things to do than to go with me to a mantua maker's."

"Get one with military styling," Charlotte advised. "Those are the first stare of fashion."

Tabby nodded. "I'll try, but on short notice, I may have to take something else."

"You might pay Cecile to produce something quickly. She has been known to work miracles, if she receives the right amount of cash."

"I shall contrive," Tabby pledged and directed the conversation away from expenditures for the rest of the evening.

In the morning, glad that she did not have to reckon with Thomas and Charlotte, Tabby found a rather ill-fitting riding habit at the shop of an unknown dressmaker who was just entering the profession. She thought she could tailor it in places, but she was wrong. The ensemble was so poorly cut that she could do little to help matters. Nor could Evans do anything with it. "It's a disaster, my lady," she denounced. "Belongs in the dust bin."

"I didn't wish to spend a great deal," Tabby defended,

unhappily eyeing herself in the mirror. "What if I don't like riding?"

The abigail shrugged. "Madam, where are your boots?"

"Oh, my Lord, I forgot!" she gasped. "What shall I do? Perhaps sturdy street shoes would suffice. The duchess will be here any minute!"

Evans sent her a withering look. "Let me see what I can do."

The dresser left the room and came back with a shining pair of boots. "They belong to one of the footmen. He didn't like lending them, for they are his best, but I told him you would amply reward him. You will, won't you, my lady?"

Tabby sighed. "Very well. I have little choice."

The boots were a bit large, but Evans stuffed them with rags until they fit. Tabby felt miserable. When she descended the stairs, she knew she must look like a veritable troll.

Charlotte had arrived and was waiting with Thomas in the entrance hall. Behind them stood a footman, wearing such a smirk that Tabby knew he must be the one whose boots she had borrowed. She wished she could flee.

"What in God's name . . ." Thomas began.

"Hush, brother," Charlotte admonished.

"I know I look awful," Tabby managed, teetering on the edge of weeping.

"Where in the hell did you get such an antidote?" he demanded.

Her temper flared. After all, saving money was to his benefit. "I didn't exactly have a great choice, given short notice. And since when did you become an authority on ladies' fashions?"

"I know what looks nice," he maintained, "and that looks like the very devil."

She set her jaw. "Thank you, Thomas. I do so enjoy your compliments."

"Come, Tabitha." Charlotte clasped Tabby's arm and fairly dragged her from the town house.

"I did the best I could," she said.

"I know, dear. Now let us be away from here. Please assist Lady Maxfield," she ordered her groom.

The man gave Tabby such a colossal toss up that she nearly fell off the other side.

"I'm not going to be good at this," she groaned, righting herself. "I am not athletically inclined."

"But you are graceful," Charlotte professed. "A good equestrienne must be fluid. When you ride, pretend you are dancing with the horse. Now, here is the way you hold the reins."

Maud was quiet and patient, the very epitome of a beginner's horse. Tabby quickly gained confidence, until she was even willing to try a slow trot. Charlotte, rejoicing, proclaimed her a 'natural'.

The outing would have been deemed a triumph, if they hadn't met Mr. Frederick Gates, a dandy who always noticed and blatantly prattled about everyone's attire. He was a very insulting figure, who should have been snubbed by the whole *ton*, but who was considered an eccentric and, therefore, put up with. He gaped at Tabby and raised his quizzing glass.

"My, what have we here? A dowdy marchioness? Goodness, there should be a law against such an eyesore."

"Mind your own business," Charlotte snapped. "That costume you're wearing is enough to put one's eyes *out*, let alone make them sore."

"Whew!" He fanned his face with his hand. "The Duchess of Dragons breathes fire!"

"I'll breathe more than fire in a moment," she vied. "I'll dust your face with my riding crop."

"Ooh, I'd best escape while I can," he grimaced.

Tabby could scarcely believe Charlotte's sharp tongue.

"Namby-pamby. Woman in man's clothing. Come along,

Tabitha, and avoid this insult to mankind." Charlotte started past him. When her horse's rump was even with Gates's leg, she neatly nudged the animal with her heel. The well-trained animal obeyed the signal and set his hindquarters against Gates's limb, squashing it hard.

"Ouch!" screeched Gates pitifully. "You did that on purpose!"

"Go play with your dolls," the duchess cast over her shoulder.

Horrified, Tabby propelled Maud into a jog to catch up with her. "Charlotte, he will cause the worst of scandals!"

"Balderdash! Who cares?"

"I care! What will people think?" She could picture Thomas in a horrible rage over gossip about his wife.

"Nobody listens to him," Thomas's sister passed off. "Tabitha, my goodness! You've started to trot, all by yourself!"

"I'm trying to escape Mr. Gates," she said grimly.

Charlotte pealed with laughter. "Then we'll have to include Gates in your lessons. This is the best I've seen you do all morning!"

Shortly thereafter, they ended the lesson and rode home. When they neared Maxfield House, they saw an elegant carriage drawn up in front. An equally elegant woman was descending.

"It's Cecile!" Charlotte hooted. "I see that Thomas has taken matters in hand. You'll soon have an admirable riding habit, Tabitha. La, just think how much my brother is paying for this actual visit by the paragon of London fashion!"

Tabby moaned. "Such an expense isn't necessary. This is ridiculous!"

"Nonsense! Spend Tom's money! Let him spoil you! You shouldn't be embarrassed."

"But I don't want . . ."

Behind them, another appreciated the marquess's largess. "Ha-ha! Ha-ha! The eyesore will soon be remedied!" heckled Mr. Frederick Gates.

"This is terrible," Tabby lamented. Charlotte could say all she wanted, but she was totally mortified. In addition, she was worried. Economy must be practiced. But how could she manage efficiently if her husband continued to spend?

She forced a smile and invited Charlotte in to help with the order. It was a mistake. Charlotte proudly bragged to Thomas about Tabby's great equestrian skill. As a result, Cecile took orders for two riding habits and promised to set all other designing aside and to hire two extra seamstresses so that she would have them ready for Tabby's next outing. They would even work through the night.

"That's the thing!" Charlotte encouraged.

Tabby softly groaned.

Two

Cecile was as good as her word. She personally delivered the two riding habits—one an indigo blue and the other a deep rust— practically overnight. Tabby could only imagine what the exorbitant bill must be. It was apparently delivered to Thomas, so she never saw it. Just the thought of it, however, made her attack the household structure with greater zeal. Economies must be initiated at Maxfield House, and they must be put into effect immediately.

First, Tabby called Mrs. Dobbs to the morning room to discuss her ideas. To make possible a smooth transition, she must have the housekeeper's support. Although she expected some opposition, she hadn't anticipated it to be quite as strong.

In order to make their meeting as pleasant as possible, Tabby ordered a tea tray. When it arrived, she poured two cups of the steaming brew and invited Mrs. Dobbs to help herself to the biscuits. "I hope to make our conferences pleasant, for we have much to do."

The housekeeper nodded, but sat rather stiffly beside Tabby's desk.

"I have not been at Maxfield House very long," Tabby began, "but I have noticed an overabundance of staff."

Mrs. Dobbs eyed her warily.

"It seems that I frequently encounter servants with absolutely nothing to do. That does not seem to me to be very efficient."

"On the surface, that might appear to be true, my lady," the housekeeper explained. "However, I assure you that all of our people are necessary."

Tabby arched an eyebrow. "Why?"

"In order to provide fine service, of course," she said mildly.

"I don't understand."

Mrs. Dobbs sighed in a manner that indicated long suffering. "If the servants are physically working when you or his lordship summon, their response time is longer. Therefore, people must be instantly available to answer your summons."

Tabby smiled. "Such speed is not necessary. It doesn't hurt anyone to be a bit patient."

Mrs. Dobbs glanced doubtfully at her. "But if the jobs they were undertaking were filthy, they would have to wash up first, perhaps even change their clothes, or report in an unclean condition."

"It would seem to be unusual for all the servants to be engaged in dirty work," Tabby contested. "I doubt that would happen frequently."

The housekeeper drew herself up ramrod straight in her chair. "Once is too often, my lady."

"I realize that you must take pride in such things," Tabby said sympathetically.

Mrs. Dobbs nodded vigorously. "Maxfield House has always run smoothly, with not so much as a ripple on our peaceful waters. My aunt was housekeeper before me, madam. I trained under her, and I have always followed in her flawless footsteps. In all our combined years, no Maxfield family member has *ever* complained."

"I am not precisely complaining," Tabby said carefully. "I am merely offering what I consider to be a more efficient way. The sum total of the staff's salaries is prohibitive. Perhaps in your aunt's time, wages were cheaper."

"Money isn't the object," the woman muttered.

Tabby set her jaw. A disregard of cash! That was the root of every problem at Maxfield House. Everyone went on as if a day of reckoning would never come. The household had a huge, bulky budget, and by Jove, she was going to trim it! Of course the housekeeper did not wish to reduce staff. That would require more proficient planning, which if she had been following her aunt's guidelines, Mrs. Dobbs probably didn't know how to do. Tabby did, and she would teach her.

"We must thin out the number of servants," she directed firmly. "There are entirely too many."

The housekeeper was not going to fall into this scheme without protest. "Most of our people have been with the Maxfield family for generations. The employment of kin has always been taken for granted."

"Not anymore," Tabby countered. "That practice will cease. I am determined to carry out my plan of efficiency."

Mrs. Dobbs pursed her lips. "My lady, I know you mean well, but I just do not see how we can dismiss any of the staff. They are needed. They are necessary! Please leave such matters to me. I am a professional in my field. I know how things should be done."

Aha! That was the crux of the matter! Mrs. Dobbs didn't believe that Tabby knew what she was doing, which was entirely understandable. Few young ladies of the *ton* had been trained in such a high level of housekeeping as she.

"Mrs. Dobbs," she commenced slowly, folding her hands and studying them. "My mother instructed me in the fine points of housekeeping. She is an expert in the art. She truly should write a book about it."

The housekeeper blinked.

"In order for you to understand, I must speak very personally. I do not wish my comments to leave this room."

Mrs. Dobbs looked very interested, leaning forward to catch every word. "Lady Maxfield, your secrets will *die* with me."

"Very well. To continue . . . you must know that my family is far, far from wealthy, and yet we must hold our place in the *ton.*" She paused for dramatic effect. "My mother's model of efficiency is so skillful that she can fool the sharpest observers of social appearance. In short, she has tricked everyone into thinking that the Kinsdales are just as well-to-do as many others. But it is sham, Mrs. Dobbs, sham."

The woman took a long moment to digest that; then she licked her lips as if relishing what she was to say. "My lady, I'm sure that your mother must set an admirable example."

"She does," Tabby agreed, "and she has tutored me in every facet. So you see, I am not like the average bride. I have learned enough to be highly qualified for being a housekeeper myself."

"I believe that you are. But, my sweet lady, you needn't bother your pretty head about it. Leave everything to me!"

Tabby nodded happily. Evidently, Mrs. Dobbs would prune those household positions that were superfluous. "I am glad to hear you say that, Mrs. Dobbs."

"Just leave it all to me," she repeated.

"Thank you. I am glad that you and I see eye to eye. I am certain that we will enjoy working together to make Maxfield House the most efficient, well-oiled household in the kingdom!" She rose. "Now I wish you to show me the linen room. We have not ventured there before."

Mrs. Dobbs scrambled to her feet. "But, madam, it isn't necessary. You see one linen closet, you see them all!"

"Still, I intend to observe it."

"As you wish," the housekeeper said rather tightly.

They exited the morning room and climbed the stairs to the second floor, turning down the hall of the rear ell. Several servants, standing about, hastened to leap through the door to the back stairs. Tabby lifted an eyebrow and glanced at Mrs. Dobbs.

"Do consider, my lady, that employees must take respite once in a while," she explained.

Ha, Tabby thought. They were dallying. But if the housekeeper had taken Tabby's words to heart, that sort of thing would soon be remedied.

They entered the linen room. As Mrs. Dobbs said, it looked similar to the Kinsdale alcove, but it was a great deal larger. She was pleased to see that it was very neat, with bedding, toweling, extra pillows, feather beds, and tablecloths and napkins all arranged in order on the many shelves. Lifting the lid of a barrel, Tabby saw that it was filled with feathers for replumping stuffed items. A trunk contained quilt scraps and partially constructed quilts. She raised the lid of a very huge chest. Within was a bundle of miscellaneous sheets, comforters, and pillowcases.

"What is this?" she asked.

"Oh, those are worn-out articles. We cut them for rags, give them to staff, or donate them to charities," Mrs. Dobbs said offhandedly. "They are nothing to be concerned about."

As she spoke, the door opened and a young maid entered, dipping dumbfoundly into a hasty curtsy.

"This is Meg. She's the linen maid," Mrs. Dobbs introduced.

Tabby smiled, but her mind instantly registered such a position as nonessential. At the Kinsdale residence, the single laundry maid also managed the linens and did the ironing and mending, too. It was a full-time job, but the girl was not overworked.

"Mrs. Dobbs is acquainting me with the running of Maxfield House, Meg," she said. "Will you describe your job to me?"

"Yes'm." She eyed Tabby nervously. "I take the things and put 'em on the shelves where they belong."

"What about mending?" she asked.

"Oh, there ain't none of that."

"There isn't?" Tabby inquired in wonderment. "And what of the ironing? I can see that these goods are very nicely pressed."

"The ironing maids does that, ma'am." Meg shuffled from foot to foot. "I just do what I'm told."

"I'm sure you do," she said to put the girl at ease. She did as she was asked, and no one had told her to do anything else. Well, Meg could keep her job, but her duties would be expanded.

Tabby pulled a pillowcase from the chest of discards. There was a small tear along the seam. "Why is this here?"

Mrs. Dobbs gazed at her as if she'd lost her senses. "Why, it's damaged, my lady."

"But it's practically new!"

The housekeeper shook her head and clicked her tongue. "The shoddy workmanship these days."

"But why is it tossed among the scraps?" Tabby frowned, pulling out a sheet that was barely marred by a very small rend. "And why is this here?"

"It's torn, Lady Maxfield." Mrs. Dobbs gaped at her as if she had lost her mind. "It's ruined."

"It can be mended! I can scarcely believe this! I have never seen such waste!" In a frenzy she pulled piece after piece from the container, only to find them in a similar state as the first two. "Meg, fetch your needle and thread."

"I ain't got one," she sniveled.

"Mrs. Dobbs," Tabby ordered, "see that she gets the wherewithal to repair these materials."

"But I can't sew!" Meg wailed. Dropping to her knees, she twisted Tabby's skirt hem through her fingers. "Don't fire me, my lady! I'll learn. Somehow I'll learn!"

Tabby felt miserable. Dismissing people was an unhappy business. She'd honestly hoped that she could put it off on Mrs. Dobbs, but evidently she would have to lower the ax herself, in some cases. But she couldn't discharge poor, pleading Meg. Actually, one of the ironing maids (they clearly were plural!) would have to go.

"Stand up, Meg," she directed. "If you are willing to learn, you will not lose your job."

"I'll do it!" Meg cried.

"Good! Mrs. Dobbs, I require one of the ironing maids to teach Meg how to press these linens. *And* a seamstress can teach her to mend them."

The housekeeper chewed her upper lip. "My lady, your garments are attended by Evans; his lordship's are mended by his valet. We have no seamstress on staff."

That was amazing. Tabby had estimated that they had a surplus of them, too.

"Evans and Morton are far too busy to teach this girl to sew," went on the housekeeper.

Tabby could have debated that, but she let the statement stand. "Then I shall teach her."

"*You,* my lady?"

"The Kinsdale women are noted for their needlework," Tabby said proudly.

"But *mending,* Lady Maxfield?" Mrs. Dobbs gasped.

"It won't be the first time." Tabby selected several pieces from the batch of so-called ruined linens. "If you will be so good as to fetch my workbasket from my chamber, Mrs. Dobbs, we shall commence immediately."

Mrs. Dobbs still stood in place, gawking at her.

"My workbasket?" she prompted.

The housekeeper's expression of amazement turned to one of disapproval.

"Please do as I ask," Tabby stressed, meeting Mrs. Dobbs' ogle with a set jaw of determination. "Meg and I will be in the morning room. Come, Meg."

She swept from the linen room to leave Mrs. Dobbs stewing in her own juices. Descending the stairs with the linen maid respectfully trodding behind her, she reflected upon the morning's work. She was certain she'd made her position clear. Only time would tell if the housekeeper would comply. And if she refused? Tabby gritted her teeth. She would have to dismiss Mrs. Dobbs as well and find someone who *would* carry out her wishes. Maxfield House would run properly, if she had to fire everyone and start over again.

I will take charge, she vowed to herself. *Neither Mrs. Dobbs nor anyone else will get the best of me!*

For the next few days, Tabby tutored Meg on the fine art of mending. Accomplishment was slow. Though the girl showed promise, it was difficult for her to catch up with skills Tabby had accumulated since she was a little girl. When it seemed that they would never reach the bottom of the chest of torn linens, she decided to take matters into her own hands. Instead of doing pretty work while she and Thomas relaxed before a fire in the evenings, she brought a supply of pillowcases.

"What are you doing?" her husband asked one day.

"Mending," Tabby replied. "I found a great stock of linens which needed repair. The linen maid did not know how to sew."

"Well, I don't know what a linen maid is, or what she is supposed to do, but I assume that ours was deficient?"

Tabby nodded vigorously. "I am teaching her."

"Wouldn't you rather hire someone to do it?" He grinned. "I imagine you'd rather be doing your fancy work than common sewing like this."

"Of course, but it needs to be done. And it would not be efficient to hire someone to school Meg. That would defeat the purpose of logical economy."

He laughed. "We wouldn't want to be uneconomical!"

"Certainly not!" she agreed, glad that he recognized the need to save money.

It was about time that he acknowledged such a practice. The day before, he had brought home a costly diamond pendant for her. To be polite, she'd pretended enthusiasm, but the time was fast approaching when she would be forced outright to deplore his gifts in order to make him take a long, hard look at such matters. Now that he seemed to be getting the idea of economizing, she hoped she would not have to do that.

Bolstered by this spark of approval, Tabby set out the following day to visit the laundry and ironing area. Arriving there without even the notice of Mrs. Dobbs, she thoroughly surprised the staff. The huge wash boilers were empty and dry, and there were no fabrics hanging on the drying racks. The sadirons were cold and stacked on a countertop. The maids themselves were sitting on the broad windowsills, eating apples.

"What is this?" Tabby cried. "It isn't lunchtime."

The servants leapt up, their cheeks crimson. One, in particular, seemed anxious to hide her face from her mistress. She was unsuccessful.

"Betsy?" Tabby sputtered. "What are you doing here?"

The one-time assistant of her personal maid wrung her hands and bowed her head. "Miz Dobbs put me to work here, my lady. She said there was plenty of work in the laundry, and I'm doin' a good job, too!"

"It doesn't look like the batch of you are doing any job whatsoever," she accused.

"We're waitin' for the chambermaids to bring down the linens," one of Betsy's coworkers explained.

"Well then, shouldn't you be heating the water in preparation?"

"Oh, no, my lady! First, you put in the things. Then you add water and soap and set them over the fire."

"I have never heard anything so ridiculous!" Tabby said severely. "That procedure allows for nothing but idleness.

Get busy and put water on to boil! Betsy, you come with me."

"My lady, I didn't do nothing wrong! Mrs. Dobbs said she could use an extra pair of hands in the laundry, so I asked if I could do it."

"I am truly sorry, Betsy, but it seems to me that there are already too many hands in the laundry." Tabby sailed upstairs with the whimpering maid in her wake, and she barely paused to rap on the housekeeper's office door before opening it.

Mrs. Dobbs and French, the butler, started, setting aside cups of tea.

Tabby frowned her displeasure. "I dismissed this girl, and now I find her still employed."

Betsy noisily broke into tears. "What'll happen to me? Oh, dear Lord, help me!"

French fled.

"Lord, look down on me from Heaven," Betsy moaned.

"Goodness, Betsy," said Tabby, "I'm not intending to *murder* you."

"What'll I do without a job? London eats up girls like me!"

"Please, Lady Maxfield," Mrs. Dobbs interjected. "Do sit down and allow me to handle this."

"There are too many maids in this house," Tabby warned.

"Yes, yes. Never fear. I won't waste precious money on wages." She hustled Betsy from the room and, when they were both outside, carefully closed the door.

"Betsy," the housekeeper whispered, "stop your sniveling. This is what you must do."

The maid wiped her eyes with the hem of her apron and hopefully glanced at Mrs. Dobbs.

"I will give you money for transportation to take you back to the country, to Maxfield Hall. You will carry a letter from me to the steward, explaining what has happened and requesting him to hire you there."

Betsy sniffled. "You will? And he will?"

"Indeed so," she assured. "Why, your people have always worked for the family."

"What'll I do when *she* comes there?"

"You'll simply stay out of her sight. Everyone will assist you."

Betsy sighed deeply. "I tried to make her like me."

"It isn't that she dislikes you." Mrs. Dobbs patted her cheek. "Our new marchioness has some sort of bee in her bonnet to save money. I have no earthly idea why! But she'll come round in time. Now go pack your bags."

When the housekeeper returned, Tabby had calmed, but she was still adamant. "I feel terribly sorry for Betsy and the others, but we cannot hire everyone we pity. That goes beyond compassion."

"Yes, my lady," Mrs. Dobbs said shortly.

"You *have* been reducing staff, haven't you?" she quizzed.

The other woman lowered her gaze. "I . . . I have been reviewing the situation."

Tabby lost her patience. The housekeeper had not dismissed one excess employee. She fixed her hands on her hips.

"Mrs. Dobbs, you are driving me to my wit's end. I expect to see reductions, and I expect to see them quickly. You may start with the laundry. Furthermore, I intend to pry into every aspect of domestic work at this house. I had best witness efficiency."

"Yes, my lady, yes! I shall act speedily!"

As Tabby left the housekeeper's domain, she thought she heard a soft giggle, but she didn't wish to return to find out. Let Dobbs laugh all she wished. That mutineer would soon find out that Tabby meant what she said.

Entering the main hall, she intercepted Thomas as he

came in from an outing. Thoughts of domestic matters bolted from her mind. She smiled happily.

"Tabitha!" he said with delight. "I'm glad you're right here. I have a surprise for you."

Oh, no, she thought, *another expenditure.*

He took her arm and led her out onto the front stoop. Along with Thomas's mount, grooms were holding two other sleek horses. She realized he'd been to Tattersall's.

"What do you think of her, Tabitha? The gray mare." He was almost boyish in his enthusiasm.

As usual, Tabby couldn't help mentally calculating the price. The horse was beautiful, but she could have continued to ride Maud. She forced a smile.

"She is splendid, Thomas," she said in a lackluster voice.

His excitement palled. "You don't like her."

"No! It isn't that!" she tried to amend, despising the necessity of drowning his elation. "I think she is perfectly divine. I was only concerned with her price and the cost of her upkeep. I wondered if my riding ability merited such an expenditure."

"It's a mere trifle," he surmised.

"But . . ."

"Never mind, Tabitha. The mare is top drawer. I'm sure I can easily find a buyer." Turning on his heel, he returned to the house.

"Thomas!" she cried, hurrying after him. "I adore the horse! It's just that . . ."

He whirled. "Do spare me your pretense, madam."

She halted, unhappy and flustered. "It isn't . . ."

He strode into the library and slammed the door.

She was suddenly aware of being ogled by French and one of his footmen. *Drat it all!* Why must there be witnesses to this unfortunate event?

"Oh, dear," she murmured, her eyes hazing with tears. Lifting the hem of her skirt, she dashed up the stairs to her chamber.

* * *

"Damn!" Thomas swore and crossed the room to his liquor cabinet, pouring himself a great draft of brandy. What could he do to please his wife? The situation was beyond his comprehension.

She didn't like flowers. She'd made that obvious.

She didn't want fashionable clothes. She'd made that plain when she appeared to suffer greatly under Cecile's ministrations. Didn't she realize that, as his marchioness, she had a certain appearance to uphold? That damn Frederick Gates had made her a laughingstock at the gentlemen's clubs, because of that ugly riding habit. And it had reflected back on Thomas.

She had hated that diamond pendant that had cost him so dearly. In his desk drawer, he had matching earrings, but he was afraid to present them to her for fear of rejection. Bloody damn!

Now she obviously disliked the mare. Maybe she didn't like gray. Maybe she didn't like female equines. Maybe she didn't even like to ride and was doing it only to please Charlotte. Who knew? She was unlike any woman he'd ever met!

With a short sigh that was almost a snort, he drained his glass and refilled it. In essence, she seemed to loathe every gift he had given her. She'd abhorred them so much that she couldn't even hide her displeasure. His taste and hers must be poles apart.

Feeling totally defeated, he sat down at his desk. His gaze fell, at once, on a report from his man of business. His investments on the Exchange had reaped royal rewards. What difference did that make? Who cared for great wealth if he couldn't use it to please the woman he loved? Angrily, he swept the papers onto the floor.

The irate gesture somewhat soothed his shattered feelings. At the same time, he realized that wrath would not solve his enigma. Somehow he must discover *something* she liked. Something besides mending that cursed, torn-up bedding! Who the hell wanted to do tiresome tasks like that?

He searched his brain. She appeared to set great store in domestic matters. Perhaps she would like a treasure for the house . . . like a fine painting or an exquisite porcelain.

His spirits revived. That was what he'd try. This very afternoon, he'd make a tour of the galleries and find such a rarity.

Nodding to himself, he rose from his chair and went to the bellpull to ring for French. He'd have his lunch served here. Alone. Although he felt encouraged about the situation with his wife, he still wasn't in complete charity with her as yet.

Looking dawn the long table to the empty place at its head, Tabby had never been so miserable. Oh, why hadn't she been able to conjure up more pleasure when she'd seen the gray mare? She had hurt Thomas dreadfully, and she didn't know what to do about it. He had bought her just too many expensive gifts. She dearly loved each one of them, but she couldn't bear to encourage him to buy more. Oh, the money that he spent! They'd end up in debtor's prison.

Ever since she had been a little girl old enough to wish for toys, she had coveted the fine French dolls that the squire's daughters received each year for Christmas. Tabby had one tiny china doll, not nearly so beautiful as theirs, and each Christmas, she received new clothes for it. She realized now that her mother had designed the fashions. They were perfectly exquisite, but to Tabby, they didn't hold a candle to the European toys. So the holidays always brought disappointment.

When she was old enough, her mama had explained that they were poor, and then she understood why she did not receive the kind of gifts her friends acquired. Almost immediately, Mrs. Kinsdale had begun to teach her how to stretch a guinea as far as it would go. They made a game of it, reporting economic coups and savoring their triumphs. Now . . . Tabby sighed. Why didn't everyone view waste and unnecessary spending as the colossal enemy it was? Why couldn't Thomas . . . ?

Unshed tears prickled her eyes. Why couldn't he simply tell her he loved her? He didn't have to prove it by buying expensive things.

She pushed her untouched plate away and felt bad for wasting food as well. There was too huge a surfeit of edibles at Maxfield House. She would have to address that topic next.

But oh, Thomas! He was so angry. He'd never acted this way before.

She put down her napkin and rose from the lonely table. She must think of something to regain his favor! The whole predicament made her veritably nauseous. Leaving the dining room, she proceeded to the garden in the rear of the house. Perhaps the fresh air would ease her malady and chase the cobwebs from her brain so that she could come up with a remedy for this unhappy occasion.

Mrs. Dobbs and Mr. French stole time in the middle of the afternoon to sip a glass of sherry in his office. They had not felt the need for such a conference since the eve of his lordship's arrival home with his bride. Now they had a problem with that very lady. Well, French had not had a direct dilemma as yet, but they both recognized that it was only a matter of time until the marchioness attacked his domain. Moreover, when his lordship was overset, *everyone* had a problem.

"I have dismissed staff today." Mrs. Dobbs rolled her eyes heavenward. "To risk a pun, let us say that she cleaned up the laundry. I wonder which sphere in the household is next."

Mr. French twitched his nose. "Such a sad business, and such a perilous one, if she continues these reductions. What will we do?"

"I'll resign before I'm demoted to ironing sheets!"

"I do not blame you. That would certainly be far beneath your status. She'll have to do it herself!"

They laughed, but there was a grimness about their mirth.

"What will she do to me?" French wondered morosely.

"Fire footmen," Mrs. Dobbs predicted. "Instruct your people to behave busily whenever she is nearby."

"But she must know that footmen often must stand in waiting, ready to respond instantly to a summons."

"One would think she'd be aware of that, but I would put nothing past her. Frankly, she just does not know how a grand house is run." She clicked her tongue. "Each member of this staff is essential. In addition, nearly all are practically part of the family! They've been serving the Maxfields for generations."

"So what shall we do about it? Go to his lordship?" He bit his lip. "I'd hate to be forced to do that."

"Maybe she'll come to her senses in time, especially with his lordship's birthday approaching."

French shuddered. "I'd forgotten that."

"Not I," moaned the housekeeper. "With further reductions in staff, that annual fete will be more of a challenge than I want to face!"

"What did you do about the dismissed staff?"

"Luckily, they were all from the country, so I sent them home to be employed at Maxfield Hall." Mrs. Dobbs lifted a shoulder with dismay. "Maybe she'll cease this nonsense soon. It could be that she's merely testing her authority as the new mistress."

"Let us hope," he said fervently.

Mrs. Dobbs finished her wine and rose. Lady Maxfield was spending much of the afternoon in the garden. But she could come in at any moment and recommence her meddling in the domestic realm. The housekeeper did not want to appear inactive. Lady Maxfield might take a notion to dismiss her and assume the role herself!

Though the shadows had grown long and the brilliant fall day was ending, Tabby was still in the garden when Thomas returned home. She hadn't thought of a thing to say to repair his hurt feelings. When she heard the masterful step that could not belong to a servant, she nearly panicked.

"Tabitha?"

"Here," she squeaked, rising.

He turned through the trellis entrance of the rose bower, where she had cloistered herself. "Darling Tabitha."

Her heart soaring, she ran to him. "Oh, Thomas, I am so . . . so *dreadfully* sorry!"

He caught her in his arms and drew her close, raining kisses on the top of her head.

"I do love the mare! Really I do!" The words came in a rush. All thoughts of economy and inspiring him to greater saving flew from her mind. Unfortunately, she did adore the horse, and she wanted her. She would just cut the household budget further to make up for it.

"Are you certain?" he queried. "Be honest, love. I don't wish to give you a gift you abhor."

She tilted her chin to be kissed. "I'm positive."

He lowered his lips to hers, gently at first, and then with more ardor. Tabby savored each sweet moment until he lifted his head and looked down at her, his eyes dark with feeling.

"Oh, Thomas, let us never, *ever*, have harsh words between us."

He brushed a soft wispy curl from her cheek and grinned. "An admirable plan, my darling. But if we fail in this vow, let us promise to rectify matters in just such a pleasurable way as this."

Tabby, ready to take the initiative and claim his mouth, happened to look up at the house and saw the ample form of Mrs. Dobbs dart away from a window. She stepped back. "I fear we are observed."

Thomas turned and glanced quickly. "Servants! I don't know what we would do without every one of them, but they certainly are an inconvenience at times."

She would show him just how well they could manage without every one! And he would be ever so happy at the money she saved. She slipped her arm through his. "My bower is not so secluded as I thought, but come, can we look at my new horse now?"

"Of course." He led her from the rose bower through the garden to an iron gate.

"I've never been back here," she mused interestedly.

"There is no reason for you to go to the mews. If you wish to ride, simply tell me or French. A groom will bring the mare round." He disengaged the latch and showed her into an alleyway. The tidy brick stable and small courtyard lay beyond.

"I have never had a horse of my own," Tabby told him as they entered the immaculate building.

"The mare comes highly recommended, but if she does not suit you, we shall find another. She belonged to the wife of a friend of mine who decided she did not want to ride anymore."

"Then I'm sure she'll be fine," Tabby concurred.

Thomas nodded. "You probably want to continue to

ride with Charlotte, but you and I can ride together, too. Would you enjoy that?"

She laughed. "If you vow you will not go too fast."

"I promise."

Seeing their lord and lady enter the mews caused great excitement among the staff. With grooms and stableboys snapping to attention, the coachman and head groom walked forward. "Good afternoon, my lord, madam," the head groom welcomed, bowing deeply.

Thomas and Tabby acknowledged the greeting.

"How may we serve you?" beseeched the coachman.

"My lady desires to see her new mare," the marquess told them.

"We shall fetch her immediately." The head groom turned to his row of assistants.

"No, don't bother," Tabby told him. "I can just look at her in her stall."

"If you please to follow me, madam." He spun smartly and strode toward the rear of the line of stalls.

Tabby trailed him, deeply breathing the combined aromas of fresh hay, saddle soap, and horseflesh. It was a new experience. Having had little to do with horses, she had seldom been in a stable.

"Everything is so clean," she murmured to her husband.

"It had better be," he answered. "I employ a large staff to keep it so."

As usual, she wondered if all these people were truly necessary. If they worked no harder than the household staff, it would take two of them to accomplish one task. The mews, however, were beyond her domain. From what she had learned of her husband, she doubted if he would dismiss any of them. She'd best forget it and mind her own matters.

Her new mare was munching hay when they arrived at her stall. She lifted her head, whuffled at them, then went back to her meal. The groom started to put a halter on her, but Tabby waved him away.

"Do not disturb her. I can see her well enough." Tabby smiled at Thomas. "What is her name?"

"They called her Frosty Morning, but you may name her whatever you please."

"That name will be fine. I'll call her Frosty." She stepped in the stall to stroke the mare's silky neck. "Thank you, my lord. I'm certain that we'll become fast friends."

When they returned to the house, Thomas drew her toward the salon. "I have something else for you, something for the house."

Tabby's heart fell to her toes. More largess! Would it never cease?

The marquess was watching her closely as he directed her toward the sofa, upon which sat a framed, scenic painting. "By Constable," he said. "Do you like his works?"

She looked at the rural landscape. The artist's depiction of a mill, stream, and ancient old oaks was as lifelike as any vista she'd ever seen. Constable was much revered, and therefore, his art must be costly. She sighed. Would Thomas never cease to spend money?

"You don't like it," he guessed.

"No!" she protested, recalling how, just this morning, she had hurt his feelings regarding the mare. "It's lovely."

"You look troubled."

"Oh, no. I *do* like it. I am only in a quandary over where to hang it," she fibbed, hurriedly deliberating. "The breakfast room, maybe?"

He eyed her suspiciously. "Are you certain?"

"Well, do you think it would be pleasant in that room?"

"I am speaking of whether or not you care for it."

"Thomas, I positively relish it." She tried to inject delight into her voice. "Please give me your opinion of where it should hang."

"The breakfast room is fine, but if you don't want it . . ."

"I do!" She would be forced to drastically cut staff, but what other choice did she have? First thing in the morning, she would speak with Mrs. Dobbs.

When Tabby came downstairs to breakfast, dressed in her riding togs for a ride with Charlotte, she found Thomas had donned his.

"I thought I'd ride with you ladies, if you do not mind," he informed her. "I'd like to see Frosty in action and make sure she is suitable for you."

"We'll enjoy your company," Tabby said cheerfully, anxious to gain his approval for her newly acquired equestrian skills.

When she filled her plate, she saw that the Constable painting hung over the sideboard. It looked quite pretty there. She paused to admire it.

Thomas noticed her regard. "What do you think, my dear?"

"It's lovely," she assented and joined him at the table, appreciating the fine appearance he presented in his expertly tailored riding coat. She peered down at her food and wished she hadn't helped herself to so large an amount. Her stomach, somewhat queasy yesterday, had not righted itself. She merely picked at her meal.

"Are you ill?" her husband inquired.

Why did he scrutinize her so closely? Or were her feelings so plainly written on her face? She sighed.

"I am in excellent health." She speedily changed the subject. "Will you be satisfied with a ride so tame as a jaunt in the park?"

"Any time spent with you is enjoyable."

She lightly blushed. "I could say the very same thing."

He grinned. "You *are* happy, my love?"

"Ecstatically so," she laughed, nodding to a footman to

remove her plate. She would be even more joyful if she could further trim the budget.

"Splendid." He, too, laid aside his napkin. "Remember what I told your family?"

"What is that?"

"I said that I fully intended to spoil you dreadfully. I am determined to carry that out." He drained his cup and signaled for more. "I want you to have everything in the world."

A rising lump in her throat threatened to strangle her. She slowly shook her head. "I already have all I've ever dreamed of. You need not think you must continually buy me gifts, Thomas. *You* are enough."

"Prettily said, my darling, but I have yet to know a lady who doesn't wish for trinkets."

"Trinkets? My goodness! The things you have given me are far from that. They are treasures." She smiled sweetly. "And they are already enough to last a lifetime."

"Humor me, won't you?" He slipped a hand in his coat and drew forth a small jewelry box.

Oh, no! Tabby felt like wailing.

He opened the case and extended it to her. "They match the pendant."

The earrings glittered in the bright beam of autumn sunlight streaming through the window. Like everything Thomas purchased, they were exquisite. He was spending a fortune!

Tabby burst into tears.

"My darling!" Thomas gathered her into his arms. "If the earrings are so repulsive—"

"No! No! They're beautiful," she sobbed. "It's just that I . . . Oh, I cannot explain!"

Thomas pressed his handkerchief into her hand. "Don't cry, love. Tell me what I can do to ease your distress."

Managing to gain control of herself, she blew mightily

into the cloth. "I don't know what is wrong with me. I do love the earrings."

She lifted one of the drops from its velvet cushion. The rays sparkled through the gem, emitting a rainbow of color. "They are so very beautiful."

"But never as stunning as you," he acclaimed.

"Thank you." She flushed, warm with anxiety. Bending her head so that he might not see the concern on her brow, she returned the earring to its box and closed the lid. Dear heavens, she was going to have to trim the staff to skeleton strength!

"I will save the pendant and earrings for a very special event," she murmured. That occasion might be the day she had to pawn the jewels for enough capital to have him released from debtors' prison.

"Very well, then. Shall we ask for our horses to be brought round? I sent Charlotte a note saying that we would ride by her house when we were ready. Are you sure you feel like going?"

"Yes, just give me a few moments." She stood. "I must confer with Mrs. Dobbs about the day's chores."

"All right. I shall await you in the library."

"Perhaps you'd best put these in the vault." After giving him the jewelry, she scurried from the room.

Mrs. Dobbs was awaiting her for their daily discourse, menus in her hand.

Tabby scanned the paper and dipped her pen in the inkwell to cross off the expensive items. "In the future, we will dine more modestly. Also, there is entirely too much food prepared. It is a waste."

"No, ma'am, not garbage!" Mrs. Dobbs apprised. "The few servants who live in London take the excess home to feed their families."

Tabby frowned. "Do we not pay them enough to take care of such things?"

"Why, yes, but they have grown to expect it."

"They must learn to live within their budget, just like everyone else," she stated.

Mrs. Dobbs lowered her gaze. "Yes, my lady. Is that all?"

"The staff must be cut. I must see . . ." She considered. "I must see a twenty-five percent reduction in the number of servants, both in your bailiwick and in Mr. French's."

"Twenty-five percent!" the housekeeper cried. "Lady Maxfield, it will be impossible to maintain our usual level of service!"

"Mrs. Dobbs, I must disagree," Tabby said in a voice that did not brook dissension. "I see too many idle hands. Now will you so instruct Mr. French, or shall I?"

"I'll do it," she mumbled.

"I appreciate that, for I am in a hurry." Tabby got up. "I expect the two of you to attend to the matter today. We will not prolong the process."

"Yes, madam," she said tightly, "but . . ."

"Yes?"

"Lady Maxfield, if I may speak plainly?"

"You may," Tabby permitted, hesitating.

"Mark my words, you and his lordship will not be pleased with the results," she blurted.

"Mrs. Dobbs, the other servants will simply be required to provide an honest day's work, without lackadaisical lounging around. You and Mr. French will probably have to keep after them at first, but soon all will run smoothly again."

"I am compelled to say that I must disagree," she asserted.

"Well, we'll just see about that. In the meantime, please do it." Tabby turned and left the room, closing the door before she heard the housekeeper's grumble of aggravation.

* * *

Charlotte and Thomas were highly delighted by Frosty Morning's performance, but not nearly so much as Tabby was.

"She is an angel!" she thrilled only moments into their excursion. Frosty's gaits were much smoother than Maud's, and her mouth and sides were decidedly more responsive. Tabby could not have asked for a better mount.

"Tabby is a veritable angel on her back," Charlotte complimented.

"So she is," Thomas agreed. "My dear, I did not dream that you had progressed so rapidly. Perhaps the gray mare is a bit too tame for you."

"No." Tabby shook her head. "I like quiet, fully trained horses. I doubt that I'll ever want to train young animals, like you and Charlotte."

Her husband's restive colt, the one he'd bought when he'd purchased the mare, danced nervously. "It's a great challenge."

"Nevertheless, it is one I shall leave to you." She smiled, appreciative of his skill in sitting so calmly. She probably would have been on the ground by now.

She was silently pleased, however, with Thomas's admiration of her beginning ability. Every time she glanced at him, she found him looking at her. Of course, the expensive riding habit enhanced her appearance, even though it seemed to be a bit tight in the waist. Well, she would soon lose the few pounds she'd gained, now that the plenteous amount of food would be reduced and the meals would become more simplified.

She returned her mind to the ride and saw that Charlotte and Thomas had gotten some distance ahead of her. Touching her heel to Frosty's side, she jogged to catch up. The mare's gait was smooth even at this tempo, delighting her to no end. The horse was perfect. She was superbly worth the loss of some cream puffs.

"Talking about me?" she joked as she intercepted them.

"No, we were speaking of Tom," Charlotte answered, "and his upcoming birthday."

"Oh?" Her ears perked up.

"Ever since Tom has been the marquess, the whole family has gathered to celebrate his birthday at Maxfield House," Charlotte explained. "I hope you are ready to assume the role of hostess."

"Of course!" Tabby said brightly. "I would love to arrange a party."

Charlotte looked pleased. "There are certain traditions to uphold."

"Just advise me what they are."

Thomas grinned. "The only tradition I value is that of my delicious, special cake. I've always had that for my birthday, even before I became marquess."

"Then I shall be sure to instruct the chef," Tabby vowed. "This variety of cake would have been baked before his regime. I assume he has the receipt."

"Oh, yes," Charlotte replied. "When our old family cook died, your chef got all of her recipes."

"Good! Then there should be no problem with that. Tell me more," Tabby implored. "I wish to do everything just right!"

"Of course Mama will come from the country," Charlotte went on, "but you need not worry about that. She is a very easy guest to accommodate. So are the others, except for Aunt Thelma, but don't be concerned about her. It is impossible to please her."

"Mrs. Dobbs is well accustomed to what is expected," Thomas put in. "Leave all the household arrangements to her."

Tabby nodded. Mrs. Dobbs certainly would be a big help, but she planned to put her own finishing touches to everything. She would impress them all as being a worthy wife and marchioness.

"Let us discontinue discussion of the event," Thomas

appealed. "Remember, I shall be another year older and *that* is not so sweet. Shall we canter?"

"Tabitha?" Charlotte queried.

"I am only just learning that pace," she said apologetically to her husband, "but if you are willing to put up with me, I shall try."

"I like putting up with you." He flashed his dimples at her.

"Very well then." Tabby signaled Frosty as Charlotte had taught her, and she was happy that the mare responded so beautifully. Again, she caught Thomas's adoring eye. She laughed with satisfaction. All was going well, and now that the household matters should be getting in order, things would be even better.

Three

Domestic trouble surfaced within days of Tabby's order to cut staff and trim expenses. One morning, when Tabby consulted with the housekeeper about the daily activities, she was surprised to see Jean-Michel, the French chef, stomping along after the woman. His face was stark white, with the exception of scarlet touches high on his cheekbones. Tense muscles rippled along his jaw. His mouth was drawn so taut that one could scarcely discern his lips. Jean-Michel was angry. Very angry.

He backhanded the door shut with a loud slam. "Lady Maxfield!" he boomed, elbowing Mrs. Dobbs out of the way. "I will not take such commands. I will not!"

Tabby gaped. "My goodness, what is wrong?"

"No one will tell Jean-Michel how to cook! No one!" he shouted.

"Mind your manners in front of her ladyship," Mrs. Dobbs scolded.

"Shut up!" he cried. "I am not your underling! I am a law unto myself!"

That was certainly true. Tabby had never seen such a display from an employee. Jean-Michel was an Original.

She scanned her memory to come up with what might have disturbed him. She had sent him a note to inform him to be prepared to make the special birthday cake, but why should that have irritated him? She'd asked him to prepare simplified meals, but that reduction in labor should have pleased him. Something else must have happened.

"What is wrong, Jean-Michel?" she asked. "What is bothering you?"

He clicked his teeth like a vicious dog. "I have come to give warning. If you, my lady, continue to disrupt my kitchen, I shall leave immediately."

Disrupt his kitchen? Tabby lifted a questioning eyebrow. She had made several short visits to that hallowed establishment, but that shouldn't constitute disruption.

"I do not understand," she said.

"These . . . these . . . what do you say? *Economies!* I cannot create my artistry when I am so hampered!" His jaw jutted forward and backward in agitation.

Tabby choked back laughter at his comical facial gesturing, but she was unable to hide the mirth in her dancing eyes.

Jean-Michel saw it and became even angrier. His entire face glowed fiery red. "So you think this is funny, madam?"

"No." She harshly bit her inner lip to gain restraint. "Which of the economies do you dislike?"

"All of them!" he bellowed. "I do not make simple food! I must have the very finest of ingredients!"

"Please calm yourself, Jean-Michel," Tabby soothed, "so that we may rationally discuss this. Do be seated."

Still seething, he dropped unceremoniously into a chair and regaled her with a long, frenzied paragraph in French.

Tabby looked at Mrs. Dobbs for explanation, but the housekeeper merely shook her head.

"Jean-Michel," Tabby stated, "if you wish us to comprehend your disagreement, you must speak English."

"Faugh on the English! I will go home to France, where I am understood and appreciated!"

"Now, Jean-Michel, you must know that we enjoy your creations."

"That is falsehood!" he raved. "If you did, you wouldn't order plain roasted beef!"

"That will be enough!" Mrs. Dobbs cautioned. "You will not speak to the marchioness in such a way, or I will fire you!"

"Do it, you old bag of wind! Just try! *You* are not my boss, and neither is that buffoon, French!"

"Cease this tantrum, Jean-Michel!" Tabby decreed. "Or *I* will dismiss you. You may be disturbed, but I will not have such talk in this house. I believe it would be best if you returned to the kitchen. When you are able to control yourself, you may come back and discuss your complaints with me."

His eyes flashed murderously. "You throw me out?"

"Until you are rational, yes."

"Very well, Lady Maxfield! I'll go!" Jumping to his feet, he tramped from the room.

"Whew," breathed Tabby. "What an exhibit."

"The Gallic temperament, doubled by being a chef. He has always been difficult, refusing to take orders from anyone but his lordship."

Tabby hoped that he wouldn't take his quarrel to Thomas. "Those times are gone. My lord has given me complete authority in domestic affairs."

"Yes, my lady. Of course." Mrs. Dobbs extended a paper. "While we are on the subject of kitchen matters, here is Jean-Michel's menu for today."

Tabby quickly surveyed it, frowning at the elaborate offerings. "He has not paid one bit of attention to my desires." The housekeeper shrugged.

Tabby took her pen and mercilessly crossed off all but the simple dishes. "My chef must not dictate to me, Mrs. Dobbs."

"Please do not blame me, my lady."

"I don't. Not at all! I can verily see what a handful he is." She smiled kindly. "May we continue? I have been anxious to go over the arrangements for our house party. Have you made lists?"

"Yes, madam. I have written down the names of the usual guests and have made sample chamber assignments." Mrs. Dobbs laid the pages on Tabby's desk. "You, of course, must make the final decisions."

Tabby gaped at the long roster. "My, but the house will be filled! Tell me, does anyone ever stay with the duke and duchess?"

"Oh, yes, madam. Usually the couples with children, since Her Grace already has her nursery and playroom set up."

Tabby nodded and pointed to two names. "Is this couple married? They are assigned separate rooms."

Mrs. Dobbs chuckled. "My lord's aunt and uncle intensely dislike each other. If we put them together, the resulting outrage would not be unlike that of Jean-Michel!"

Tabby laughed. "Well, we cannot have that! One malcontent in the house is quite enough, thank you!"

They continued on for an hour, with Mrs. Dobbs providing a lesson in Maxfield genealogy as well as arranging the house for the birthday party. Tabby was overwhelmingly grateful to have the longtime retainer. As Charlotte and Thomas had said, the woman knew just what to expect.

When they were almost finished, there was a soft scratch at the door. A young maid, who Tabby remembered from her visits to the kitchen, entered. She curtsied awkwardly.

"Yes?" Tabby asked.

"There's something awful happened in the kitchen," she murmured, staring at the floor.

"What is it, girl?" Mrs. Dobbs prompted.

"Jean-Michel's gone. Packed up 'is bags and left." She winced. "Said he was goin' back to the Continent."

Tabby's heart fell to her toes. What would they do with

the house party coming? It might take time to find a satisfactory, new chef. But if Jean-Michel refused to follow orders, he was useless. Besides, the servants who'd always assisted him should know enough to prepare the simple meals she requested. Perhaps one of them should be elevated to the role. If there was something they were not sure of, they could follow receipts.

"Who was second to Jean-Michel in the kitchen?" she asked.

"I guess that'd be me," said the maid. "Flo was, but she retired last year."

"All right. What is your name?" Tabby queried.

"Delores, ma'am."

"You shall now be in charge, Delores. Can you read?"

"A little bit, ma'am." She lifted her head so that Tabby could see intelligent blue eyes. "Enough, I guess."

"Here is today's menu." She handed Delores the page. "Read it over and tell me if you have any questions."

The girl perused it. "No, ma'am. It ain't difficult."

"Good'! Then that will be all."

"Yes, my lady." She curtsied and left the room.

"I don't feel very comfortable about Jean-Michel leaving," Mrs. Dobbs ventured. "Not with the party so near."

"We will give Delores a chance," Tabby directed. "If it doesn't work out, we shall go to an employment agency. But I believe it's only fair to promote employees whenever possible."

"Yes, I agree," said the housekeeper. "I worked my way up into this position. It's just that . . . the house party. Ah well, it shall be as you say, Lady Maxfield. Probably all will be well. Maybe I'm overly cautious."

"Let us hope for the best." She laughed lightly. "At least, I shall save a great deal of money. Jean-Michel's wage was outlandish!"

* * *

When Mrs. Dobbs left her conference with Lady Maxfield, she went at once to apprise Mr. French of the latest events. "Jean-Michel has departed in a huff."

The butler paused in his polishing of a gigantic silver epergne. "He quit?"

"That he did. He viewed my lady's economies as a threat to his artistry." She lifted a shoulder. "Personally, I never cared for Jean-Michel, but I do not know what we will do without him, so near to my lord's birthday party. Especially since Lady Maxfield has installed Delores in his place."

"Delores!" He slowly shook his head. "She cannot handle such an affair. You should have advised . . ."

Mrs. Dobbs threw up her hands. "I have *advised* until I was blue in the face, but Lady Maxfield will not listen! She is determined to prove that this house can be run on a shoestring. Our ship is sinking, Mr. French, and when all those houseguests arrive, she will founder for sure."

"You are oh, so right. Jean-Michel's leaving drives the last nail into the coffin." He sighed. "Look at me. I am forced to do *all* the cleaning of the silver. The few footmen I have are polishing the brasses throughout the house. If my lord or lady rings for service, God knows who will answer. And now that the weather is cooling, there will be fires on every hearth. That requires an enormous amount of wood. I myself will be forced to carry some of it. I! The butler!"

"I know," she said grimly. "I will be pitching in to do some of the actual labor of cleaning the chambers. To say nothing of the rest of the house! We will be unable to maintain its current spotlessness."

They both stared unhappily at each other, half starting when a bell rang.

French glanced up at the bell panel on the wall. "It's his lordship in the library."

"You will have to go."

"Yes, and look at my hands." He turned them over and

back, sadly eyeing the black tarnish stains. "I feel like tendering my resignation. If I had not been with the family so long, I would!"

"So would I," Mrs. Dobbs mourned. "I too had best be on my way. We've begun cleaning the guest chambers today, and I must wield my feather duster!"

"Maybe Lady Maxfield will soon come to her senses."

"Maybe, but I doubt that she does it before this party."

Her shoulders slumped, she left the butler's pantry. There had been commiseration enough. Now was the time for action, for her to commence scrubbing hearths like the lowliness of maids.

Thomas looked up in surprise to see none but the butler himself entering the library. "Oh, it's you, French."

"My lord." He bowed. "How may I serve you?"

"Please send one of your footmen to break off that branch outside the window. It's windy, and the limb is rattling the glass in a most distracting manner."

"At once, sir." He moved to depart.

"And also, French?" Thomas halted him.

"My lord?"

"Do dispatch a footman to bring wood and stoke up the fire. It's rather chilly today, isn't it?" he asked.

"Not for me, my lord." He shrugged. "I am too busy to become cold."

Thomas smiled. "I suppose everyone is getting ready for the party."

"Indeed, sir."

"I am looking forward to the gathering. It will be good to see all my relatives again," he said cheerfully, "although I imagine it creates a great deal of work for the staff."

"Oh, yes. Yes, it does." French studied his feet. "My lord, there is a problem. We . . ."

"Yes?" Thomas urged.

The butler chewed his lip as if seriously debating his reply. "Never mind, my lord. It is nothing that I cannot work out."

That was odd. French certainly had something on his mind, but he couldn't bring himself to discuss it. Furthermore, Thomas probably couldn't do anything about it anyway.

"Very well, French, but do let me know if there is anything I can do to solve your dilemma."

"Yes, my lord." He quietly departed.

Thomas thought no more of it until the butler returned with an armload of firewood, placed it neatly on the hearth, and bent to stoke the fire. The marquess was amazed. In all the years he had known French, the butler had never stooped to such a demeaning role.

Thomas was doubly bewildered when he looked out the window and saw French on a ladder sawing away at the offending branch. Were the footmen ill? Was there some sort of epidemic decimating the staff?

When Thomas went to the dining room for lunch, French was present as usual, but he had no footmen to aid him. As a result, the butler dashed back and forth to the kitchen, fetching bowls and platters of food himself. The marquess couldn't imagine what was going on.

"Tabitha?" he asked when the butler had raced from the room to fetch a different wine that Thomas had requested. "What is afoot? Are the footmen ill? French seems to be running this house single-handedly."

"I do not know," she said simply.

"I wouldn't say it in front of him, but he is too old to do such flying about." He frowned. "I wondered if there was illness among the servants."

"I don't think so." Tabitha considered. "I earlier witnessed several footmen polishing the brasses. Perhaps French has them busy elsewhere, preparing for the party."

"I've never seen them too busy to serve." Thomas

dropped the subject at the butler's return and began picking at his meal.

The food wasn't up to its usual quality either. The center of the luncheon was individual chicken pie, and it was a disaster. The chunks of fowl were rather undercooked, and the crust was heavy and soggy. Thomas took several bites of his and set it aside, concentrating on the fruit, which was good, and the bread, which was burnt on the bottom.

"It isn't good, is it?" his wife fretted.

"I've had better. Jean-Michel must be off his stride."

Tabby opened her mouth as if to explain, then apparently thought better of it and returned to stirring her nearly inedible chicken pie. "I am not hungry anyway. My stomach is somewhat unsettled."

As time went by, Thomas said no more, deciding that an illness must be spreading throughout the house. Service had become poor; the food improved, though not up to Jean-Michel's usual standard; and his wife seemed frequently unhinged and turned down all riding invitations. He didn't prod her. She was likely concerned with preparing for her first house party.

As the day approached, Thomas grew very concerned with the looming entertainment. His well-oiled household had become outright slovenly. Tabitha went around with her brow knitted in worry, and when they retired to bed for the night, she quickly, fell asleep exhausted with no response to his caresses. He did not question her for fear of having his head snapped off. Something was very, very wrong, but he could only wait until she came to him for assistance. He began spending time at his club, both for jovial company and to get a good meal. If indeed his wife noticed, she said nothing about his absence.

Tabby was glad that Thomas was seeking his club. Without his presence, she was much more free to engage in assisting the chambermaids in their frantic cleaning. It was tiring work, truly sheer drudgery, and nothing like she'd experienced at home. Maxfield House was huge and filled with beautiful things, all of which needed monstrous care. She, Mr. French, Mrs. Dobbs, and their minions could scarcely keep up with the normal daily tasks, let alone prepare for a house party, but each day they did seem somehow to gain a greater foothold. Tabby knew in her heart, however, that she had been wrong. She had cut too many corners, caused too many servants to be dismissed, and oversimplified the food. She was in the midst of a disaster, and there was no one to blame but herself.

It was too late to hire more employees. There wasn't time to install them properly. She could only work harder herself, and such slavery was taking its toll. She was tired all the time, and her stomach continually revolted. Could matters be any worse?

They could. One morning, Delores requested an interview. Tabby regarded the new cook with trepidation.

"I've got trouble, my lady," she began.

Haven't we all? Tabby felt like snapping, but she held her frazzled temper. "Can I help?"

"I don't know, ma'am. That Jean-Michel took all the receipts with him when he left."

Tabby's heart sank to her toes, but she was quickly cheered by a new idea. She would throw herself on her mother's mercy, briefly trade Delores for Molly, the Kinsdale cook, and dine well again. After the party, she would address the problem. With relief, she suggested the revelation to Delores.

"That'll be fine, my lady. One kitchen's same as the other, I guess. Really, I'm glad not to have these worries." The lines relaxed in the girl's face and she looked her age again.

"I shall call on my mother at once," Tabby vowed.

"Thankee, Lady Maxfield." Delores curtsied deeply. "I

was afraid I'd have to try to figger out how to make that cake his lordship likes."

Oh, God. Tabby had forgotten all about that special confection. "Jean-Michel took *all* the receipts?"

"Yes'm, and to my way of lookin', they wasn't his property. Some of 'em were real old. They'd been in the family for a long time."

Tears sprang to Tabby's eyes.

"Don't fret, my lady." Delores actually put a comforting hand on her shoulder. "It can't be too hard for an experienced cook. It's just a pound cake, all buttery and full of eggs."

Tabby gave a mighty snuffle. "Then why is it so special?"

"Must be the lemon," Delores guessed.

"Lemon?" Tabby cried. "I've never eaten lemon pound cake."

"It's real good, ma'am," she said cheerfully.

"Yes, I imagine it is, but . . ." Tabby burst into tears.

"My lady!" the girl wailed. "It ain't so bad!"

"Everything's wrong! Oh, I have caused such a muddle!" she wept. "Thomas will hate me!"

"No, he won't, my lady." Delores awkwardly patted her shoulder. "Everyone says he's crazy over you."

"No longer! I know all will fail, and I shall appear a numskull in front of his entire family. Oh, what shall I do?" She folded her arms on her desk, laid her head on them, and sobbed.

Tabby wept for a long time, with Delores sympathetically standing in waiting and rubbing her back.

"Shall I send for your abigail, ma'am?" Delores finally cooed.

"No." Tabby drew herself together and sniffled, removing a handkerchief from her reticule. "I must begin solving this problem. Have French send for the carriage. I will go, at once, to my mother."

Surely, Mrs. Kinsdale could help. Her mother was never at a loss on what to do. She would contrive some solution.

Hurriedly dressing for visiting, Tabby was ready to hasten to the carriage as soon as it appeared. In moments, she arrived at her parents' house. Mournfully, she entered, pouring out the story, almost before she and her mother had seated themselves.

"Of course, I shall lend Molly," Mrs. Kinsdale agreed. "That should go a long way toward solving the dilemma. Do you want chambermaids, too?"

"I believe we can manage without, but what shall I do about the cake?"

"Molly knows how to make a basic pound cake. You will merely have to experiment with adding lemon juice."

"But I don't even know how it is supposed to taste!" Tabby moaned.

"Your servants should know. Have them taste samples and . . . Aha!" she cried. "I have the perfect remedy!"

"Do tell," Tabby begged anxiously.

"You will go to Lord Maxfield's sister. Tell her that your chef left you in a lurch and implore her to help with the tasting!"

Tabby considered. "What if she tells Thomas? I can't bear up under his questioning."

"Swear her to secrecy. Explain that you do not wish to cause him concern on his birthday." Mrs. Kinsdale leaned forward to clasp her daughter's hands. "I feel sure that she'll understand. She seems to care a great deal about him."

"Very well. I'll do it." She groaned. "Oh, Mama, I have made such a tangle of everything."

"Frankly, my dear, you look terrible. You must get more rest." Mrs. Kinsdale frowned. "Promise me that you will."

"How can I? I have only a few days before guests will arrive." Tears again prickled her eyes, but Tabby fought successfully against weeping. "After this is concluded, I shall hire more help and take a good, long rest."

Her mother narrowed her eyes and painstakingly surveyed her. "You are not in an interesting condition, are you?"

"No," Tabby said miserably. "I am merely tired."

"If you say so," Mrs. Kinsdale said doubtfully, "but I am not so certain. You have a particular look about you. . . . Ah, there's no time to think of that now. First, we shall rise to *this* occasion."

"Yes, Mama." Standing, Tabby hugged her tightly. "I'd best return to my chaos."

Mrs. Kinsdale accompanied her to the door. "I shall immediately dispatch Molly, and I don't need Delores. Let her stay on as Molly's assistant. We shall get along. I sometimes think your father does not know what he eats anyway. Especially if he is deep in the midst of a study."

"Thank you. What would I do without you?" Tabby kissed her cheek.

"You would contrive. Didn't I teach you to be inventive?"

Tabby nodded. "But everything seemed to come at me from all directions. Now I feel much relieved."

"All will be well," her mother said confidently. "I know it will!"

Tabby certainly hoped so. Thomas's family would stringently judge her. She must not fail.

On her way home, she stopped by Charlotte's and gained her compassion and assistance. When she reached Maxfield House, her troubles seemed greatly lessened. She was ready to rise to the challenge.

It was well that she was. Thomas was waiting for her. In his hand was a jewelry box.

Tabby felt like crying again, but forcing a smile, she lifted the lid. In it was a diamond bracelet to go with her pendant and earrings. She peered at it, too jaded to react.

"Thank you," she woodenly stated.

"I thought you would enjoy wearing the full set on the night of the party," he remarked.

"Oh, yes." The glittering jewels grew blurry. Tabby crumpled to the floor in a dead faint.

"I do not need a doctor," Tabby proclaimed, looking up at Thomas from the sofa. "I shall be fine."

Frowning, he bathed her cheeks with a cool washcloth. "By the lack of smelling salts in this house, I must infer that you are not in the habit of fainting, my love."

"I am merely up in the boughs about the house party," she shrugged off. "I don't need a fuss."

Thomas deepened his scowl. He knew that the weaker sex was subject to such frailties, but his marvelous wife had never given any indication that she was so prone. He was worried, almost to the point of being fearful for her.

"Darling, please allow me to call in a professional," he implored. "You should not diagnose yourself. After all, it has seemed like many of the servants have been afflicted recently. Some of them still must be under the weather, for I have not seen them return to work."

"No, I shall be all right." She weakly sat up, then clapped a hand over her mouth, swallowing several times.

"Darling . . ."

She pretended to giggle. "My stomach has been stirred up by the incident. In a moment, the sickness will pass."

"Dammit!" He had to convince her to seek aid! "Tabitha, do not expect me to stand by and watch you grow sicker and sicker. I am going to send for the doctor."

"No!" Tears shone in her eyes. "All I need is some fresh air and a bit of rest. I shall go to the garden."

"Not alone, you won't." He stood and swept her up in his arms.

"Thomas! You will injure your back!" she protested.

"Be still, love. You are light as a feather."

Her hovering abigail rushed in front of them to open the doors. Once outside, he dismissed her. "You may wait upon Lady Maxfield in her room. I shall bring her there shortly."

She dipped a curtsy and left.

"Thomas, you need not send me to bed." Tabby gazed up at him, her blue eyes wide with pleading. "I have much to do today."

"I think not. You will have your fresh air, and then you will go to bed. *Or* I will send for the doctor." He was adamant, and he would remain so. She would dodge him no further.

"All right," she murmured, "but . . ."

"No buts."

"Thomas, our guests will arrive in just a few days!" she wailed.

"Let them. The staff can handle matters." He sat down on a stone bench and gathered her comfortably in his lap. "You will rest, if I have to stand over you."

"Very well," she sighed, and promptly fell asleep, her head sweetly lolling on his shoulder.

When Thomas was certain she was napping heavily, he carried her up to her room.

"Take good care of her, Evans," he instructed her abigail. "I want her to doze for the rest of the day. If she tries to get up, send for me."

"Yes, my lord." She affectionately gazed at her charge. "Poor lady. She will not take care of herself."

"That's correct. I have another idea, Evans. Do you have some laudanum?"

"No, my lord. My lady never takes medicine."

"Then send a footman to purchase some. When Lady Maxfield awakens, give her tea laced with laudanum. That will keep her in bed." He drew a hand across his brow. "She must stay in bed."

"Yes, my lord. I will see to everything," she vowed. "You need not worry."

"But you know I will. If anything happened to her . . ." He left with the sentence unfinished. If anything happened to Tabitha, life would not be worth living. She filled a gaping void that he hadn't known existed. He would be empty without her.

Tabby arose well rested from a very long sleep. According to Evans, she had reposed a day and a half. The thought of it made her nearly panic, but she hid it well. If Thomas saw her harried, he might impose more respite. She certainly didn't have time for that! The date of the guests' arrival was fast approaching.

From the delicious taste of her breakfast, served to her on a tray, she realized that Molly was in command of the kitchen. She hoped the elderly Kinsdale cook would pass on her wealth of knowledge to Delores. It would be nice (and cheaper!) to employ the girl as chef rather than to find another.

After eating, Tabby got up, donned a worn housedress, and went on a survey of the guest chambers. Although there were several still to be cleaned, things seemed to be coming together quite well. She was surprised to pass Daphne, a Kinsdale maid, in the hall.

"Good morning, Miss Tabby, uh, Lady Maxfield."

"Daphne! What are you doing here?"

"Miz Kinsdale sent me, Miss . . ." She grinned.

"How kind of her. Are you getting along all right?" Tabby felt a profound sense of relief. Her mother had taken up the reins. All would be well.

She descended the stairs and went immediately to the kitchen. The room was enveloped in a frenzy of activity, much of it centered around the huge worktable where Molly wielded a spoon in a large bowl. Mr. French, Mrs.

Dobbs, and several servants, also with spoons, stood nearby.

"Good morning, Miss Tabby." Molly squeezed a lemon into her mixture and stirred. "All right, everybody. Taste it."

They crowded round, dipping their spoons in the batter.

"How about it?" Molly bellowed.

"Very good."

"Almost."

"Maybe when it's baked."

"Well, we'll just bake this up," the old cook decided. "Want to take a taste, Miss Tabby?"

"If you think my opinion is valuable." She joined the group, stuck her finger in the mix, and tasted. "It's excellent, but I don't know how it's supposed to be."

"We'll soon find out." Molly poured the batter into the waiting pan. "Let's all keep our fingers crossed!"

As she spoke, a bell jangled. At its first peal, every servant glanced up at the huge panel of bells that dominated the kitchen wall by the door. Tabby saw that her husband was ringing from the library. French dashed toward the door, removing his apron as the bell rang again. Gad, but Thomas was a demanding man! Did he not realize that people needed time to get themselves from one part of the house to another?

The bell ringing ceased. French or a footman, galloping at top speed, must have finally achieved the library. Those in the kitchen relaxed.

Moments later, a red-faced footman sprinted in. "My lady, my lord wishes to see you. He's been searching for you."

Fustian! Thank heavens he hadn't dreamed of looking in the kitchen. He would not have appreciated her servile attire.

"Very well," she said briskly. "I'll return as soon as I can."

"Yes'm." Molly went on with her task. "Maybe the cake'll be ready for tasting by then."

When Tabby departed, two maids critically stared after her. "Marchioness! In the kitchen! That's a sad sight for ya. I've a notion to put in my application at an employment agency. I'm tired of her nosing in my business," one spat.

"That's a good idea. I think I'll do the same. Get some position where the mistress knows her place."

"Shut up!" shouted Molly, picking up a cleaver and shaking it at them. "Miss Tabby's the finest mistress you'll ever have. But go on. Quit! She deserves better than the likes of you!"

"There will be no more slurs on her ladyship," seconded Mrs. Dobbs. "Go on about your chores!"

"Cleaning more chambers," one groaned.

"Get on with ya!" Molly started toward them, weapon in hand.

The two maids skittered away.

"Troublesome bits o' muslin," Molly grumbled and went back to her baking.

Unaware of this mutiny, Tabby fled up the servants' stair. Reaching the second floor, she peeped cautiously from the doorway. Only a chambermaid bearing a stack of bed linens and looking weary dragged her footsore legs down the hall.

Tabby darted through the door and closed it behind her. She felt sure that Thomas was still in the library awaiting her, but it didn't pay to take chances. Not in this shabby attire! Hurriedly, she started toward her room.

Hearing footsteps, the maid turned, regarding her mistress with a gloomy gaze. "I've almost got another room done, m'lady."

"Excellent!" Tabby praised. "I knew I could depend upon you."

"Well, maybe so, but I'm going to have to take a lie-down for a while, 'fore I can go on." The servant shifted her bundle and wiped her arm across her perspiring forehead. "M'back hurts bad."

In all conscientiousness, Tabby couldn't attempt to persuade her to carry on, but she deplored any delay. She sighed demonstrably and nodded. "Very well, Margaret. I know you are doing your utmost."

The chambermaid hid her sour expression until her lady had passed. "I'm goin' home to Maxfield Hall," she muttered. "His lordship's steward'll hire me there. Or I'll go to his lordship's mother. She'll understand!"

"Shut your mouth or I'll mash it." Daphne poked her head from a guest chamber into the hall. "Miss Tabby's the best of mistresses. She's sweet and kind and loving. If you go off and leave her, I'll send m'beau after you, and he'll beat you to a pulp."

Heedless of the further subversion, Tabby entered her room to find her abigail carefully folding lingerie and placing it in a drawer. The fragrance of the lavender sachet blossomed forth, but its sweet scent failed to ease her. She had scarcely been up out of bed, but already her back ached dreadfully. There was nothing to do about it though. She must join Thomas in the library.

Evans, looking disgusting fresh and unruffled, assessed the dishevelment of her mistress. "Have you come for refreshment, my lady? Perhaps for a long soak in the tub?"

"I haven't time." She briefly closed her eyes, imagining the soothing warm water flowing about her weary body. "I wish I could."

The servant slowly shook her head. "A marchioness . . ."

"What about it?" Tabby snapped.

Evans was too grand to be intimidated by the sharp note in her mistress's voice. She arched an eyebrow, her disapproval patently obvious.

"Please just make me presentable," Tabby murmured.

The dresser sniffed. "Madam smells of the kitchen."

"Use cologne."

Evans obeyed. She bathed Tabby's face, arms, bosom, and neck in lavender water, then helped her into a clean sprigged violet dress. She lightly dusted her mistress's face with talcum and naughtily added a touch of rouge to her cheeks and lips. She brushed Tabby's golden tresses into a delicate knot on the crown of her head. When she finished, Tabby felt becalmed and refreshed.

"Thank you, Evans. You have worked a miracle." She rose from the dressing table bench.

Leaving the dressing room, Tabby glanced at the clock on her bedroom mantel and saw that she'd left Thomas cooling his heels for far too long. Her revitalization evaporated. Once again feeling like the devil was chasing her, she rushed from the chamber.

Her husband was seated on the sofa, impatiently tapping his foot. "Where in God's name have you been?"

Tabby swallowed with difficulty. He had never, ever, spoken to her in that tone. "I . . . I was occupied with a household task. I'm sorry, Thomas. I came as swiftly as I could."

"You engage yourself too thoroughly in domestic matters. That's why we have servants, my dear. Besides, I thought you were going to rest." Although he had tempered the statement with an endearment, his words were an admonition.

She felt like bursting into tears. "I . . . I . . ."

"Might your husband claim a trifle of your time?" he went on. "I realize you are readying the house for the party, but really, Tabitha, you are setting too great an emphasis on it. Don't worry so. I don't want you fainting again."

"I want everything to be right." She bent her head and clasped her hands behind her back. "Everyone will be judging me."

"Not as harshly as you evidently seem to believe," he contended. "Everyone knows you are new to your role. They'll understand."

How could he be more wrong? The *ton,* family or no,

were stern critics. They would be greedily waiting for her to make the smallest misstep. Then they would fly in like a big goose, beating its wings and flogging its victim. No, there would be no kind compassion.

But she didn't defend herself. In the first place, Thomas didn't know that she'd dismissed half the staff. Secondly, he was not aware of the further economies she had instituted. She didn't want him to realize.

"You must give our people more credit for being able to prepare for a gathering of this nature. Truly, Tabitha, you need only to give them the simplest of orders."

That was unequivocally false! Tabby's anger flared. Her lips twisted spontaneously into a thin line of animosity.

Thomas was too newly married to recognize the signs. He plunged on. "Actually, my dear, you should pay no more attention to the details. If you wish, I'll call Mrs. Dobbs in and tell her to handle the entire matter, thus freeing you from all responsibility."

Tabby's temper overflowed. She jerked up her head and treated him to the most withering look imaginable. "Whether you believe it or not, I am totally responsible for this affair, and people will, very definitely, blame me if anything goes wrong! What is wrong with you? Have you been bumbling along blind all these many years?"

The marquess gaped at her, dumbfounded.

"This entire festivity makes me so furious, I could spit! Why wasn't I warned in advance? Does everyone take me for granted?" She wildly threw up her hands in consternation. "And, my lord, you could not be more wrong! Everyone *will* judge me!"

His mouth dropped open, giving him all the appearance of a simpleton.

"I have had enough!" Tabby whirled on her heel and started toward the door.

"Tabitha!" Thomas gathered enough of his wits to leap in pursuit.

As Tabby turned the doorknob (which, she immediately noticed, needed a drop of oil), she glanced back in time to see her husband catch his toe on the carpet and sprawl full length to the floor.

"Oh, my!" She hurried to him, kneeling down. "Thomas, are you all right?"

He looked balefully up at her, then with a lightning gesture, caught her arm and toppled her down beside him. "No, I am not all right. Not with my wife taking up partnership with the Furies."

Her ire flowed away. "Oh, Thomas, my temper ignited beyond all belief. I had no call to—"

"Hush." He laid a finger across her lips. "It is all my fault. I had no business making light of your position. Of course you wish to impress my family."

"But . . ." She formed the word in spite of his suppression.

Thomas decided to resort to stronger measures to buy her silence. Upside down or not, his lips sought hers. Tabby's protest was quelled, but he could not allay the giggle that rose in her throat.

Kissing her husband topsy-turvy was a totally new experience and, though unique, was not as pleasurable as a kiss in the proper direction. Breaking away from his lips, she rolled toward him. "Is this not better, my darling?"

"Indubitably." He gathered her into a closer embrace and once again sought her mouth.

A footman, having heard Tabitha jiggling the doorknob, remembered that it sometimes stuck. Clutching it in his strong fist, he grandly opened it with a flourish, revealing his lord and lady clasped in a highly warm cuddle on the floor, of all places! With a loud gulp, he yanked the door shut. His mistress might be a strict taskmaster, but she was certainly not puritanical. With a chuckle, he dashed off to tell all the others.

Tabby wrenched upward when she heard the door, but

her delay in responding prevented her from identifying the witness. Drat! The tale of this escapade would be swiftly circulated throughout the house. It would undermine her authority. What to do? She had no choice of action. Thomas drew her down and turned her on her back, grinning mischievously at her.

"So we were perused? The staff will be rampant with such a scandal. We may as well carry on."

"No!" she gasped. "This is . . . is . . . highly irregular!"

He laughed. "I believe it to be a quite normal event in the life of a married couple."

"Not on the library floor!" she professed. "What will the servants think of me?"

"Unfortunately, that is part and parcel of having a large staff, my dear. Now and then, one is inadvertently spied upon."

"I am mortified." Tabby eased free and sat up. "I cannot go on."

"Very well." He sighed, rising and extending a hand to help her up. "I cannot continue without you."

"Well, it is broad daylight," she began.

Before that short sentence left her mouth, he picked her up into his arms and started toward the door. "The time of day has nothing to do with it. We'll finish this in the bedroom."

Tabby shrieked. "This is even more improper! Surely you do not intend to carry me up the stairs!"

"I intend to carry you all the way, darling. I believe you need some more rest."

"What you are intending is definitely not restful! Put me down!" She valiantly kicked her legs and pushed against his solid chest. "Oh, Thomas, you cannot do this!"

"Just watch me." With a chuckle, he carried out his mission, striding past ogling servants in the hall, climbing the stairs, and entering Tabby's bedroom, where an agitated Evans fairly flew from the chamber. When they were alone, he firmly kicked he door shut and gently deposited his now giggling wife on the bed.

"There now, my love. Was that not so bad?"

When Thomas dozed, Tabby arose, bathed, and sneaked hurriedly down to the kitchen. As she entered, she could scarcely believe the delicious odor that assailed her nostrils. Centered on the table, circled by excited servants, was the cake.

"Come, Miss Tabby, and have a bite," Molly proudly offered.

"I'm almost afraid." Tabby bravely sauntered forth. Plucking a bit of the golden concoction, she placed it in her mouth, rolling it round her tongue like a connoisseur tasting wine. Suddenly, she gripped the table. She ate a bite more, studying.

"That has to be it!" she cried. "This just *has* to be the correct taste! It is very buttery with a marvelous touch of lemon. No wonder Lord Maxfield appreciates it so! I vow it's the best pound cake I've ever eaten!"

Molly and the staff drew a collective breath of relief. Maybe the ordeal was over. They'd finished the cleaning today. They'd performed all the little extras that would make the house nice for guests. Maybe now their addle-pated marchioness would be satisfied.

"Bring me a box, someone, and fetch a footman. We'll send a piece straightway to the duchess, who has the final say. Oh, I do pray she will give it her approval. I so want Lord Maxfield's birthday to be perfect."

"As do we all!" said Mrs. Dobbs with heartfelt desire. "And now, my lady, may you and I confer? I do believe we are ready for guests, and not a day too soon!"

"Thank God," was all Tabby could think of to say.

* * *

Charlotte not only approved of her sample of cake. She, along with her husband, carried her report in person. When the butler showed them into the salon that evening, Tabby found herself holding her breath.

"I know it isn't proper to call at this hour, but we are family so it shouldn't matter," Thomas's sister announced.

Her husband nodded. "Thought we might scare up a game of piquet, but it looks as if Tabitha is otherwise occupied."

"No, that is quite all right." Tabby set aside the pillowcase she was mending.

Thomas chuckled. "I believe my wife is a perfectionist. She does not trust the tedious tasks to servants."

Tabby flushed.

"Yes," the marquess summed up. "Tabitha is most particular in overseeing the staff. Only the best will do."

His sister smiled admiringly. "Dear Tabitha, I do applaud such virtuosity. I am not so domestically inclined."

The duke guffawed. "That is certain! If it weren't for our housekeeper, the whole house would be a total shambles at all times!"

"For shame, love," Charlotte chided with spirit. "I am responsible for *some* matters."

"Such as?" he gloated.

"I approve the menus."

The duke laughed heartily. "Yes, my sweet, we are quite aware of where your greatest domestic interest lies. In what you eat!"

Tabby smiled. Charlotte was one of those lucky souls who could consume what she wished and never grow plump. Her sister-in-law's figure was willowy and not enticingly curved like Tabby's, but Cotty didn't seem to mind. Indeed, it was obvious that he was wonderfully in love with his wife. She wondered how she and Thomas appeared to others. Immediately, her cheeks burned, as she vividly remembered their late afternoon. Suddenly she felt everyone's gaze upon her. The feverish flush spread down her neck to her bosom.

Charlotte cocked her head sideways. "My goodness, Tabitha. What *are* you visualizing?"

Her brother grinned broadly.

"Very well," she said with a simper. "I shan't tease you further. Perhaps we'd best turn our conversation to food again."

Tabby hoped she was disguising the hope in her eyes.

"As a matter of fact, that piece of cake you sent me today," said Charlotte, "was as delicious as anything I can remember. You must give me the reciept, Tabitha."

"Cake?" Thomas queried. "We had no cake today. Only pie."

"It was an experiment," Tabby told him. "I did not wish to serve it until I was certain of its flawlessness. Knowing that Charlotte has such an educated palate, I sent her a sample and asked her opinion."

Her husband looked askance at her, so Tabby babbled on. "I only wish the best for you, Thomas. I do have my pride, you know."

He lifted an eyebrow.

"It's true," she maintained.

"You strive too unremittingly," he countered.

Charlotte glanced back and forth from one to another. "Do let's change the topic. This is becoming tiresome. Suffice it to say that Tabitha intends to be a commendable wife, and you, Thomas, will become dreadfully spoiled. Now cease this tit for tat!"

"I agree." Thomas stood. "Come, Cotty. Let us go to the billiard room. We'll have a brandy and a game. I have the feeling that our ladies would rather chat than play piquet."

The duke concurred, rising to join him.

"Good!" Tabby exclaimed when the gentlemen had departed. "Do tell, Charlotte. Was the morsel I sent as good as the original?"

"Even better!" she enthused. "I am ecstatic!"

"Not nearly so much as I," Tabby sighed.

"I still think you should have told the entire story to Thomas. He would have understood. And this mending . . ." Charlotte shrugged. "Aren't you taking on a bit too much?"

Tabby proceeded carefully. Thomas's sister didn't know the half of the tangle she'd gotten herself into, and she wanted to keep it that way. If Charlotte had the slightest suspicion that her sister-in-law was doing servants' work, she'd promptly tattle, and then . . . Tabby didn't want to think about that scene. It would be terrible, and that was that.

"Now that I have solved the problem of the cake, I shall not be so occupied," Tabby said lightly. "No preparations will be left for me, save approving the final arrangements."

"I am happy to hear that all is well now." Charlotte tilted her head and observed Tabby closely. "I do have one other question, and I hope you will not consider me impertinent for asking. I am only interested in your welfare."

Tabby dipped her head. "Please continue."

Thomas's sister blushed ever so faintly. "Are you well, Tabitha? You seem a bit pale."

"I am fine, and I do wish people would cease worrying about me."

"I was only concerned," Charlotte repeated. "If there is a problem . . ."

Knowing the house was ready, Tabby smiled almost brightly. "Nothing is wrong. Things couldn't be better."

"Good! Oh, my, I cannot wait till your party! I shall so enjoy seeing everyone again."

Even though the house was sparkling and there was competent help in the kitchen, Tabby wished she had never heard of the entertainment. There were still dilemmas to solve. Minor ones, maybe, but obstacles nevertheless.

Soon after the guests had arrived and the house party was in full sway, Tabby discovered that the minor problems she had anticipated were actually major ones. In short, Thomas's family was a demanding lot. The servants couldn't keep up with their requests, and chaos reigned. Tabby, of course, couldn't answer a bell, but she toiled in the background, assisting Molly in the kitchen, helping French wash the delicate crystal, and collaborating with Mrs. Dobbs. When she played hostess to the visitors, she was so weary she could scarcely stay awake. The dual role was so exhausting that it showed.

"Love?" Thomas caught her just as she was heading toward the green baize door that separated the service section from the rest of the house.

She paused.

"What are you doing? You seem to be everywhere at once, and you look as if you've been run off your feet."

Tabby forced a smile. "There is much for a hostess to do."

His brow creased with concern. "Not *this* much, surely. Don't worry so. Relax and spend more time with my family. Enjoy yourself!"

She felt like hitting him. More time with his relations? Very well, she could do that!

"You're right, Thomas," she said sweetly. "Perhaps I am trying too hard."

She doubled her load, taking the only time left from her sleep. She grew pale overnight. Dizziness and nausea became her constant companions.

Finally, Evans intervened. "My lady, you must cease this drudgery. In your condition, it isn't safe."

Tabby sat down on her bed, leaning against the post. "I shall rest when this party is ended."

The abigail violently shook her head. "You must slacken now. It isn't good for the babe."

"What?" Tabby cried.

Evans chuckled. "I thought you'd been too busy to notice. You are increasing, my lady. You are in the family way."

"Impossible!" Tabby shrilled.

"Lady Maxfield, I am sure," she went on. "You haven't had your monthly in a very long time, and you have all the signs. Now, if you do not begin to take it easy, I shall tattle to his lordship."

Tabby stared speechlessly at her. "Do . . . do you really think?"

"I *know.*"

"Oh, my goodness! What shall I do?"

"You will rest, my lady. *Now.* I'll tell Mrs. Dobbs what is happening and that she must not count on you anymore." Evans turned down the covers and reached around Tabby to unfasten her dress.

"But . . ." Tabby began, but a wave of dizziness swept over her. "Well, just for a few moments."

She allowed Evans her ministrations and soon was in bed, bundled under the blankets. She fell asleep immediately. She awoke the next morning, when Thomas lightly kissed her cheek, and found herself in his arms.

"My dear Lord!" she wailed, when she realized what had happened. "The party! The guests!"

He laughed. "Everyone understood your weariness, and they think you're magnificent."

"But this is the next day! I nearly slept round the clock!" She bounded from the bed. "I have much to do. It's . . . it's . . . Oh, Thomas, it's your birthday!"

"That's right, and it seems that a man could cuddle his

wife on his birthday." He scolded, but his eyes were brimming with laughter. "Come here, my darling. It's early yet."

She smiled sweetly and complied, but her heart was pounding with stress. This time of day was so busy for the servants. And there was no one free to fix the breakfast trays. She hoped Thomas would never learn of the mayhem. He wouldn't want to caress her then!

It was late when she arrived in the kitchen, and the breakfast trays had already been sent up.

"We were slow in serving," Mrs. Dobbs said, mopping perspiration from her face. "We can't keep up, my lady. Frankly, we've given up trying."

"I'm so sorry!" Tabby burst into tears.

"My lady!" she exclaimed, shocked.

"Miss Tabby." Old Molly wrapped her big arms around her. "It's all right, Miss Tabby. Molly will make it all right. What matter about these people! You've got yourself to look after. If they don't like you round here, we'll just go home."

The suggestion sounded heavenly, but Tabby knew she must face the trouble. After all, she had caused it. She allowed Molly to wipe her tears on her apron.

"It is my fault," she told the gaping servants, who seemed to materialize out of nowhere. "It is all my fault. I thought I knew what I was doing, but I didn't. I was just so worried about money."

"Sweet lady." Mrs. Dobbs squeezed her hand. "Don't you know that his lordship is rich beyond all belief? He has so much money he probably doesn't even know the grand total."

Tabby started to weep again. "I didn't know. I have always been accustomed to economy."

"You needn't worry your pretty head." Mrs. Dobbs patted her cheek. "You just take good care of yourself."

There was general agreement among the servants. "We can manage!" boomed Mr. French.

Again, Molly wiped Tabby's face. "See, Miss Tabby? Everyone understands."

"As soon as possible," Tabby vowed, "I will seek out all the servants I had dismissed, if they can be found, and reinstate them, if they so wish."

Mrs. Dobbs chortled. "Most of them can be found, my lady. Their families have served the Maxfields for generations. They simply went home to work at Maxfield Hall."

"I hope you aren't angry about it," Mr. French added.

"No. I'm glad," she said with relief. "Thank you. Thank you *all* for putting up with me."

"Just take care of that baby!" several advised.

She started. "My, does everyone know about that?"

They grinned. "We guessed, Miss Tabby. Then Evans told us," Molly said.

Tabby beamed. "You probably knew of it as soon as I did. And yes, I shall take good care of him. I promise you."

Though everyone worked doubly hard, it was still a difficult day. Tabby was tired when at last she descended the stairs to join the assembly of guests in the drawing room as they awaited dinner. Thanks to Evans and her rouge, she thought she looked almost her best, especially with the magnificent diamonds Thomas had given her. She was in for a horrid surprise, however. All of Thomas's relations carried gifts, which they placed on a corner table. Tabby, horrified, realized that, in her travail, she'd forgotten entirely to buy him a present.

There was another nasty jolt, too. Midway through the meal, a footman bent close to her ear. "Madam, you must come to the kitchen."

Oh, dear! What now? She hastily excused herself and dashed after him to find Molly and Delores gawking miserably at a burnt cake.

"I did it, my lady," Delores sobbed. "In all the confusion, I forgot."

Tabby, also, felt like weeping, but that would not correct

the situation. She had no birthday gift and no special cake. She was a failure.

"I've mixed up another cake, but I'm havin' trouble with that newfangled oven," Molly said tightly. "I'll do my best, Miss Tabby. That's all I can do."

"That's all anyone can do, and, Delores . . ." Tabby patted the girl's shoulder. "These things happen, especially when there is so much confusion. Please think no more of it."

Unhappy, she returned to the table. Thinking of how she had failed kept her on the verge of weeping. What would Thomas think when he received no gift from her? How disappointed would he be when he had no special cake? When the next course was served, she hastened to the kitchen, amid questioning stares from her company.

"How is it, Molly?" she anxiously queried.

The old cook peered at her. "Don't cry, Miss Tabby. It'll be all right."

"No. Never." She shook her head. "I've ruined his birthday. I even forgot to buy him a gift!"

"But you have the best gift of all," Molly soothed. "A baby!"

"I didn't think of that!" Tabby gasped.

"Of what?"

She whirled to find her husband leaning against the doorjamb. "Thomas!"

"What the hell is going on?" he demanded.

"Don't you get mad at her," Molly decreed. "You might be a fancy marquess, but you're a lucky man to have such a wife."

Tabby, awaiting his wrath, was surprised to see him grin.

"I know that," he stated. "I also know that something is bothering you, Tabitha. Please tell me why you keep running to the kitchen."

She hung her head, a tear sliding down her cheek. "I've made a muddle of everything."

"Impossible." He strode forward and took her in his arms.

"I tried to economize," she murmured. "I dismissed too many employees. I made Jean-Michel angry, and he quit. I . . . When I realized my mistake, I tried to make up for it by helping the servants."

"Shh. It's all right." He gently stroked her back.

"No, it's awful!" she moaned. "All the gifts you gave me . . . I truly did love them, but I was afraid they were far too expensive."

"Darling, you needn't fret about that. I have a great deal of money." He took his handkerchief and dried her tears. "I wish you had come to me. You must always come to me."

"I shall," she whispered. "But your special cake . . ."

He tilted her chin with his forefinger. "All right now? And what of the cake? I smell something mouth-watering."

"Here is your cake, my lord." Molly proudly carried it from the oven. "Hope you don't mind eating it a bit warm."

"It might even be better. Please give me a sample."

He savored the thin slice she offered. "It is better than ever. You are a good cook. Better than Jean-Michel! I hope you are in our employ for many years to come."

Molly blushed with delight.

"Molly is Mama's cook," Tabby explained. "I borrowed her."

Thomas lifted an eyebrow. "Perhaps I can pay her a larger wage and steal her. The food has been uncommonly good of late."

"No need," Molly cackled. "I'm teachin' your Delores all I know."

He winked. "That might be so, but keep it in mind. Now, Tabitha, we'd best be returning to our guests."

"Don't forget your gift, Miss Tabby," Molly reminded.

"What about a gift?" Thomas asked as they went down the corridor.

"I . . . uh . . ." She paused, blushing. "I have a unique birthday remembrance, my lord. You see, in all my bustle, I forgot to buy a gift, so . . ."

"You are prize enough, my love," he said quickly.

"No, I . . . I think we are going to have a child, Thomas," she whispered.

"Did I hear correctly?" he shouted.

She nodded happily.

He drew her close. "Tabitha, you are an absolute marvel! That's the best gift I could ever have!"

"Do you really feel that way?"

"Certainly!"

Tabby hugged him joyfully.

"You will take good care of yourself, my love. No hard work! And we will increase the staff to normal," he proclaimed, "and to hell with the cost!"

"But, Thomas, economy . . ."

She could not finish the sentence. Her husband, totally ignoring economy, had silenced her with a long, sweet kiss.

OLD ENGLISH POUND CAKE

2 sticks margarine
1/2 C Crisco
3 C sugar
5 eggs
3 C flour
1 1/4 C milk
1 Tbsp vanilla
1 Tbsp lemon extract
1 Tsp baking powder

Cream margarine, Crisco, sugar, and eggs until fluffy. Add vanilla and lemon extract. Alternately add flour and milk. Last, add baking powder. Pour into greased and floured tube or Bundt pan. Place in cold oven. Then bake at 300 degrees for one hour or a bit longer, depending on pan used and oven. Let cool in pan for approx. fifteen minutes before removing.

A MATTER OF TASTE

by
Alana Clayton

One

"Do try to control yourself, Edwina," advised Fiona, patting her friend on the arm. "You will take ill if you continue."

"I am ruined," wailed Edwina Hayden, Lady Hamilton, staring down the drive at the departing coach.

Lady Fiona Atterly also watched the cloud of dust kicked up by the horses' hooves as they conveyed Edwina's temperamental French chef away from the Hamilton estate. "It couldn't be so hopeless as to throw you into such an uproar," soothed Fiona. The two young women had been lifelong friends, and Fiona wished she could say more to alleviate Edwina's distress.

"I'll be the laughingstock of all England, and John will never forgive me."

"Stuff and nonsense. John loves you. He would never blame you for something that is beyond your control."

Edwina dabbed at her eyes with a fragile scrap of lace-edged handkerchief. Everything about her seemed wilted in the summer's heat. Her red hair, which normally had a life all its own, lay in dispirited tendrils around her face. Her green eyes were pink edged and watery from her tears. Even her gown seemed to droop on her tall, willowy form.

With her petite stature and black hair, Fiona was a startling contrast to Edwina. She often wondered what had brought them together in a friendship that had endured over the years.

"Perhaps I could have avoided such a disaster if I had only held my tongue," lamented Edwina.

Fiona tended to agree, but would never tell her friend while she was in such a taking. "He seemed a bit overly sensitive," she offered, hoping her judgment would afford a bit of solace to Edwina.

"But I fretted over the menus so. Then, once they were set, I changed them time and again. And I kept reminding him how important this house party was to me. I don't think he cared for it at all."

"Perhaps you shouldn't have questioned whether he was equal to the occasion," said Fiona gently. "You know, chefs are exceedingly fragile when it comes to their art."

"But this house party is my first as a married woman, and I wanted to impress John and his friends with my ability to carry out a perfect event. Now I'm left with a houseful of people due to arrive tomorrow and no one to cook for them." Edwina's eyes threatened to overflow again.

"Stop being such a watering pot," scolded Fiona. "We will be able to contrive something adequate, I'm certain. There must be passable cooks in the area. Perhaps you could borrow one from one of your neighbors."

"Heavens no! It wouldn't be long before the entire neighborhood would know I was unable to run my own household. I would never be able to overcome the embarrassment."

"Then we will send to London for a new chef."

"It's far too late," countered Fiona. "The guests arrive tomorrow, and it would be a sennight or more before a new chef could be here."

"Then you must make do with a local cook," replied Fiona, exasperated with her friend's unwillingness to accept an alternative.

"I couldn't allow our guests to face such country fare."

Edwina thought a moment; then her expressive face lit up. "But I do know where there's a chef equal to the demands of John's friends."

"Good," said Fiona, glad to have the dilemma solved so quickly. "We shall send a message immediately. Is this chef close enough to arrive by tomorrow?"

"Oh, I believe so," replied Edwina, smiling for the first time that day. "It is you."

It was a moment before Fiona recovered her power of speech. "No! Absolutely not, Edwina! You have led me into all manner of schemes, but I will not allow you to convince me of this shatter-brained idea."

"You have done the same to me," charged Edwina stubbornly.

"That may be true," Fiona admitted. "But nothing equal to this."

"What is so wrong?" asked Edwina, an appealing expression on her face. "You're an excellent cook. It's been your passion since you were old enough to squeeze dough between your fingers. When you're at home, you cook nearly every day. You told me so yourself."

"That is among my family only. My mother would swoon from humiliation if she knew I was cooking for a house party."

"She need never know," replied Edwina, growing more excited as she considered her plan. "You need not stay in the kitchen. Merely oversee it."

"That sounds far too easy," said Fiona. "I know from experience it will take more than a few minutes a day. How will I explain my disappearances to the other guests?"

"We shall contrive," asserted Edwina confidently. "No one will be watching you closely. People will be scattered all over the house and grounds engaged in various activities. They won't know where you are or what you're doing."

Fiona had to admit the offer was tempting. Edwina had spoken the truth: She had been enthralled with cooking since childhood. Recipes intrigued her as much as Gothic novels fascinated most other young women. She was in rapture when she found the perfect ingredients for her recipes; and when she successfully invented a new dish, she was happier than if the Prince Regent had asked her to dance.

At first, Fiona's mother, Lady Banning, had not been unduly alarmed when her young daughter seemed to revel in the kitchen. Her own mother had been a cook of some renown until she married and her husband implored her not to arrive in the drawing room covered with flour. Now, it seemed her talent had been passed on to her granddaughter, and Lady Banning worried that no man would want a woman with such an inferior interest.

Lady Banning offered stitchery, art, and music in an attempt to draw Fiona's attention away from the kitchen. Lord Banning taught her to ride to the hounds. But nothing diverted Fiona from her interest in cooking. Her family finally bowed to fate. The servants were all sworn to secrecy and the household enjoyed some of the best dining in town.

"You have long wanted to try your recipes on people other than your family," said Edwina, interrupting Fiona's thoughts. "Now would be an excellent time. Your mother isn't here to keep you from it, and you would have a free hand in the kitchen."

Fiona was tempted beyond belief. It was true she had never been able to offer her dishes for anyone's consumption other than her own household. How she longed to judge the reaction of others to her creations. And without doubt, Edwina was faced with a crisis of monumental proportions, rationalized Fiona.

On the other hand, her parents would find it too lowering by half if they discovered what she was up to.

"If it were not for causing my mother and father embarrassment, I would agree," said Fiona. "But if I were found out, they would both be in high dudgeon; and I could not blame them."

"I promise no one will ever know your part in all this. Not even John."

"How will you be able to keep it from him?"

"Politics has taken over his life so completely that he barely acknowledges I exist any longer," replied Edwina sadly. "He will no doubt be so involved with the men he has invited that the house could burn down without his notice unless it interrupted his precious meetings."

Fiona had never heard her speak so bitterly. "You know he loves you, Edwina. Perhaps he doesn't realize he's ignoring you. Have you told him how you feel?"

"I will not demean myself by begging for his attention. If he cares so little, then perhaps I was wrong to marry him."

"Never say that, Edwina. He is the only man you've ever cared about. This is just a small misunderstanding, I'm sure."

Edwina sighed heavily. "That was why I wanted this house party to be perfect. I thought it would make him take notice of me again."

Fiona could not allow Edwina to suffer as long as she could do something to help ease her pain. Knowing she most likely would regret it, she allowed her sympathy for Edwina and her own desire to win out over good sense. "All right. I will do as you ask."

"Oh, Fiona. I knew you wouldn't let me down!" said Edwina, her face bright with joy.

"But there must be precautions," warned Fiona.

"I'll do whatever you say," promised Edwina. "I'm convinced everything is going to be perfect. My house party will be flawless, and John will be so pleased he will spend more time with me. Things will be as they once were."

Fiona had no desire to ruin her friend's elation, but she thought Edwina depended too heavily on her success as a hostess to bring her happiness.

The rest of the day was taken up with planning Fiona's secret life. She would arrive in the kitchen early each morning to direct the staff and make preparations for some of her special dishes. The kitchen staff were skeptical of a lady so closely overseeing them, but they were loyal to their young mistress and were willing to do whatever it took to make the house party a success.

The most experienced of the staff was given the title of cook and would be in charge of seeing that the everyday dishes were served as usual. Another was designated to sound a warning if a guest should approach the kitchen while Fiona was there.

Fiona retired at the end of the day thinking they had planned as well as possible. But she knew from experience that there was never a plan that covered every contingency that might arise. She only hoped that whatever might occur could be handled before any damage was done to either Edwina or herself.

Galen Sheffield, Lord Burke, approached the Hamilton estate with mixed feelings. He was pleased the long journey to York was nearly over. The weather had been hot and dry. Dust had been thick on the road from London, and the usual shine on his black traveling coach was dulled by a considerable layer of the dirty powder. Nor had he escaped its reach, and he brushed at the sleeve of his well-tailored jacket with little success. His valet had his work cut out for him once they reached Hamilton House.

Though Galen was thankful he would soon be arriving at his destination, it only brought him closer to the difficult mission with which the Prince Regent had charged him.

A short while later, after Galen had washed away the dust of the road, he descended to the sitting room for a drink before dinner. John, Lord Hamilton, was already in the room, and he came forward to greet Galen.

"Galen, I apologize for being absent when you arrived, but Lord Huxley and I were riding at the time."

"I suppose he's still after that black of yours."

"He never gives up," said John with a grin. "At all events, I allow him to ride the animal when he's here. It only whets his appetite. It's good for him to know his money can't buy everything. Our other guests will be down shortly, but I'm glad we have a few minutes to ourselves."

"I'm sorry to bring the Prince Regent's problem along with me," apologized Galen. "But there was nothing else I could do. The issue must be resolved and quickly. Prinny asked me to convey his appreciation for your cooperation."

"I'm honored to be allowed a small part in aiding the Prince Regent," said John. "Now what can I do."

"You've already done what's been needed. I assume you've invited the people whose names I sent to you."

"Yes, and they all accepted."

"I thought they would. The racing at York is too convenient for them to refuse," replied Galen thoughtfully.

"Can you tell me what this is all about?"

"Not one word must go beyond the two of us or it could be the end of my investigation, and the end of my relationship with the Prince Regent."

"Your secret will be entirely safe with me," assured John.

"There's been an outbreak of race fixing at the courses lately," Galen revealed, "and Prinny is extremely sensitive about that."

"Lord, yes. I expect he would be. I remember my father talking about the furor that arose when the Prince was suspected of race fixing himself. Said his horse, Escape, had been on a wining streak. Then, one afternoon, he lost a race, which raised the odds. The very next day the horse won handily, allowing the Prince to win a substantial sum at greatly increased odds."

Galen nodded in agreement. "That's true. The Jockey Club ruled against Chifney, the Prince's jockey, and he was forced to do away with the man's services. The Prince withdrew entirely from racing at that time, but still supports it. I don't think he wants it said he overlooks race fixing of any kind or it might reflect poorly on him. Make everyone think those charges might have been true."

"And he expects you to find the culprit and bring him to justice?"

"That's what he's asked. I've identified certain suspects. All of them have the ability to arrange the fixes. My man of business is inquiring as to whether any of their pockets are to let. In the meantime, your house party affords me the chance to observe them close at hand. It also puts them near the race course—a temptation the guilty party will be hard put to resist. It's my hope I'll be able to catch him in the act so there will be no question of his culpability."

"If I can help with anything else, be sure and let me know," said John. "Ah, here are Edwina and Fiona."

Galen turned to greet the ladies as they entered the room. He was immediately struck by the difference between the two women. Edwina's tall, willowy form, with her red hair and green eyes, was in stark contrast to the petite young woman standing beside her.

"Galen, I'm so pleased you could accept our invitation," said Edwina as they approached. "This is my good friend Lady Fiona Atterly. Fiona, this is Lord Burke, a longtime acquaintance of John's."

Galen greeted the ladies, quickly appraising Lady Fiona. As he had first observed, she was shorter than average height, but it did not diminish her presence. Her hair was black as a raven's wing, and it gleamed with a luster as rich as silk. But it was her eyes that startled him as he met her gaze. They were an unusual violet color that he had never encountered before. He had an odd feeling they would haunt his dreams that night.

It didn't surprise Galen that he was seated next to Lady Fiona at the dinner table. John was often amused by his wife's matchmaking schemes. Evidently Lady Hamilton had decided he and her friend would match. Galen had to admit Lady Fiona was appealing, but he was not ready to commit himself to any particular lady. More than one woman had attempted to catch him in parson's mousetrap, but he had avoided them all. Besides, for the next fortnight, he must devote himself to finding the race fixer for the Prince Regent.

However, midway through dinner, Galen found himself in a curious state of mind. Lady Fiona had not, as he had expected, sought to occupy his full attention. Instead, he had found it extremely difficult to attract her notice for more than a few words of polite conversation.

Galen surreptitiously observed her as she examined each dish before she tasted it. Closing her eyes, she chewed slowly before swallowing. "Is something wrong with your food, Lady Fiona?"

"What? Oh, no, my lord. I merely appreciate a good dish," Fiona replied, feeling a blush rise to her cheeks. She had not meant to be so obvious in her evaluation of the meal.

"I must agree. The Cornish hen is particularly well cooked."

Suddenly he had her full attention. "What do you think of the stuffing?" she asked with an intensity more appropriate to a matter of state.

The force of her violet gaze held him silent for a moment. "I find it delicious," he replied as soon as he had recovered.

"You don't think the juniper berries too much?"

"Juniper berries?" he asked, sounding sometimes confused.

"Of course, ofttimes the taste is a bit too subtle for the ordinary palate to distinguish, but I think they add a little something extra for those who can appreciate it," mused Fiona.

"I have dined at Prinny's elbow more times than I can count," declared Galen, desiring to put her in her place. "He employs the finest chefs in England. You may take it on my authority that the juniper berries add exactly the right touch to the stuffing."

"I'm so glad you think so," said Fiona with a huge sigh of relief. "You don't know how much I have fretted about it."

"It would seem to be Lady Hamilton's place to worry about the quality of dinner," observed Galen, a puzzled expression on his face.

"It is," said Fiona, thinking she must be especially vigilant around Lord Burke. It hadn't taken him long to question her interest in the dishes being served. "But she has recently employed a new cook and has asked me to offer an opinion on her ability."

"Well, to my way of thinking, she has nothing to worry about. Dinner has been delightful," said Galen.

"Thank you," said Fiona, favoring him with a huge smile. "Edwina will be pleased to hear your favorable comments."

It was certainly a different kind of dinner, thought Galen. He had not had to utter one flattering word during the entire course of the meal, except to commend the juniper berries, of course. Perhaps he would be able to pursue the Prince Regent's request uninterrupted after all. He must see to it that he continued to sit next to Lady Fiona so he would be free to observe the other guests.

"Tell me all about dinner," demanded Edwina when she found Fiona alone in the drawing room.

An expression of concentration appeared on Fiona's face. "I thought the trout a bit overdone," she replied. "I'll need to speak to the cook about that in the morning."

"I didn't mean the food. I was able to judge that for myself."

"Then what in heaven's name did you mean?" grumbled Fiona. "What else could be so important that you would hunt me down when you should be playing the perfect hostess?"

"I was speaking of Galen," explained Edwina patiently.

"Lord Burke? He enjoyed dinner very well, I believe. He particularly mentioned the juniper berries."

"Juniper berries?" echoed Edwina, wondering whether the heat of the kitchen had caused her friend to lose her wits.

"In the Cornish hen stuffing. He was able to discern the taste when many would not."

"And did you enjoy his company?"

"I liked him well enough. He did not talk overmuch, and I was able to concentrate on the dishes. He mentioned he often dined with Prinny, and I assume he is able to judge the quality of food much better than most. I hope you'll keep his place next to mine if possible."

"Oh, I believe I can arrange that," replied Edwina, an expression of satisfaction on her face.

"Did Edwina's machinations work? Have you fallen head over heels yet?" asked John when he had a moment alone with Galen.

"Surely you didn't expect me to be smelling of April and May so quickly, did you?" replied Galen with a smile.

"It's been known to happen."

"With you and Edwina as I recall."

"Just so," John agreed, glancing across the room to where his wife stood talking to Fiona.

"And you have been happy?"

"Life has never been better. Edwina is an excellent wife. She arranged this house party without a hitch," bragged John.

"And I have just partaken of a most exceptional dinner," added Galen.

"I don't know how she managed to find such a superior

cook," said John. "My mother always had a problem finding and keeping anyone but, as I said, Edwina can work miracles."

Galen found himself more than a little envious of his friend's contentment, and he decided perhaps it was time to reconsider his stand against marriage. As soon as this business with racing was over, he was going to give considerable thought to finding a bride. There was precious little he hadn't experienced as a single man; and more and more often, he found himself thinking of a family of his own: sons to teach to ride, daughters to spoil, and a wife with whom to share the rest of his life.

But now was not the time. He must not allow himself to be distracted from his mission. He must find the person responsible for fixing the races before he could attend to his personal life.

"I must leave you to play the host this evening, but I see you won't be solitary for long," said John, offering Galen a knowing grin before turning and walking away.

"Lord Burke," came a voice from behind him. "I have not been able to say so much as a word to you since dinner."

Galen recognized the voice of Lady Melissa Leander. He had often encountered her in London during the past Season. She was considered a diamond of the first water, but despite a profusion of blond curls, and a manner cultivated to please the most particular gentleman, Galen found her icy-blue eyes far too cold for his liking.

"Lady Melissa," he replied, turning to face the woman. "You look exceptionally charming this evening."

A smile of satisfaction appeared on Lady Melissa's face as she took Galen's arm and led him toward the French windows opening into the gardens.

Fiona forced her heavy eyelids open. The sun had not yet risen but she knew the kitchen staff would already be up and at their appointed tasks. She must follow through on her promise to Edwina to oversee the cooking. Without calling for her maid, Fiona struggled into a gown, pulled her hair back into a businesslike knot, and slipped down the back stairs to the kitchen.

Fiona had determined the staff could prepare the breakfast dishes without her supervision. The hot and cold breads, the egg dishes, and meats required no more than an adequate cook to see that they were served neither burnt nor raw.

Since the company preferred Town hours, there would be an informal luncheon served to fill the gap between the morning and evening meals. This, too, could be simple, for on fair weather days, the men would most likely be out and about hunting or fishing or taking in the horse racing at the nearby course.

Although Fiona wanted all the meals to be tasty, it was dinner that concerned her most. That was when she would present her special dishes for the company's consumption.

Today she must see that there would be adequate fresh fish for she wished to serve rolled fish fillets based on a recipe passed down from her grandmother. She would need herbs and spices and currants, and she hoped the kitchen held all the ingredients she needed.

Breakfast preparations were already under way when she arrived in the large kitchen. She checked to see whether her orders from yesterday were being followed. Afterward, she concentrated first on luncheon, then on the dinner dishes. Promising the nervous cook she would be back to consult with her whenever possible, Fiona made her way out into the hallway.

Leaning against the wall, she closed her eyes. Although the cook was new to her position, she had been working in the kitchen long enough as an undercook for Fiona to feel confident she could handle most things. It was the special dishes—the dishes Edwina hoped would impress her guests—that would require close supervision.

"I must return to my room," murmured Fiona. She pushed away from the wall and walked straight into a warm, firm body. Arms encircled and steadied her, and she found it a distinctly comfortable feeling.

"Is there anything amiss, my lady?"

Fiona's breath caught. She would recognize that voice anywhere. It was the same one that had complimented the juniper berries the night before. Drat! How could she explain being outside the kitchen before the sun had risen?

The distraction of his arms around her made it difficult to find a suitable reply. "Lord Burke," she finally replied brightly. "You're up early."

"But you have beaten me. What could have coaxed you from your bed at such an uncivilized hour, my lady?" His voice was low, and she felt a trace of his breath as it stirred a wayward wisp of hair.

Fiona's mind stubbornly refused to come up with a reasonable explanation. "Oh, I . . . I just couldn't sleep," she stammered.

"So you decided to take a walk to the kitchen?" he asked in an amused voice.

"I yearned for a hot muffin and thought cook might have some ready," Fiona improvised quickly, still not pulling away from his grasp as any proper young lady would do.

"That sounds tasty. Perhaps she has an extra to spare."

"No, you can't. I mean, they're still in the oven."

"How unfortunate you made the trip for nothing," he said, looking down at her.

His gaze caused Fiona to be aware of the gown she had pulled on any which way and of her hair, which was escaping the confines of her hasty knot. No doubt, she was not a pattern card of a lady of the *ton*. After seeing her in such disarray, he had probably concluded she was all about in the attic.

"You must excuse my appearance, my lord. I did not want to awaken my maid for such an inconsequential errand."

"You look absolutely charming," replied Galen courteously and—oddly enough—he thought she did. The hall was still dim, lending an intimacy to their meeting that forced his thoughts in a direction that was not suitable with someone such as Lady Fiona. But she was a desirable woman, and he was a man who just the evening before had begun thinking of taking a wife. "Absolutely charming," he murmured again, slowly lowering his head toward hers.

Suddenly a noise in the front hall echoed to the back of the house, jarring them out of the trance into which they had fallen. "I must go, my lord," Fiona said quickly, turning toward the back stairs and disappearing into the murky predawn darkness.

Galen stood a moment staring after her before continuing on his way to the stables. He wanted to select the best mount available and have the animal kept for his use only. It was important he have a horse he could rely upon should the need arise. The thought brought him back to why he was here, and it did not make pleasant thinking before the day had barely begun.

"Fiona. Fiona," whispered Edwina, shaking the shoulder of her friend. "Wake up. It's full light and you must visit the kitchen before the other guests arise."

"Must you shake me so hard?" objected Fiona, sitting up amidst the jumbled bedclothes and pushing her wayward hair back from her face.

"Yes. You know it's important you see the kitchen help first thing."

"And I have done so," said Fiona, distinctly out of curl. "Long before either you or the sun rose. I was attempting to catch up on my lost sleep, for I'm certain I'll need it before the day is over."

"I'm sorry. I wouldn't have disturbed you had I known," apologized Edwina, looking abashed. "I don't mean to make such a to-do, but I'm on pins and needles that this house party go off without a hitch, and the meals are such a great part of it."

"I know," soothed Fiona. "And I assure you there will be no need to be ashamed of the dishes that come from your kitchen."

"I don't know what I'd do without you."

"You would manage," Fiona replied, getting out of bed and ringing for her maid. "Now what is the order of the day?"

"Most of the men are going to the race course," said Edwina, wrinkling her nose. "The ladies will be staying here. Of course, Melissa wanted to accompany them, but her mother put paid to that idea very quickly."

"I noticed she hung on to Lord Burke the entire evening," commented Fiona.

"Never say you're jealous," teased Edwina.

"After one evening? I should say not."

"Well, he is certainly patient to put up with Melissa as he did."

"Now, Edwina. Perhaps he is genuinely attracted by her," suggested Fiona. "You must admit her blond hair and blue eyes are appealing, and she dresses to the nines."

"If only her character were as winning as her gowns, I would not speak one ill word of her."

"Then you must put your feelings aside for the next fortnight if you expect your house party to be a success."

"I suppose you're right," Edwina grudgingly agreed. "But I won't like it."

"It isn't necessary you do. Just keep your feelings to yourself. Now, I must get dressed. Then we'll go downstairs and see if any of your other guests are up and about yet."

* * *

It was late afternoon before the gentlemen began the journey back to Hamilton House. John and Galen were trailing the rest of the group to indulge in private conversation.

"Did anything new come to light today?" asked John.

"Not much more than I already know," replied Galen. "Duncan will bet on anything that has at least one leg and can move. Sanborn is timid when it comes to betting. Wallace and Huxley have moderate interest. Trent has, no doubt, joined us because it was the thing to do. But I saw nothing which indicated any one of them was attempting to fix a race. And I believe all the winners today were legitimate."

"It's the devil's own mess—that's for sure. How do you intend to narrow your suspects?"

"Keep watching," replied Galen. "If one of them is guilty, he'll slip up sooner or later. I only hope it's within the next fortnight. If he's too sharp to try anything here, everyone will scatter to the four winds and my opportunity will be lost."

"I'll help you as much as I can by suggesting we attend the races at every possible occasion."

"Don't overdo it," warned Galen. "I don't want to make anyone suspicious."

"Well, there is one thing we can count on, and that is being met with a delicious meal at the end of a long day," said John.

"That's true," agreed Galen. "I'm looking forward to seeing what your cook has in store for us this evening." He was also looking forward to seeing whether Lady Fiona's attention was still confined to her dinner.

Two

"Lady Fiona, I had been hoping to find you alone," said James Colter, Lord Duncan.

The men had finished their after-dinner port and rejoined the ladies in the drawing room. Fiona had been standing staring out the French windows, and Lord Duncan had made directly for her.

Fiona met his dark mesmerizing gaze and realized why ladies found him fascinating despite his tarnished reputation. He exuded a feeling of danger, and his eyes promised excitement even while he exercised his impeccable manners.

"And why is that, Lord Duncan?"

"Because I make it a point to become acquainted with lovely ladies," he replied, flattering her shamelessly.

"Lord Duncan, may I ask your opinion?" she inquired, glancing at him from beneath dark lashes.

"Of course, my lady," he said, moving closer and staring intently into her eyes.

"What did you think of the rolled fish fillets at dinner this evening?"

It took all of Fiona's willpower to contain her laughter. Lord Duncan seemed at a loss for words; a rare occurrence she would wager. But then, no doubt it wasn't often his conversation with ladies turned to fish.

Admittedly, Fiona had not been subtle in her questioning, but she desperately desired to shock the man out of his controlled countenance. And it seemed that her question had the desired effect. However, she was also sincere in wanting his opinion. How else was she to learn whether her dishes were pleasing?

"The rolled fish?" Duncan repeated once he had regained his composure.

"Yes. You see I have an interest in cooking, and I would like another opinion on the quality of the dish to see whether I should serve it when I return to Town."

Duncan cleared his throat and glanced quickly around the room. "I, ah, I would say the rolled fish was very tasty indeed. It wasn't too dry, and the herbs and spices were pleasant, but not overpowering."

"Why Lord Duncan, you sound absolutely poetic," replied Fiona, tapping his arm with her fan.

Duncan looked slightly embarrassed. "Well, it so happens you've uncovered a particular interest of mine. I've made it a pastime to dine at the best of tables, and I am fascinated at how divergent the same dish can taste when prepared by various chefs. Now, for the rolled fish," he said, relaxing in her company and seeming to enjoy the harmless conversation. "I have tasted many attempts at the same dish, and most of them were utter failures. Some were overcooked and dry as dust; others did not have the seasonings to make it interesting. The ones served this evening had sage, parsley, and thyme that I could discern."

"There was also rosemary, majoram, and savory," added Fiona.

"What exquisite taste you have," said Duncan, complimenting her. "I also believe I detected a trace of cinnamon and mace."

"Don't forget the nutmeg," added Fiona.

Duncan thought for a moment. "I do believe you're right," he admitted. "And did you notice the currants?"

Fiona leaned closer anxious to know what he had thought of the addition of currants to the recipe.

"I thought they added just the right touch of . . ."

Galen watched as Duncan's and Lady Fiona's heads drew close together, and he wondered what they could be discussing so intently. Hadn't she been warned about the danger Duncan posed for young ladies?

At dinner, Lady Fiona had once again been engrossed in the dishes that passed before them as they sat beside one another. When she did turn her attention to him, the topic generally concerned food. She had particularly sought his opinion of the bacon-wrapped venison once she found he was partial to it. She had seemed inordinately pleased when he not only praised the venison, but also the barley with wild mushrooms and chives that provided an excellent accompaniment.

"Lady Fiona is too coming by half, wouldn't you say?"

He had been unaware of Lady Melissa's approach until her comment, which was immediately followed by the clasp of her fingers around his arm. Galen felt like an animal held in a trap, but he maintained his gentlemanly aplomb and did not jerk away from her unwelcome hold.

"I see nothing different in Lady Fiona from the other ladies in the room," he remarked evenly.

"Look at the company she keeps," insisted Melissa. "I'm surprised Lord and Lady Hamilton invited him in the first place."

"Duncan may have an unflattering reputation, but he is still accepted in Society," said Galen, wondering why he was defending the man when his thoughts had been the same as Lady Melissa's only moments before.

"And it's a shame," contended Lady Melissa. "Everyone knows he frequents the gambling hells almost every night in London."

"As do many gentlemen," Galen pointed out. "Duncan's father left a reputation which isn't easy to live down. I'm not certain it's fair to judge him by that standard."

"Surely you can't approve of him?"

Galen did not want his opinion of Duncan to be a source of comment among the house guests. "I will not ruin my own reputation by having such a dull conversation with a lovely lady," he said, flashing her a brilliantly false smile. "Shall we join Lord and Lady Hamilton?"

Without waiting for an affirmative answer, he led her to where John and Edwina were conversing with Viscount Sanborn. It wasn't long before he excused himself and was at last free from Lady Melissa's grasping clutch.

"Fiona, Duncan," greeted Adam Trent as he joined the two beside the windows. "Nice place to catch a bit of fresh air."

"That it is," agreed Duncan. "But if you'll excuse me, I need to check with the groom. My mount seemed to be favoring his right front leg when we returned this afternoon." Casting a regretful look at Fiona, Duncan stepped through the French windows and disappeared into the gathering darkness.

Fiona had met Adam during the Season of her come-out. They had reached London at approximately the same time and had fast become friends. He was a little taller than she and slight of frame. His blond hair and blue eyes gave him a cherubic appearance. During the entire time of their acquaintance, she had never seen such a bleak look on his face as dwelled there now.

"You look exceedingly serious," she teased.

"I am," he replied without breaking a smile. "It's concerns Lady Catherine."

"Don't tell me you are taken by her?"

"Is it so surprising?" he demanded. "She is the loveliest,

most charming lady I have ever had the good fortune to meet."

There was more passion in his voice than was warranted thought Fiona as she glanced across the room to where Lady Catherine sat with her sister Lady Althea Emerson and with the honorable George and Corinne Wallace. The young woman was attractive to be sure, but Fiona doubted that in London she would be considered a diamond of the first water. Fiona knew, however, that love changed a person's perception of another. She had seen it time and time again as her friends fell in love and attributed extraordinary characteristics to men who seemed quite ordinary to her. She wondered whether that particular malady would strike her one day without her even being aware of it.

"She's very well favored," agreed Fiona, wondering why her comment should cause Adam to be so blue deviled.

"And she is as far removed from me as if she was on the other side of the world." He heaved a great sigh and stared morosely out into the night.

"I cannot believe she wouldn't welcome your attentions," Fiona declared loyally.

"Oh, she does," Adam said. "It's her parents. They want someone better for their daughter. Someone with a title." He did not attempt to hide his bitterness.

Fiona was well aware of Adam's background. His mother was the daughter of an earl, but she had chosen to marry an untitled man. Their union had been a happy one, and it had produced one son. Adam had never seemed discontented about his lack of a title until now. Love did not always bring joy, observed Fiona.

"Perhaps they will change their minds when they see that Catherine holds you in such high regard. She does, doesn't she?"

A flush rose to Adam's cheeks. "I believe so. However, her feelings will not matter to her father. He is determined that neither she nor her sister will marry beneath them."

"Adam, you are not beneath them!" exclaimed Fiona. "You are every bit as good as any man in England. Lord Cheswick should be pleased you want to offer for Catherine. That is your desire, isn't it?"

"Yes," he said, the flush deepening on his cheeks. "I haven't declared myself yet, but I'm certain she knows that's my intent."

"Then talk to her father as soon as you return to Town."

"I have nothing to offer her," said Adam. "When my parents died, they left me a small inheritance, but not enough to support a family. My grandfather has promised to see to my future, but nothing has come of it yet. I'm not looking for a handout," he said stiffly. "I am willing to oversee his estates or do whatever it takes to make a place for myself."

"You have a place," insisted Fiona. "Perhaps if your grandfather knew you were serious about setting up a household, he would carry through on his promise. He probably still thinks of you as in leading strings and doesn't realize you're contemplating marriage."

"Perhaps so," agreed Adam, his face brightening somewhat. "I wonder," he began, then hesitated.

"What is it, Adam? We know one another well enough that you need not stand on ceremony with me."

"Would you help us?" he asked quickly. "We cannot allow her sister to see us together too often. We thought we might meet without her knowing, but we must have a means to set up the times and places."

"Adam, you will end up in a coil if you are found out. Catherine's reputation would be ruined."

"If she were compromised, then we would be forced to marry," replied Adam, a stubborn set to his mouth. "And it would accomplish what we desire."

"Surely you don't want scandal to fall on Catherine."

"We might be a nine days' wonder, but it would be no more than that," he insisted. "Will you pass a note to her for me? You needn't know what's in it. You will be innocent in the entire matter if it ever comes to light."

Fiona sighed. It was useless to argue with Adam. He had his mind set on a course of action. She did not agree with his decision, but he was her friend and she would help him if possible, even if they both ended up in the suds.

"I will do what I can," she said.

Adam's face was suddenly transformed with a huge smile. "By George! I knew I could count on you. I was so certain that I wrote a note before I left my room this evening. You must get it to Catherine sometime this evening," he instructed.

He took her hand and gazed into her eyes. Fiona felt the smoothness of the paper press into her palm. She had not thought Adam would call upon her so soon. A simple house party was becoming exceedingly complicated. In how many schemes would she be entangled before the fortnight was over?

Which brought to mind the necessity of speaking to the cook about the port sauce to be served the following day. If the woman was unable to prepare it, Fiona must either change the menu or do it herself. She smiled when she thought of arriving in the dining room with splatters of port and butter on her gown.

She must stop woolgathering, thought Fiona. She had too many things to accomplish this evening. First she must get Adam's note to Catherine. Then she would slip out and visit the kitchen. Finally, she would be able to lay her weary head on her pillow. She had been up before dawn, and the tension of the day had taken its toll. She must get some rest so she could begin again tomorrow.

Galen had become adept at spying on people. It was not a talent of which he bragged, but one that had become necessary in order to carry out the Prince Regent's orders.

He had been watching Fiona and Duncan, and when Trent had taken Duncan's place at her side, he had continued to observe the two. He saw Trent take Lady Fiona's hand and easily detected the scrap of paper exchanged between them.

His interest piqued, Galen watched as Lady Fiona circulated throughout the room. His attention was drawn from her several times, and the last he saw was a quick glimpse of her back as she slipped out the door into the hallway.

He pondered what he had seen. Something strange was taking place in the household. He had found Lady Fiona near the back entrance at an extremely early hour with an excuse that didn't ring true. She and Duncan had been absorbed in one another until Trent interrupted. Then after Duncan left, Trent slipped Lady Fiona a note. Soon thereafter, the lady had stolen out of the room like a thief in the night. Was she rendezvousing with Duncan even now? Were the three of them involved in some sort of scheme, or was Lady Fiona merely a cat's paw for the men? It could take more than one person to successfully fix a race, particularly in such a small group of people.

Duncan had a reputation to be sure, and it was common knowledge Trent's pockets were not plump. But what would be Lady Fiona's incentive? Her family was wealthy, so it could not be for want of money. Did she have a *tendre* for one of the men? What else would induce such a woman to put aside a respectable upbringing but love?

Galen stepped into the hall. It was empty except for a footman stationed near the door. He caught sight of Lady Fiona again as she disappeared in the direction of the kitchen. A frown appeared between Galen's eyes. It was late—even for a lady who professed such an interest in food—to be visiting the kitchen. Was her interest in cookery also a ruse? Or was it only a cover for some other trickery?

He would wait a moment, then follow, decided Galen.

He was ready to make his way toward the back of the house when a tinkling fall of laughter claimed his attention.

"Why, Lord Burke. I was just saying if I had a gentleman to turn the pages, I'd play a tune for the company. Could I impose on your goodwill, sir?"

Galen sighed. As if long hours of spying weren't enough, he had to endure being pursued by Lady Melissa! He hoped the Crown would be suitably appreciative of his efforts. At times such as this, he could see no benefit in being a friend of the Prince Regent.

The following day was a distinct disappointment for Galen. It had rained on and off since early morning, keeping everyone inside. There were billiards and cards and reading, but Galen yearned for a brisk gallop across the countryside. However, the sky remained dark, and by afternoon, it was apparent that a ride was out of the question. Determined not to let the opportunity pass, he attempted to engage the other men of the party in conversation, hoping one of them would slip and reveal a knowledge of the seamier side of racing.

He had also hoped to find time to engage Lady Fiona in conversation. However, each time she joined the company, she disappeared before he had an opportunity to approach her. Her frequent absences only increased his suspicion, and he wondered what kept her from the party so often. On occasion, both Trent and Duncan were out of sight when she vanished, but without seeing them secretly meeting, he could only assume it was no more than coincidence.

The long, dark day finally ended, and the company gathered for dinner. At least, everyone but Lady Fiona. The members of the party were taking their seats around the table when she breathlessly appeared by his side.

"Lady Fiona, I had almost given you up."

"I was unavoidably detained," replied Fiona, thinking

of the time she had spent in the kitchen before dinner. She had wanted the pork roast to be perfect and had ended up preparing it for cooking herself. Rubbing it with oil, covering it with thyme, rosemary, and parsley, before searing it and judging it to be ready to roast. She had given close instructions to the cook about preparing the accompanying port sauce, then raced up the back stairs to change into a suitable gown for dinner.

"I had hoped we might play a hand of cards today," said Galen. "But our paths never seemed to cross."

"I took advantage of the rain to complete some correspondence."

"You must have been engrossed to have missed luncheon," he observed.

"I was. When I write to my mother, it takes all my concentration. I had a light repast in my room," she replied, then wondered why she was explaining herself to him.

"Perhaps you would care to join me tomorrow. If the weather clears, we could ride or take a walk if you prefer."

Fiona considered all the running up and down the back stairs she had been doing the past several days and shuddered when thinking of taking one step farther than was absolutely necessary. "Won't the gentlemen be attending the races?" she asked, hoping for a reprieve.

Galen was in a quandary. He craved to learn more about Lady Fiona, but his initial commitment was staying with the men in order to detect the identity of the culprit. "It's possible," he admitted. "But if we remain here, I hope you'll allow me to enjoy your company for a time."

Fiona murmured a faint, "We'll see," and attended to her dinner until the roast arrived at the table. When it did, it was browned to perfection. She was anxious to sample the final results. Putting a small bite into her mouth, she chewed thoroughly. A slight smile of satisfaction appeared on her face, and her shoulders relaxed. The roast and port sauce were perfect.

"What do you think of the roast?" she asked, anxious to get Lord Burke's opinion since he dined at the royal table.

Didn't the woman ever think of anything but food? thought Galen, stabbing at the meat on his plate as if to ensure it wouldn't rise up and walk away. Well, he was tired of their one-subject conversations. He had attempted to be agreeable since the moment they met, and she had shown no interest unless they were seated at the table discussing what was on their plates.

Galen chewed slowly and allowed his gaze to be fixed at a distant object, hoping he looked as if he were seriously considering the roast, which was the best he had ever eaten. He swallowed, then turned to Lady Fiona, who was anxiously watching him.

"The port sauce is too strong," he observed solemnly.

"What!"

"The port sauce," he repeated. "It overpowers the meat, which in itself might be over seasoned. But I can't properly judge that due to the sauce."

Galen smugly watched as bright pink slashes of color appeared on Fiona's cheekbones. She quickly took another taste of the roast. This time chewing quickly and decisively.

"The port sauce is not too strong, and the meat is not overseasoned. It is perfectly cooked."

"Perhaps I'm wrong then," said Galen, in a tone implying just the opposite. "But I had such a dish just before I left London, and they are quite dissimilar."

"Then perhaps the dish you tasted was improperly prepared," she hissed, her violet eyes sparking with anger.

"Conceivably," he replied, shrugging his shoulders beneath the blue superfine of his jacket. "But I'll keep that suggestion from the Prince Regent. He would be past all bearing if he thought his chef was inferior to Hamilton's."

"I'm not implying that at all," Fiona shot back quickly. "It's possible an undercook prepared the roast instead of the Prince Regent's chef. I only know that to my taste this dish is as it should be."

"There you have it," exclaimed Galen. "It's all a matter of taste."

Lord Burke's attention was claimed by his dinner partner on his opposite side, and Fiona was left to sit and stew in her port sauce. She consumed her entire serving and each bite she took tasted just as delicious as the last. The seasoning was discernible, but not overpowering. And to her way of thinking, the port sauce itself was absolutely not too strong. She did not speak to Lord Burke during the remainder of dinner. Instead, she pretended to be absorbed in her meal, then turned to converse with George Wallace, who sat on her other side.

Fiona trailed the ladies as they rose to leave the gentlemen to their after-dinner cigars and drinks. But instead of following them into the drawing room, she went down the hall toward the back of the house and out into the herb garden. She still simmered with indignation over Lord Burke's criticism of her recipe. She would not be confined in a room with the tasteless fool for the remainder of the evening. She was contributing far too much to the success of Edwina's house party to be governed by the usual rules of polite society.

"So here you are," said Edwina, a short time later. "It may be the mark of a poor hostess, but I had to have some time away from such inane conversation that is now taking place in the drawing room. I claimed it was necessary to meet with the staff, and no one questioned it. But why are you here?"

"I could take it no longer. Lord Burke and any other of his ilk who do not appreciate the finer points of dining can complain to one another about the port sauce," burst out Fiona, the rage she had been holding back pouring out. "But it does not mean that I am compelled to sit and listen to the taste-deprived simpletons spout their nonsense."

Edwina remained silent, completely bewildered by her friend's outburst. "I haven't heard any objections about the port sauce," she finally ventured to say. "On the contrary, there were many comments as to its excellence. John is particularly fond of the dish, but never seems to be completely satisfied with the attempts our cooks have made in preparing it. Tonight he especially commented on its superior quality and asked for a second serving."

"You saw nothing wrong with it?"

"Nothing whatsoever," confirmed Edwina.

"That odious man," gritted out Fiona between clenched teeth. "It was all a hum to him. A joke he could repeat over dinner at other tables. Perhaps to the Prince Regent himself."

"Fiona, what kind of gibberish are you spouting?"

"Lord Burke," spat out Fiona. "He passes himself off as a connoisseur of the finest dishes served in England. Then because I would not agree to walk with him on the morrow, he tells me the roast might be overseasoned, but he couldn't definitely decide because the port sauce was too strong."

"I can't believe it of him. He's such a gentleman."

"You've only seen his best side," declared Fiona. "A man devious enough to complain about my roast and port sauce would stop at nothing to obtain his desires."

"Perhaps you're making too much of it," reasoned Edwina.

"You are welcome to your own opinion, but mine is made up. I will have nothing more to do with him."

"You cannot carry on a feud with him," said Edwina. "It will ruin the house party, and you know how important it is to me that it be a success."

"Piffle! Your party would be an *on-dit* once we returned to London."

"That's just what I don't want," wailed Edwina. "John would be utterly furious, and I so want to please him."

The tears pooling in Edwina's eyes convinced Fiona to take a more rational approach to her problem. "All right," she agreed. "I shall be extremely circumspect when it comes to Lord Burke. I will avoid him when possible and be exceedingly polite when we happen to be thrown together. Will that please you?"

"Thank you, Fiona. I'm aware of how much I'm asking of you, and I appreciate it more than you know."

"Then do a favor for me."

"Anything," replied Edwina fervently.

"Move Lord Burke's seating at the dinner table."

"What? How could I explain that?"

"Then move mine," said Fiona.

"I would still have the same problem of explaining."

Silence fell over the herb garden for a short time before Fiona spoke again. If it had been full light, Edwina would have seen a mischievous smile appear on her friend's face. "Put Lady Melissa in my place."

"I don't think Galen would enjoy his meals with Melissa at his elbow."

"All the more reason to do it. If he cannot abide the cooking, then he deserves a distraction. Lady Melissa should more than fulfill that need."

"I couldn't do that to Galen. He's John's friend."

"Edwina, I am doing all I can to ensure your house party is a success. But I vow if my seat is not moved from beside Lord Burke, your next dinner will live forever in the minds of your guests as the worst meal they've ever eaten."

Edwina did not know whether Fiona's threat was all a hum, but she decided not to chance it.

Three

It was difficult for Galen to conceal his surprise the next evening at dinner when Lady Melissa took the seat beside him. Looking around the table, he located Lady Fiona sitting between Adam Trent and Lord Duncan. Had she requested her seat be changed in order to more easily conspire with the two men? He did not have time to dwell on the subject because, at that moment, Lady Melissa demanded his attention.

Dinner was an ordeal Galen did not like to consider repeating. Lady Fiona's discussion of dishes being served would have sounded like a choir of angels compared to Lady Melissa's boring chatter. What rankled even more was looking down the table and seeing the lively conversation going on between Lady Fiona and her dinner companions. Lady Melissa would not even leave him in enough peace to enjoy the meal, which included some of his favorite dishes.

Venison, tender enough to eat without benefit of a knife, was served that evening, along with rosemary potatoes that raised the common root vegetable to new heights. One of the desserts offered rivaled any he had tasted. The bottom of the dish was covered in brandied cherries rolled in sugar and covered by a layer of rich custard. The dish had been garnished by Naples biscuits and rose-colored whipped cream flavored with brandy.

Even with his growing suspicion of Lady Fiona, Galen found himself missing their culinary discussions. Instead, he was called upon to describe his country estate to Lady Melissa—a conversation he viewed with distrust. A lady was usually interested in a house when she intended to make it her home. He did his best to guide the discussion into safer waters.

In the meantime, Fiona was vastly enjoying her new dinner companions. Since all was going smoothly, she had become less concerned about the menu. The kitchen staff was working well and following her instructions to the letter. The guests—other than Lord Burke—had nothing but compliments for the fare served at each meal. Some were saying Edwina set the best table in England.

Edwina, of course, was extremely happy, John was proud, and Fiona hoped Lord Burke was miserable. When she glanced down the table at dinner, his face was one of composed politeness, which usually meant a gentleman was bored beyond words. Fiona stifled a sudden urge to laugh out loud. She would wager if Lord Burke had known what had instigated the change in seating he would never again complain about anyone's port sauce, although he probably had no idea why she had taken it so personally.

"What the deuce did Edwina mean by seating Lady Melissa beside me?" asked Galen as soon as he was private with John.

"You mean you don't enjoy the fair Melissa's attributes?"

"She's easy on the eyes, I'll admit, but as soon as she speaks the illusion is shattered."

"I know of several men who have offered for her."

"And they're welcome to her," commented Galen.

"Most of them didn't carry a title, but her father would probably have forgiven that if they had enough blunt. However, none of them was plump enough in the pocket for Lord Huxley. I hear he's fallen on hard times, but I haven't seen any sign of it yet," revealed John.

"Do you think you could speak with Edwina? Convince her to make another seating change?"

"I'll try, but I won't promise anything. She usually has a good reason for everything she does. But how goes your investigation?" asked John, in order to detract Galen from his complaint. "Are you making any progress?"

"Not much at all," confessed Galen. "I had hoped to have eliminated at least one man by now, but if the malefactor is here, he's being inordinately cautious."

"It looks as if the rainy days are behind us," observed John. "We'll arrange as many visits to the races as possible. There shouldn't be any complaints since most of the men enjoy watching a good piece of horseflesh run."

"Good, I'm ready to get this over with and put it behind me. In the meantime, would you see what you can do?" Galen asked again.

"I'll do my best," promised John without a great deal of enthusiasm.

Adam had given Fiona another note to deliver to Lady Catherine. Although she did not approve of the furtiveness surrounding their relationship, she had given her word to Adam, and she would not break it. Catherine was at the pianoforte considering the selection of music when Fiona approached and took a seat by her side on the bench.

"I have a message from Adam," she said, quickly passing the paper to Catherine.

Catherine's eyes sparkled and her cheeks took on a faint blush. "Oh, thank you. I don't know what we would do without your help."

"I've warned Adam to be extremely careful. If the two of you are caught meeting in secret it will mean the loss of your reputation."

Catherine's face took on the same stubborn expression as Adam's when Fiona had broached the subject to him.

"It's the only thing we can do. Adam is a fine man, but my parents expect a better match. They want a title and a fortune for me, as if that is more important than love," she declared passionately.

Fiona did not smile at Catherine's intensity. Her feelings were real, no matter what her age. "Just be cautious," Fiona warned again as she began to rise.

"Oh, Lady Fiona . . ."

"Please, since we are fellow conspirators, I believe we should be on a first-name basis," said Fiona, smiling.

Catherine nodded in agreement. "I only wanted to thank you again."

"You can repay me by heeding my advice," admonished Fiona as she rose and moved away.

Galen had renewed his determination to narrow the field of suspects as quickly as possible, and today he would have them all together at the races. The ladies had decided to join the gentlemen, and the party consisted of several carriages and a coach filled with two servants and baskets of food for the group.

It would be more difficult to watch everyone, but Galen hoped the larger group would provide the guilty person with a sense of confidence that he would go unnoticed. The early races were of lesser consequence, but the afternoon offered several matches that were sure to attract large stakes being bet on the outcome. It was then he must be particularly vigilant.

Fiona had instructed that the plate of biscuits be placed in front of her and she guarded them carefully. They were a new recipe and she did not want them to go to the entire company until she sampled them herself. She had passed the recipe to the cook the night before and had not had time to see whether they met her rigid standards.

"Isn't it lovely today?" asked Catherine as she took a seat beside Fiona. "I'm not a race fan, but Adam seems to be enjoying himself, so I suppose I should develop a liking for it."

"It never hurts to have something in common with the man you admire," said Fiona. She immediately felt a twinge of guilt, for Lord Burke's appreciation of food had driven them apart instead of bringing them together. But that was quite different. Fiona absolutely did not aspire to an attraction developing between them. Although she was often aware of being the object of Lord Burke's attention since her place at dinner had been moved, she had managed to avoid him.

"Then I must find Adam and show him how much I am enjoying the day," said Catherine, her eyes twinkling. "I'll take some biscuits for the horses. That should impress him."

"You shouldn't be feeding them biscuits," warned Fiona, not offering her the plate. "Particularly before a race."

"Oh pshaw! One little biscuit could never hurt such a huge animal."

Before Fiona could object further, Catherine had swept several biscuits from the plate and wrapped them in her lace-edged handkerchief.

"If they're as delicious as everything else, the horses will be begging for more." Catherine giggled and started off in search of Adam before Fiona could come up with an appropriate excuse to retrieve the biscuits.

Since he was attempting to follow as many of the house party's movements as possible, Galen took note of Lady Fiona's and Lady Catherine's exchange. They spoke

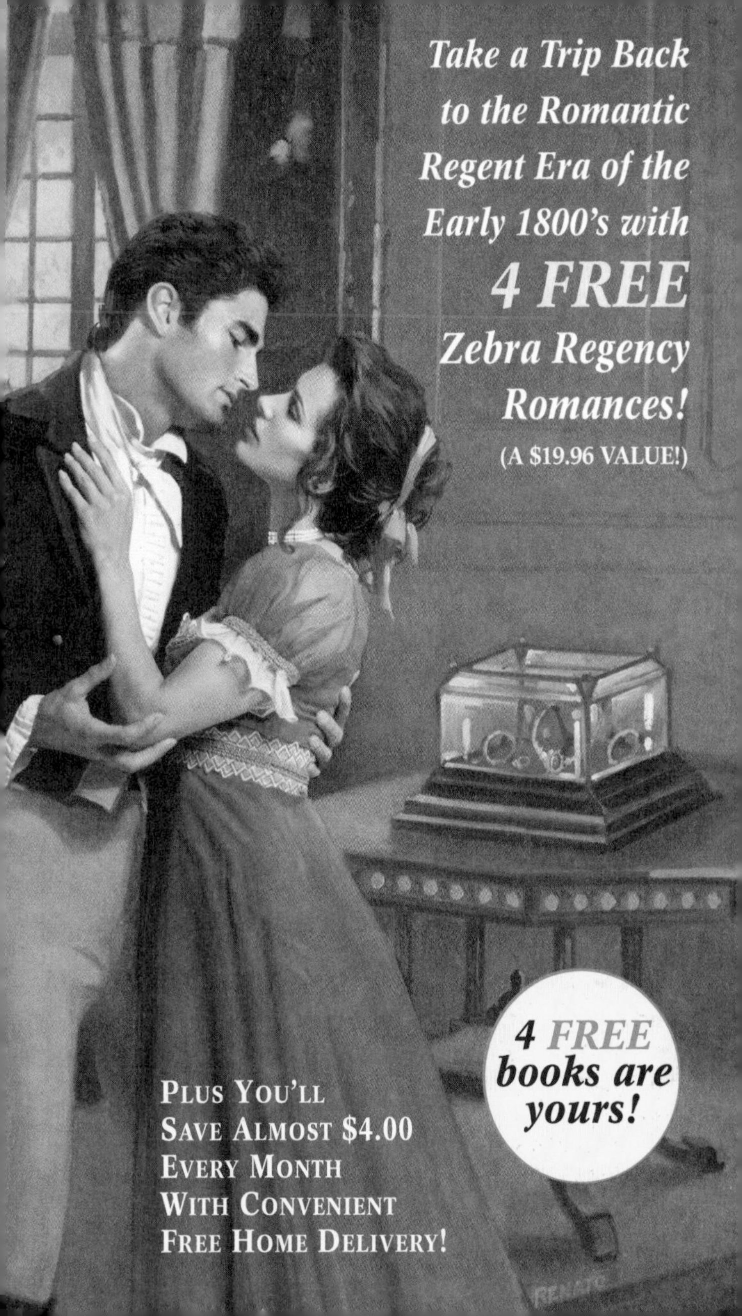
Take a Trip Back
to the Romantic
Regent Era of the
Early 1800's with
4 FREE
Zebra Regency
Romances!
(A $19.96 VALUE!)
4 FREE
books are
yours!
PLUS YOU'LL
SAVE ALMOST $4.00
EVERY MONTH
WITH CONVENIENT
FREE HOME DELIVERY!

briefly; then Lady Catherine wrapped several biscuits in her handkerchief. She smiled at Lady Fiona and wandered off toward the area where the horses were kept. Lady Fiona stared after her. The worried frown on her face raised Galen's curiosity.

He followed, watching as Lady Catherine approached one of the horses running in the afternoon's races. The groom's back was turned as she unwrapped the biscuits and held them out toward the inquisitive animal on the flat of her palm. The horse sniffed, then lifted them from her hand with the deftness of the most proficient pickpocket.

Galen started forward to prevent Lady Catherine from feeding the biscuits to the horse, but he was too late. He only hoped the animal suffered no ill effects from eating such an unusual food before running.

The next race was nearly ready to begin, and most of the people had gravitated toward the racecourse. Lady Fiona sat alone, and Galen thought it a perfect time to mend the breach with her. Dinner had become a torture for him since he had to sit next to Lady Melissa. Perhaps he could ask Lady Fiona to appeal to Edwina to reinstate their original seating. Evidently, he could not depend upon John, who had been unsuccessful thus far.

He had almost reached Lady Fiona when he heard the roar of the crowd as the race began. Just as quickly he heard a chorus of cries of alarm, and he turned, hurrying toward the racecourse.

The main body of horses were continuing the race, but everyone's attention was focused on a horse that stood, head hanging, legs splayed, near the beginning of the course. The jockey was standing by the animal's side, and men were running toward the horse, who was, quite evidently, in distress. Upon second glance, Galen recognized it as the same horse that had eaten the biscuits.

* * *

"Oh, Fiona. It was absolute terrible. That poor horse. And to think he was just fine when I fed him the biscuits," said Catherine as the two women walked toward the carriages standing ready to take them back to Hamilton House. "Could I have caused his condition?"

"I can't say," replied Fiona sharply. "I warned you about the results, so you shouldn't be surprised."

"I know, but I wanted to impress Adam, to show him I wasn't afraid. I never thought to harm the animal. I tried not to cry in front of Adam. I don't want him to think I'm a watering pot," Catherine said bravely.

"You did a good job of it," relented Fiona, patting her hand. She should not be too harsh on Catherine, for it was not yet certain that the biscuits had anything to do with the animal's affliction.

Galen heard only snatches of Lady Catherine's and Lady Fiona's conversation as he followed them to the carriages. It was obvious Catherine was upset over what had occurred, but Fiona was exceedingly composed. He heard her praising the younger woman for doing a good job. Had Lady Fiona put something in the biscuits? She was in and out of the kitchen constantly and it would be very easy for her to do so. Further, convincing Lady Catherine to feed it to the horse removed Lady Fiona from the vicinity and any blame in the matter.

Lady Fiona had even gotten rid of any remaining evidence. After the horse had broken down, she had taken the plate of biscuits to a small ornamental lake near the racecourse and thrown them in. Galen wondered whether there would be dead fish floating to the top if he returned in a few hours time.

That evening at dinner Galen watched Fiona closely, eating only what she chose for her own plate. But by the end of the meal, he felt a little foolish, for no one had fallen gasping from the table. If she had been involved in the trouble at the racecourse, she had saved her poisonous fare for the horses.

It was a relief for Fiona to leave the dining room that evening. Lord Burke had cast dark glances at her all evening, which made it impossible for her to enjoy her food. He should have been happy, she thought. He had the lovely Melissa by his side, and it was quite apparent the angelic-looking blond woman was bestowing her entire attention on him. Shrugging aside the troublesome feeling, she followed the women into the drawing room. For once, she did not resent joining the ladies. At times, there was safety in numbers, and she felt she the necessity of protection this evening.

"Oh, I feel so much better," said Catherine immediately upon approaching Fiona. "Adam told me the horse is recovering. And it wasn't my fault after all."

"How does he know?"

"Lord Duncan stayed for a time after our party left. He said a water trough was tainted with arsenic, and that caused the animal to become ill. I'm relieved the biscuits I gave him had nothing to do with it."

"So am I," Fiona replied fervently, relaxing for the first time since they had left the racecourse.

"Arsenic?" repeated Galen, staring at Duncan across the dining room table, where the men were enjoying their after-dinner drinks and cigars.

"That's what I was told," said Duncan, taking a sip of port. "Two other horses suffered minor problems before they located a water trough that was the source of the trouble."

Galen was annoyed by the feeling of relief that swept

over him. It should not matter a whit to him whether Lady Fiona was guilty or not. In fact, who was to say the biscuits could not have been laced with arsenic also? The watering trough could have been just a coincidence. As soon as the thought crossed his mind, he discarded it. He sounded like a caper-witted fool. He was allowing the seating arrangement at dinner and Lady Fiona's continued avoidance of him to aggravate him more than they should. Melissa was proving to be an irritating companion, but he could not let her prattling drive him to accuse someone of a crime he or she did not commit.

He should be concentrating on the obvious. Perhaps the arsenic in the watering trough had not been a natural occurrence, but had been added. No, it would have been too risky, he decided. There would be no way to judge which horse would drink from the trough. Today's incident must have been exactly what it appeared to be—an unfortunate accident.

"Edwina, my love."

A ripple of pleasure and hope ran through Edwina. It had been some time since John had greeted her with such an endearment. Perhaps he had completed his political discussions with Lord Huxley and realized how much he had missed their closeness. Turning, she held out her hand to her husband.

Taking it, John raised it to his lips, pressing a kiss to the soft skin. It reminded him he had spent too many nights in masculine debate, and the thought of Edwina alone in her bed brought an urgent need to his body. He tightened his grip on her hand and moved as close as polite society would allow, even for a man and wife.

"John," murmured Edwina, a warning in her voice that held little force. She was secretly elated with his obvious amorous intent. It was not good for a man to develop such a single-minded purpose, as he had of late.

His wife was charming, thought John. The faint blush on her cheeks, and her green eyes taking on that beguiling look, made it difficult for him to keep his mind on the business at hand. But first things first. His own wants must take second place for the time being.

Keeping her hand in his, he looked down at her and smiled. "I don't think I'm being prejudiced in saying this house party is one of the best I've attended."

Edwina gave a slight laugh. "Well, perhaps you're a bit partial, but I'll thank you all the same."

"Balderdash! There's not a hostess in all of England who could have done it better. Except for the rain—and I won't hold you accountable for that—everything has been perfect. Particularly the food. There isn't a person who hasn't commented on the excellence of the meals. I don't know where you found the cook, but you must keep her at all costs."

Edwina felt a pang of guilt, then pushed it away. Not only was this house party important to John's political aspirations, but it was also exceedingly crucial in solidifying her position as a hostess who could offer her guests unparalleled comfort and entertainment. The success of this party would spread when they returned to London and few, if any, would decline their invitations. Edwina envisioned a future with John as an important political figure and herself as hostess to all manner of influential guests.

"I'll do my best to keep the cook, but I'm certain they would have enjoyed themselves all the same. After all, you are an excellent host," she teased.

"There is one thing," he said.

"What is it? Did someone complain?" she asked anxiously.

"No, no, nothing like that," he soothed. "Well, not exactly. Do you remember the other evening when I asked you about the seating arrangement for dinner?"

"Yes," replied Edwina cautiously. She had quickly changed the subject when he had brought the matter up earlier; however, it looked as if he was not going to give up so easily.

"I was wondering whether you had considered changing the seating back to its original plan? For Galen's sake, if no other."

Edwina was unable to explain her decision without giving away the secret of the arrangement she had with Fiona. "I don't see how. If I did, it would embarrass Melissa. Everyone would think Galen had requested the change because he could not tolerate her."

"Well, it is the truth," said John, keeping his voice low so they couldn't be overheard.

"But it isn't for public consumption," declared Edwina, glancing around to see whether anyone was near.

"I know, I know. But surely there is some way you can undo such a mistake."

"Mistake," said Edwina, pulling her hand from his grasp. "You just told me the party had been perfection itself."

"It has, but Galen is an old friend, and he cannot fully enjoy those wonderful meals sitting by Melissa," replied John, attempting to cajole her with his most flattering smile.

"If he's such an old friend, then he should understand someone must sit next to Melissa."

"But why him?" asked John. "There are others here who would welcome her company. Sanborn desperately needs a rich wife, and Duncan would not be averse to a closer acquaintance with her, I'm certain. Then there's Trent. While he might not be in dun territory, I don't think he would turn down such a pretty face and what is rumored to be a substantial dowry."

"I didn't know you equated marriage so strongly with

money," replied Edwina stiffly. "Is that why you married me? For money and a hostess?"

"It's always a consideration," said John, meaning to follow up his comment with protestations of love. But Edwina didn't give him a chance.

"How could you tell me you don't love me in front of all these people?" hissed Edwina, looking around the room once again to see whether they were drawing the attention of any of their guests.

John was dumfounded by her accusation. It took a moment for him to form a reply. "I never said that at all," he protested. "I only meant—"

"I know very well what you meant," interrupted Edwina. "If I had not brought a considerable dowry to the marriage, if my father's name was not well known in political circles, then I would not be here tonight endowed with the honor of being a hostess for a house party all for your benefit."

Her hurt feelings translated into a bitter tone, which John had never heard fall from her lips before. Perhaps he had misspoken and had not been as subtle as he should have been, but surely such a minor offense did not warrant a reply as cutting as hers. If she had but given him time he would have expressed how much he loved her and appreciated her patience with his involvement in politics. He would have described the trip he had planned for them so they could enjoy time together. But, no, she had flown up into the boughs and given him no time to explain at all. She had accused him of only marrying her for money and her name. He was hurt she thought it of him. Too hurt to attempt to mend the argument. Giving a small, sharp bow, he left her standing alone.

Oh, Lord, thought Edwina, *I've ruined my marriage all because of a silly seating arrangement.* No, it was more than that. John had admitted why he had married her and it had not included one word about love. She stiffened her shoulders and blinked away her unshed tears. She had a house to run and guests to attend to. She would keep her feelings in check until she was alone with her misery. And John's dear friend, Lord Burke, could suffer with the lovely Lady Melissa until the last bite he took on this earth, as far as she was concerned.

"How did your luck run today?" asked Galen as he and Duncan stood near the French doors enjoying the evening air.

"Better than usual," replied Duncan.

"I noticed your choice won the race when the favorite was taken ill with arsenic poisoning."

"That's true. I'd taken a chance and wagered against the favorite. Luck was with me this time."

"Shame the horse had to suffer," remarked Galen.

"An unfortunate accident," agreed Duncan.

Not a trace of guilt appeared on Duncan's face or in his voice. He was either a consummate liar or he was innocent. At the moment, there was no way Galen could prove which was true. It had not been a good day and he yearned for the seclusion of his room, but first he must evade Lady Melissa's clutches.

Her constant chatter at dinner had distracted him from the quails that had been served. The birds had been stuffed and seasoned, covered in pastry, and cooked to perfection. Forgetting for the moment his suspicions, he reflected that, if Lady Fiona had been by his side, they could have discussed the ingredients of the stuffing and the quality of pastry. But Lady Melissa seemed unable to converse on any subject that did not involve herself in one way or another.

He was certain Lady Melissa was waiting for her chance to catch him in her snare for the remainder of the evening. And the others seemed to be cooperating with her. Evidently the seating change had given the party the idea that the two were interested in one another, and once Lady Melissa appeared at his side they were, for the most part, left to themselves.

"I hope my luck continues to hold," said Duncan, bringing Galen back to the conversation at hand.

"Does it usually?"

"I'm considered to be fairly proficient at picking winners," replied Duncan modestly. "I suppose it runs in the family. My father introduced me to racing before I could walk. There were times when I was younger that I lost more than I won, but those periods are long past."

"It's amazing you win so consistently," said Galen, hoping to draw him out.

"It's all a matter of being familiar with the animals that are running and the jockeys who ride them. It takes a certain amount of dedication, but if a person admires the sport then it's no chore at all."

A man as well known at the racecourses as Duncan could move about freely without raising suspicion, thought Galen. Duncan had just solidified himself as a possible candidate for the guilty party.

Galen left Duncan by the door and began to make his way toward the hall, hoping to get away without notice. But before he could reach safety, John approached with a dark look on his face.

"The prospect of getting you away from Melissa at dinner doesn't seem encouraging at this point. I tried to talk to Edwina about it, and we ended up in an argument. She has some sort of harebrained idea that I only married her for convenience' sake and won't listen to anything I say."

Galen could see John's exasperation and did his best to hide his disappointment. "Well, it's not the worst thing in the world," he replied philosophically. "Lady Melissa is considered a diamond of the first water. If only she would eat more and talk less, but she takes pride in how little she consumes. I wonder whether she sneaks down to the kitchen at night?"

The thought drew a smile from John. "More like she sends her maid. I doubt Lady Melissa would be caught in such a common position as sneaking into the kitchen to nibble on a leg of lamb. Think of what it would do to her consequence." His expression became serious. "I'm sorry, Galen. I didn't anticipate a problem with Edwina."

"No matter. She has a lot on her plate, seeing to the guests while we all enjoy ourselves."

"That's true," agreed John, seeming pleased to be able to place the blame somewhere other than himself. "This is her first house party since we've been married, and I know she's excessively concerned everything goes well."

"Of course, she is," said Galen. "And I shouldn't bother her with such a small thing as where I sit for dinner."

Fiona watched as Melissa made her way toward Lord Burke and John. The two men were engrossed in their conversation, oblivious to everyone else in the room. Melissa grasped Lord Burke's arm to gain his attention. A flicker of irritation flashed quickly across his face before he assumed a mask of civility. John promptly excused himself, leaving Galen and Melissa alone.

Fiona turned away. A well of discontent grew inside her and she became anxious to leave the company and retire to the privacy of her room.

Galen gave only part of his attention to Lady Melissa while observing Fiona's approach to the door leading into the hallway. She did not walk directly to the door, nor did she bid anyone good night as she inched in a roundabout way toward the hall. He wondered whether she was slipping away to meet Trent or Duncan. Some of the men were on the terrace blowing a cloud. However, they were only shadowy figures outside the French doors, and he couldn't tell who was there.

His distraction must have been apparent, for Melissa renewed her effort to engage his attention. He smiled and nodded at her remarks and was vastly relieved when Viscount Sanborn joined them. The man was not only timid when betting, but he was naturally quiet at all times. However, he had not hidden the fact that he admired Lady Melissa, and Galen wished him the best of luck. As soon as courtesy allowed, he excused himself and went in search of Fiona, who had by now disappeared from the room.

Galen told himself it was not just that he had a desire to see her, but that he had done her a disservice when he had thought her guilty of inflicting damage to the racehorse. Even though she could in no way have known his thoughts, he felt a need to seek her out and attempt to close the gap that had widened between them since the night he had criticized that damnable port sauce.

He still could not understand why she was up in arms about his remarks. It was not her dinner, nor her cook, nor even her house party. There was no reason in the world why she should have taken his observation so personally. He supposed it was because of her close friendship with Edwina.

If she hadn't taken offense so quickly, he would have told her it was just a hum—a harmless joke—and they could have laughed together. But, no. Lady Fiona had gone off in a huff, had removed herself from his side at dinner, and had pointedly ignored him since that evening.

It was uncomfortable for Galen to be in such close proximity to a woman who refused to admit his existence. He was accustomed to being able to select a companion from a long list of females. Evidently, he thought with a grim smile, Lady Fiona was not one of that list.

The situation had gone on long enough, he decided as he stepped into the hall. He and Lady Fiona would be on speaking terms before the night was over, and they would be dinner partners the very next evening if he had anything to say about it. His step was confident as he walked toward the back of the house.

He found her, not having an assignation with Duncan or Trent in the garden, but in the kitchen huddled over the table with the cook. Lady Fiona was speaking intently and the cook was nodding at intervals. There was a vast social distance between the two women, but the kitchen made them equals for the moment. He stepped farther into the room, drawing their attention.

"My Lord Burke," said Fiona, startled by his sudden appearance.

"My lady," he replied with a brief nod. "And is this the cook who has served up such delicious meals?"

The woman lowered her eyes and blushed, giving a quick bob in his direction.

"Yes, my lord, this is Mary. She's a bit shy, but that doesn't hurt her cooking."

"I should say not. If you ever want a new position, Mary, you may have one with me anytime."

"Thank you, my lord."

"That's all, Mary," said Fiona. "Get some rest. Tomorrow morning comes soon enough."

As soon as Mary left, Fiona turned to face Lord Burke. "Is there something you want, my lord?"

With any other woman, Galen might have spoken of the particular attractiveness of her gown or hair. But he knew that would not do with Lady Fiona.

"I've been thinking of you since the stuffed quail this evening."

"You have?" she replied cautiously.

"Absolutely. The stuffing outdid any other I have ever tasted."

Pleasure flowed through Fiona's body. "Do you mean

that?" She prevented herself from sighing with rapture. It wouldn't do to let him see how his words affected her.

"I'm absolutely sincere. I've never said that to anyone else," he vowed, moving closer and placing his hand over his heart.

Fiona felt like a green girl allowing his flattery to erase the ill will that had occurred between them. But how could she hold a grudge against someone who spoke so glowingly of her stuffed quail? "My lord, you don't know how much your words mean to me. Someone with your experience . . ."

"And that is not all," he said, taking a step nearer, his intent gaze holding hers. "The pastry covering the birds was baked to perfection, and it was so light I am convinced it would have floated right off the table if it had not been attached to the quail."

Fiona attempted to rekindle her resentment against Lord Burke, but found its significance rapidly vanishing. "You say too much," she objected, her cheeks flushing a delicate pink.

"No, not enough," he replied, covering the remaining distance to her side. "I believe you're the inspiration behind the meals being served. No, don't deny it," he said as she opened her mouth to do that very thing. "John is amazed Edwina found such an excellent cook, and I won't be the one to tell him any differently. But I know it is all your doing." He grew bold and reached out to touch the flawless skin of her cheek. She did not object as his finger traced the line of her neck to the softness of her shoulder. He did not know what came over him when he was close to her. All his suspicions seemed to vanish, but he did not stop to ponder the reason for this mysterious event. He tipped her chin up and placed a light kiss on her soft lips. "I wish I were free to tell everyone of your extraordinary talent," he said, staring into the dark violet depths of her eyes. "However, I will keep it to myself. Only know how greatly I admire you." Galen was surprised at his rhetoric. He had not meant to carry gallantry to such an extent.

Fiona was overwhelmed by Lord Burke's praise. She had kept her secret so long it felt odd talking to a near stranger about her passion. Lord Burke escorted her to the bottom of the stairs, and before she knew it, she had agreed to a picnic on the morrow. She was in bed with the candles extinguished before she remembered she had sworn to have nothing to do with the gentleman.

Four

"She is still abed, my lord," advised Haynes, Lord Burke's valet.

"Are you certain? She's usually up before the kitchen staff."

"That is what her maid told me. I did not press her further."

"Yesterday was overly long with the trip to the racecourse," he mused. "She's probably resting from the journey. I will write a note, Haynes, and you must see that she receives it as soon as she rises. If there is no other way, sit outside her door and place it in her hand yourself. You must not fail me on this."

"You may trust me completely, my lord," replied the servant, a satisfied glint in his eye. Perhaps his master had finally met his match.

Fiona had been up earlier than usual, giving orders for a very special picnic luncheon to be packed for her outing with Lord Burke later in the day. She told herself it was not because she was looking forward to the picnic, but that she wanted to hear him admit again to the quality of the dishes that were served. She had returned to her room for a quick nap and awakened to see her maid looking out the window.

"What is it, Kate?"

"The gentlemen, miss. They're off to the races, I'd wager."

"No doubt," agreed Fiona, sitting up in her bed. "Some of them seem to be there every day. I wonder that they all aren't without a rag to their name by now."

"That's for sure, miss," agreed Kate. "Especially Lord Burke. He's always ready to watch the horses run."

Fiona froze in the middle of her stretch. "Is he with the company now?" she asked in a stiff voice.

"Oh, yes, miss," said the maid, staring out the window and missing the expression of coldness on her mistress's face. "He makes a fine figure on that big animal he rides."

"I'm certain he believes so," murmured Fiona.

"What did you say, miss?" asked Kate, turning from the window to help Fiona with her wrap.

"Nothing. Nothing at all. Have the gentlemen left yet?"

"No, they're gathering at the stables just now."

Fiona rose quickly and hurried to the small desk in the corner of the room. "I want you to deliver a note to Lord Duncan immediately. You'll need to rush to catch him before he leaves. Wait to see if he has a reply. Then bring me coffee and a roll. I won't be going down to breakfast this morning."

"Yes, miss," said Kate, taking the note Fiona handed her and moving quickly to the door. As she stepped outside, she was surprised to see Haynes, Lord Burke's valet.

"I have a . . ."

"Whatever it is, it must wait," said Kate over her shoulder as she hurried away.

Haynes breathed deeply and settled in for a longer wait.

Galen strolled into the stable, feeling a stab of remorse as he thought of the day he could have been sharing with Lady Fiona. He had dreamed of her during the night and had even been so unromantic as to wonder what she would order for their picnic luncheon. He had looked forward to putting aside all thoughts of fixed horse races and concentrating on pure pleasure for the length of a few hours.

Then Duncan had suggested they attend the races and he could do nothing but go along with the group if he ever hoped to get to the bottom of the mystery.

His attention was drawn to a groom who was polishing a saddle to a high gloss. "You've certainly worked up a shine. What is that you're using?"

"It's my own mixture, my lord," replied the man in a somewhat surly manner.

"You're using a sponge to apply it. I've never seen that done before."

"The mixture's a little thin. So the sponge is better than cloth," the groom explained.

"Do you work for Lord Hamilton?" asked Galen.

"No, my lord. I work for Mr. Trent."

Galen walked away, wondering whether his groom could get the directions for the oil the man was using. His saddle could use a polish of that quality.

He looked toward the upper windows of Hamilton House. Had Lady Fiona received his note? There had been no way he could adequately explain the reason he chose horse racing over a picnic with her. He grimaced, thinking of her reaction when she learned of his desertion. Prinny owed him a great deal for this favor.

"Lord Duncan said he would be pleased to join you, miss," said Kate as she entered the room some time later carrying a tray.

"Good." Fiona was pleased with his acceptance. It proved that certain gentlemen would put aside a day at the races in order to spend time with a lady.

"Oh, and Lord Burke's valet gave this to me. He made me vow I would give it to you immediately." She handed

Fiona a piece of buff-colored paper, the same Fiona had used when writing her note to Lord Duncan.

Fiona read the message and tossed it on the desk with an unladylike snort of disgust. So he had something he must attend to, did he? she thought. Well, she would not sit and wait until he had spare time to squeeze her in between his trips to the racecourse. Her picnic luncheon would not go to waste. Lord Duncan had the ability to appreciate the fare, and she was certain she would enjoy his company much more than she would have Lord Burke's. She ignored the imp who sat on her shoulder and said, "Ah," in amusement.

"I want to wear a particularly flattering gown today, Kate. I think the blue one will do very nicely."

"I noticed your man polishing your saddle earlier," said Galen to Adam Trent. "He told me he used a special oil on it."

"Some concoction of his own," replied Adam. "Caused me some trouble yesterday. He ran out of sponges and said he couldn't apply it with anything else. I was able to beg a few from one of the ladies. Damned embarrassing, too."

"Do you think he'd give the directions for the oil to my groom?"

"I'll see, but he's not too pleasant a fellow. I took him on because Duncan asked me to. Said he had to let him go and didn't want to turn him out on the street. The man's got a good reputation with animals and such, but doesn't get along with people very well."

"He sounds like the perfect groom, except for his manner."

"He is. He has a passion for the racecourse, and he works cheap as long as I allow him to accompany me. It's little enough to ask, I suppose."

"Well, don't worry about the oil. It isn't important enough to overset him."

The animals were brought out then, and the two men were separated by the business of getting mounted and ready to begin the journey.

Galen remembered his note to Lady Fiona. He was hopeful that she would accept his apology until he could further explain when they met at dinner.

"I may not need your assistance in regaining my dinner partner, John," said Galen, a bit smugly, as they rode down the drive away from Hamilton House. "I believe I'm finally making progress with Lady Fiona."

"By Jupiter! I'm glad to hear it. I was feeling a bit guilty about not being able to help."

"No need," Galen assured him, thinking of the evening before. "It's merely a matter of time—and not long at that—until we'll be back on good terms."

John smiled, relieved that the problem was solved. "Are you ready to determine the guilty party today?" he asked.

Galen was reluctant to change the subject, for there was more he had hoped to learn about Fiona from John, but that could wait until the ride home. "There is no assurance, but I hope something gives him away. I'm tired of this sordid business. If it weren't for Prinny I'd give the whole thing up."

"Surely whoever is doing it will make a move soon."

"I'm going to make a special effort to keep my eye on Duncan today. As pleasant as he is, I don't trust the man," said Galen, remembering how closely he had been in contact with Lady Fiona.

"Then you'll need to wait until another day."

"What do you mean?" Galen turned and searched the men riding in a group behind them. Duncan was not one of them. "Where is he? He was in the stable yard with the rest of us. I saw him myself."

"He received a note, then told me he had changed his mind about going."

"But he was the one who suggested it. I can't imagine what would be important enough to keep him away. I wonder whether he's fixed a race and doesn't want to be there so he won't be suspect," said Galen.

"He mentioned going on a picnic with a lovely lady. So perhaps you're wrong. Perhaps there is something more important to him than horses," said John with a devilish grin.

Galen did not want to believe what he was thinking. "Did he say with whom?"

"No, but I've noticed him paying particular attention to Fiona the last several days, and I'm surprised. Duncan isn't a man prone to doing that." John was completely satisfied with Galen's silence. Perhaps if he helped Edwina with her matchmaking she would forgive him more readily.

Galen was in no better mood when he came down for dinner that evening. The day had been completely wasted. The races had gone off as planned, and none of the men in his party had indicated they were intent upon preventing them from doing so.

During the ride to and from the racecourse, Galen had given himself over to imagining Duncan beside Fiona in some picturesque setting, enjoying the pleasurable fare that had been intended for him. The image did nothing to improve his mood, and his face was a dark expression of discontent as he entered the drawing room. Seeing Fiona and Duncan together only tended to deepen the frown that creased his brow, and he hesitated, wondering whether to approach them in his present ill humor.

* * *

"My dear Fiona," said Duncan—for they had agreed to be on a first-name basis during the picnic. "I must tell you again how much I enjoyed our day."

"There is no need to empty the butter boat," replied Fiona. "You have praised our meal quite enough. Remember, I did not do the preparation myself."

"I can never say enough," he replied. "Besides, you did the planning of the entire event. You may pass along whatever thanks you want to the staff, but for myself, I will limit my praises to you. The dishes were exquisite—and beautiful in their presentation as well as being delicious."

Fiona knew Duncan was a great flatterer, but she was pleased nonetheless. It was extremely gratifying to have a man admire her after Lord Burke's callous indifference that morning. She favored Duncan with one of her most brilliant smiles.

Galen could only catch snippets of Duncan's remarks over the chatter from the other guests. But his hearing was sharp enough to catch the words *exquisite, inspiration,* and *beautiful.* And his eyesight was good enough to see the smile Fiona lavished on the blackguard. He fought the sneer that threatened to curl his lip in disdain.

At that moment, Duncan was called away by Lady Huxley, and Galen wasted no time in reaching Fiona's side before anyone could vie for her attention.

"Lady Fiona, I hope you received my note this morning," he said, attempting to lighten his mood.

"Indeed I did, my lord, and I completely understand the importance of the races over a picnic," she replied, smiling sweetly.

She looked particularly lovely this evening, thought Galen, all shiny with her silvery dress and matching ribbons in her midnight black hair, which was pulled back into a glossy fall of curls. A delicate necklace of diamonds glittered against the porcelain tone of her skin. Altogether, she was an extremely striking woman—one with whom any man would be proud of being seen.

"It was not like that at all," he protested.

"What was it like, my lord?" She continued smiling just as sweetly, her eyes glittering as fiercely as her diamonds.

Devil take it! There was nothing he could say in his defense. He could not reveal his true motive in going to the races, and he could come up with nothing else that would sound believable to her ears.

The air between them was stiff with indignation and Galen found he could not blame Lady Fiona at all. In her eyes, he had thrown her over for a bunch of horses and a crowd of men wagering until their pockets were to let. His resentment melted, leaving him feeling like a wilted cravat that needed to be starched.

"I cannot explain at the moment," was all he could think of to say.

"Don't worry, Lord Burke. I spent a very enjoyable day with Lord Duncan. The longer I know him, the more I find to admire about him. Now, if you will excuse me, I believe we're ready to go in to dinner."

Galen was the last to seat himself at the table. It took every ounce of fortitude he could summon up to turn and smile at Lady Melissa.

Galen's disastrous day rendered him completely impervious to his dinner partner that evening. He was devising possible plots to speed up his investigation while the gentlemen were having their port and cigars. Then John took matters into his own hands.

"Saw a friend of mine at the races today," began John. "He said there had been an alarming amount of race fixing going on."

"Bad thing that," remarked Viscount Sanborn. "Anything of that sort going on at York?"

"Not as yet," replied John. "But I'll be bound, it's to be expected. This is a large race meet with a great deal of blunt being wagered."

"I expect they're keeping an eye out for anything untoward," contributed Adam Trent.

"It's difficult to catch someone at the game," said Duncan. "You never know what the culprit is going to try, nor when. With the crowd milling about as it does it's nearly impossible to safeguard every animal all the time."

"Don't forget the jockeys," said Lord Huxley. "They're the fellows to keep your eye on. Most of you are too young to remember the scandal with Prinny, but I was there. And the jockey got the blame."

"I was a child," said Duncan, "but I was there, too. I'll never forget it. My father lost everything on that wager. Nearly broke him."

Galen kept quiet. Although he didn't approve of John's tactic, he might as well see if it bore fruit.

George Wallace removed his cigar from his mouth and studied its glowing point. "I was out of the country at the time. Was it as bad as they say?"

"Worse," replied Lord Huxley. "Like any young man, Prinny was mad about horses. He had a horse called Escape. And his jockey was a lad by the name of Chifney, who had the ability to draw every ounce of speed possible from the animal."

"My horse needed him today," said Sanborn morosely. Hearty laughter and a smattering of sympathy greeted his remark.

"No luck today?" said John.

"None any day is more like it," said Sanborn. "It's the curse of our family. My father loved the races and couldn't pick a winner for the life of him."

"Maybe your luck will change," consoled Galen.

The young man shrugged, then looked at Lord Huxley. "I interrupted your story. I'm sorry," he apologized.

"No need," said Huxley, raising his hand. "It's an old story."

"But some haven't heard it," said Duncan. "Go ahead. A good story can always be told again."

"It wasn't very good for the people who had wagered on Escape," continued Huxley. "But I'm getting ahead of myself. Prinny's horse was winning every race in which he was entered. Then, surprisingly, he lost one. Nothing seemed wrong with the horse, and everyone thought it was the end of his winning streak. He was scheduled to race the following day. Well, you can guess what happened after his loss: The odds were raised. The next day Escape ran the race of his life, winning by a greater distance than ever before. Of course, the Prince had bet heavily on his horse and won a substantial sum at greatly increased odds."

"And I'll wager Prinny swore he was innocent in the whole matter," said Wallace.

"He did," agreed Huxley. "But not many believed him. The rumors wouldn't die, and the Jockey Club finally demanded Prinny get rid of his jockey. The Prince didn't agree, but public opinion was against him. He not only turned off Chifney, but removed himself from racing completely."

"Poor sport," remarked Adam.

"Perhaps," replied Huxley. "But then the Prince has always been overly sensitive. He stayed away from racing for years. Finally, he received an apology, and his feelings were eased enough so he could once more enjoy the sport. However, he hasn't raced since."

"At the time, there was a multitude of hard feelings, and the animosity continues even to this day," added Duncan. "More than my father were hurt by the race. Many were completely ruined. Some swore vengeance, I'm told."

"Maybe their revenge was keeping the Prince from engaging in a sport he loved," observed Wallace. "But if he was guilty of the act, royalty or not, he should have been held answerable to the men his actions left destitute."

Sanborn gave a thin, harsh laugh. "Prinny has no thought of the result of his actions. He thinks only of himself and his pleasure. That's why I seldom wager at the races. I will not put myself in the same position as those fools did."

"Then we are all fools," said Duncan, a sardonic smile showing on his dark face. "For I believe we have all placed bets when we have attended the races."

"But not to the extent we would impoverish ourselves and be left destitute the rest of our lives," argued Sanborn. "Remember Sir Brograve's brother. He lost ten thousand pounds on one Derby. It wasn't long before he was overwhelmed by debt and committed suicide."

"The man was a fool," came Duncan's sharp reply. "If it hadn't been horses, it would have been the green baize table. Gambling was in his blood and he did nothing to contain it. You can't blame his death on the Prince."

"Shall we join the ladies," John suggested. "We can continue the discussion on our next trip to the races. Perhaps it will keep us from overextending ourselves."

The men laughed, cutting the tension that had built in the room. Galen was relieved to have escaped unnoticed during the discussion. He had been able to observe the others as they voiced their opinion of racing, but he was not yet certain whether it helped him or not. As he followed the others from the dining room, he wondered how much longer it was going to take to bring the guilty party to justice.

Fiona had been to bed too late, and up too early, to exhibit her usual good nature. She had spent far too long in the kitchen and was on her way back to her room to take a short nap before beginning the day. Her single-mindedness of purpose left her less than alert, and when a hand shot out from the shadows of the back hall to grasp her arm, she shrieked in surprise.

"Shush. Fiona. It's me," whispered Catherine.

"For the love of heaven! What are you doing lurking about in the shadows?" gasped Fiona, her hand pressed to her heart.

"I could think of no other way to see you. You're always playing least in sight during the day, and I couldn't risk missing you."

"What is so important it would get you out of bed this early?" asked Fiona.

"It's Adam," said Catherine, tears welling in her eyes.

Fiona heaved a heavy sigh. She had promised to help Adam and Catherine in their ill-advised romance, but she could not help wishing they could manage a few things on their own, particularly on a morning when everything was at sixes and sevens.

"Pray, tell me. What is wrong with Adam? He seemed perfectly well last night."

"Oh, he's as fine as five pence," replied Catherine. "The problem lies with me—or rather with Althea."

"What does your sister have to do with it?"

"She suspects something, I'm certain," said Catherine, once again lowering her voice to a whisper. "She's beginning to question where I'm running off to during the day. And last night she said she expects me to spend the entire day with the ladies or they may take offense at my absences."

Then they must truly be offended by me, thought Fiona. "What is it you expect me to do?"

"I was to meet Adam today," said Catherine. "That was in the note you passed to me last night. But as you can see, I can't meet him. Althea would surely find out since she's watching me so closely. I beg you to meet Adam in my stead and tell him what has occurred."

Fiona had no desire to be drawn any further into Catherine and Adam's romance, but it seemed she had no choice at the moment. However, when she confronted Adam, she intended to tell him in no uncertain terms that she was no longer willing to be the message bearer for the two.

"Where were you to meet him?" asked Fiona, resigned to playing Cupid one last time.

"Behind the hedge near the folly," replied Catherine. "We've found it's a perfect spot. No one goes there and the hedge is thick enough to shield us from the house."

"I'll do as you ask," agreed Fiona. "But you and Adam should think about bringing your attachment out into the open."

"I know," said Catherine. "I find it plaguesome myself. Sneaking around like this loses it's mystery after a time," she confessed.

"Then talk to Adam," said Fiona in a gentler voice. "He'll understand."

"Perhaps you're right. I'll do it at the very next opportunity," replied Catherine in a firm voice.

"Good. Now go back to your room and rest or else you'll be falling asleep over tea," advised Fiona.

Catherine giggled, then turned and bounded up the stairs with all the exuberance of a young woman in love.

Fiona was distinctly out of curl as she approached the hedge at the appointed meeting time. She had gotten little rest that morning, and she had spent more time with the ladies of the house party than usual in order to ally any suspicions they might harbor about her absences.

She neared the hedge and saw it was just as Catherine had described. It was impossible to see through the thick branches. She stepped around the end and collided with a substantial male body.

"Oh, my darling . . . Devil take it, Fiona! What are you doing here?" demanded Adam.

"Saving you the trouble of needlessly standing here for the next hour or so, wondering what had happened to Catherine," snapped Fiona, disengaging herself from him and straightening her skirt.

"What is it? What has happened?" he asked, his face going pale.

"You needn't alarm yourself," Fiona reassured him. "Catherine came to me this morning. It seems Althea has become suspicious of Catherine's comings and goings and has insisted she spend the day with the rest of the ladies. Catherine had no way of letting you know she couldn't meet you, so she asked me to come here in her stead."

"I didn't think Althea would get on to us so quickly."

"Come now, Adam. The company is small. How could she not miss her sister's absence?"

"I don't know. I had hoped . . ." Adam's voice trailed off, full of disappointment.

"Adam, this is bad form. You're doing a great disservice to Catherine. You both may well find yourselves in the basket if your secret meetings come to light.

"I know."

"Your actions do not suit your words," shot back Fiona, her patience at an end. "I am tempted to withhold her note from you." Fiona felt particularly strong about it since Catherine had confided she had written to arrange another secret meeting with Adam, even though it was to be their last. She tapped the note against her hand while vacillating about what to do.

The gentlemen of the party decided to forgo a trip to the racecourse that morning. Instead, they agreed upon fishing and shooting as competent entertainment. Galen found both sadly flat. Choosing to go it on his own, he started back to the stables. A long ride across the estate was what he needed. It would help get his mind off race fixing and Lady Fiona for a short time. At least he hoped it would. Visions of violet eyes continued to appear in his thoughts when he least expected it, and there seemed no way to escape them.

The day was perfect for a good gallop, thought Galen, as he walked back to the stables. The air had not grown hot and muggy as it was likely to do this time of year. The thick green sod beneath his booted feet absorbed every sound, and it was as if he were alone in an English paradise. A quiet, peaceful paradise . . .

"I am through," came the angry voice from the other side of the hedge. "I should never have started this, but I allowed my feelings for you to interfere with my good sense."

Galen stopped at the sound of the voice. It was one he would know anywhere. He wondered why Lady Fiona was so angry and who was on the receiving end of her sharp words.

"Fiona . . ." came a voice that Galen quickly identified as Adam Trent's.

"No, don't," warned Fiona. "It is far too late to attempt to cajole me into continuing with this conspiracy. I attempted to warn you of the damage that could be done with your scheme. I was a fool. I should never have allowed myself to become involved."

"If you would only help me on this one final occasion," pleaded Adam. "I promise it will be the last time I ask it of you. Please. You must give it to me."

Fiona considered his request for a long silent moment. "If I do, will you promise it will stop after this?"

"I promise. I never meant it to be a regular thing when

it began. You know my situation. If I were a wealthy man, I wouldn't have needed to ask for your help at all."

Fiona considered his request. He was a young man in love with someone out of his reach. While she sympathized with him, her conscience would no longer allow her to do anything that would jeopardize Catherine's future.

"Here," she said, thrusting the note at him. "This is what you want, but this is the last time," repeated Fiona. "I won't be a party to any further contrivances. I don't know whether to wish you luck or not. If you're caught, there could be disastrous consequences," she warned.

"I know," he said, as he unfolded the paper. "There has always been that chance, but I couldn't stop myself. I see now I should have never started."

As Adam read Catherine's note, Fiona's attitude was softened by his remorse. Adam was a good man who had the misfortune to fall in love with a woman whose parents wanted more for their daughter than he could provide. She could not leave with him thinking she was no longer his friend.

"I'm sorry I was in such a pet. You know, my feelings for you haven't changed at all."

Adam smiled ruefully. "I know. I could ask for no one truer than you. You've done more than many would have. I appreciate this," he said, holding up the note.

"Well, put it away so no one will see it," advised Fiona.

"Right," said Adam, folding the paper again and putting it in his pocket. "This is for tomorrow. The last day of my secret life."

They both laughed: Fiona with relief, Adam with carefully concealed uncertainty.

Galen quickly moved away from the hedge once it was apparent the conversation between Fiona and Adam was concluded. He certainly did not want them to know he had overheard what they had to say.

He was loath to consider the obvious interpretation of

what he had heard. If he did, he would be forced to conclude that Lady Fiona had a *tendre* for Adam and was conspiring with him in some plan. Evidently, she had become alarmed and had decided to have nothing else to do with it. However, she had passed on one last bit to him for use on the morrow.

The ploy that was foremost in Galen's mind was, of course, race fixing. At all events, he did not want to believe Lady Fiona was involved in the scheme, but her conversation with Trent seemed to confirm his worst suspicions. Finding she might be head over heels for Trent was another blow to Galen. He could not deny Trent was a fairly handsome man, but he seemed far too immature for Lady Fiona. She needed a man she could depend upon—not a young cub who must be taken to task like a schoolboy.

Briefly, he wondered about the brief kiss he had shared with Lady Fiona in the kitchen. She had not responded as if her heart was engaged elsewhere.

But that was all beyond his helping at the moment. Lady Fiona and Adam were already conspirators, and tomorrow something was to come about for the last time. The gentlemen were planning to attend the races again the next day, and Galen meant to keep a sharp eye on Trent.

Fiona turned toward the house, her steps lighter knowing Catherine and Adam's secret trysts were a thing of the past. However, her spirits were doomed to be dampened when she met Edwina sitting in the garden, a woeful expression on her face.

Fiona took a seat beside her friend. "It looks as if matters have not improved between you and John."

"He is still on his high ropes, and I suppose I am no better," Edwina admitted. "Oh, we are cordial to one another in front of the guests, but it goes no further. He completely avoids being alone with me."

"Have you approached him?"

"He gives me no chance, and I don't know whether I would even if I could." Edwina's mouth firmed into a stubborn line.

"There must have been a mistake," said Fiona. "I cannot believe that John would be cruel enough to admit he married you only for your family connection and money."

"Well, you can believe it, for that is what he said. And I am glad he did, even for all the pain he has caused me. At least I am under no misconception that he loves me."

"And it has made you miserable," said Fiona, taking Edwina's hand.

A small sob escaped Edwina's lips. "Yes, I am," she admitted. "But John must never know."

Fiona sat silently, thinking of her friend's dilemma. "Well, I have solved one problem," she said, hoping to distract Edwina from her misery.

"You have made it up with Galen?"

"No, I haven't seen the odious man." She then proceeded to tell Edwina about her part in Adam and Catherine's attachment.

"I pray she doesn't make the same mistake I did," said Edwina.

"You did not make a mistake. This is all a misunderstanding that began over the seating arrangement. The two of you were caught between your friends. Lord Burke and I wanted our own way, and you and John attempted to give it to us. So it is our fault that the two of you argued."

"I don't blame you," said Edwina. "I'm happy I found out how he feels about me now rather than after we had children."

"If you changed the seating arrangement, you might not be at daggers drawn. At least the issue that began your argument would be eliminated."

"I don't want to make up," Edwina stated obstinately.

"You and John should allow yourself an opportunity to

straighten this out. It would be just as tragic if a marriage made in love dissolved due to a simple misunderstanding."

"Do you think that is it?"

"There is only one way to find out," said Fiona. "And it must begin with the two of you talking. Now dry your eyes and let's plan the new seating arrangement for this evening."

"But what will I say?"

"You will tell everyone you didn't want them to become bored with their dinner partners, so you decided to change it all around for their enjoyment."

Five

Galen was greatly surprised to find he was once again seated beside Lady Fiona for dinner. Melissa glared down the length of the table toward him as if blaming him for the change. He attempted to send her an apologetic smile, but from her reaction, he was evidently unsuccessful.

He greeted Lady Fiona and she murmured a suitable reply. Then they each turned to their other dinner partner while the first courses were being served.

Galen had no doubt the dishes were as well prepared as they had always been, but they were bitter to his taste. He was where he had wanted to be for days now, but it gave him no pleasure after the conversation he had heard between Lady Fiona and Adam Trent that morning. If his suspicions were true, he wondered at her ability to carry on as if she had no thoughts other than to enjoy herself.

Although Fiona contained her feelings, she was curious about Lord Burke's reaction to the new seating arrangement. He had greeted her, but that had been the extent of their conversation thus far. Politeness decreed that they converse for a time during dinner. What a delight to look forward to, she thought grimly.

"You have made yourself scarce recently," Galen finally said by way of conversation.

"I've been occupied by various matters," Fiona replied

shortly, but pleasantly. She was determined Lord Burke would have no reason to complain to John.

"In the kitchen, no doubt," he said, a smile taking the sting from his words.

"I did promise Edwina, after all. And I would never let her down."

"I cannot help but think there is more to it." His sharp gaze caught and held hers as she sought an answer for his comment.

"You are too clever by far," she replied, giving him a coy glance from beneath her dark lashes.

Her presence disconcerted Galen, but he could not let her get the upper hand. "You mean there is more?"

He suspected something, Fiona thought with alarm. She must not allow him to find that she was running the kitchen for Edwina. If it got back to John it could destroy what chance he and Edwina had to repair their marriage.

"I will tell you, but you must vow not to divulge it to a soul."

"On my honor," he said, thinking he might find out the truth about Trent and whatever it was she had passed to him that afternoon.

"I am writing a book," she confessed, her eyes lowered beneath his gaze.

Galen was struck silent for a moment. He had been prepared to hear that Lady Fiona was having assignations in the kitchen, that she was mixing up poison in the large black pots that hung over the fire, throwing in frogs, snakes, and all manner of things to cause horses to lose their races. He had been prepared to accept anything that fell from her lovely lips—anything except that small five-word declaration.

"You are writing a book," he repeated, unable to come up with anything more original.

"I know you think it strange," she said in a low voice,

looking around to see that they were not attracting attention. "You must not think that I am a bluestocking."

"Of course not."

"But I have decided to compile a book of recipes and instructions on the running of a kitchen for newly married ladies," she said, decidedly pleased with herself at coming up with such an excellent reason for being in the kitchen so often. "Many of them know nothing even about the daily tasks, but when they are called upon to entertain—why they are frozen with fear. And if they do not have a competent cook—well, you can see what that could lead to." Lady Fiona's voice and expression reflected the amazement any lady should feel at such a shortcoming.

It took a great deal of self-control for Fiona to subdue the laughter that welled inside of her. It was exceedingly apparent that Lord Burke had not expected her revelation. She did not know what he suspected, but from the look on his face, it was something far more devious than a book.

"Well, what do you think?" she asked, more pleased with herself as each second passed.

"I think . . . I think it is a very noble enterprise," Galen said, recovering from the surprise of Lady Fiona's disclosure.

Fiona smiled broadly. "I am happy I confided in you. I feel so much better now." She picked up her fork and returned to her dinner, leaving Lord Burke to wonder whether he had let his imagination get the best of him.

The ladies had once again decided to join the gentlemen at the races the next day, and the party set out with the full complement of carriages, coaches, and servants to see to their comfort.

Galen enjoyed the simplicity of riding off to the races without a lot of fuss, but the ladies demanded more niceties than the gentlemen, which he accepted with as much goodwill as possible. However, after the long night he had spent tossing in his bed, his goodwill was sadly lacking.

Lady Fiona's confession that she was writing a book might very well be true. She certainly spent enough time in the kitchen and she had an extraordinary interest in food, but that was not what she and Trent were up to. They had met in secret—probably only one of many times they had done so—and she had passed an item to him. If only Galen had been able to see what it was, the mystery might already be solved. But it had been impossible to see anything through the thick hedge that had separated them.

He had closely watched both Lady Fiona and Trent last night and this morning, but other than the common courtesies nothing untoward had passed between them. He would continue his surveillance during the day in case they attempted another meeting.

After all, Lady Fiona had said she was through with Trent and their scheme. Trent had pleaded that he was not a wealthy man, and Lady Fiona had given in, passing Trent something to help him out today. What was it? Galen could only surmise it had to do with race fixing.

The race meet was a large one with huge sums of money being wagered on every race. Today would be the perfect time to pull off fixing a race that would insure the winner would become a wealthy man. Galen meant to be there to catch the culprit this time.

The company arrived at the racecourse. The men sauntered among the horses and placed wagers. The ladies watched the crowd, partook of refreshment, and gossiped. All was well until midafternoon when the most important race of the day was to be run. The crowd had grown even larger to watch the favorite, Merton's Pride, run. The people were to be disappointed, for the horse lagged behind from the moment the race began.

It was very quickly apparent that something was wrong with the animal, and he soon stumbled to a halt. The jockey leapt to the ground and ran to the horse's head. Merton's Pride stood on quivering legs, its head drooping almost to the ground and its sides heaving. A crowd of men gathered around, each venturing suggestions as to what was wrong and what should be done.

Galen observed Trent stuffing a large amount of money in his pocket. Evidently he had been able to collect his winnings without a worry for Merton's Pride.

The race had long been over. Galen had stayed behind to see if the cause of Merton's Pride's collapse would be discovered. When it was revealed, he was as shocked as every other person there. It took a cleverly diabolical mind to conceive the plan that had nearly killed the horse.

He did not like to think that Lady Fiona was involved in such a scheme and had actually passed on to Trent the object used to maim Merton's Pride. But the meeting he had overheard, and the conversation that had taken place earlier between him and Trent, weighed heavily against them.

He arrived at Hamilton House long after the others in the party and entered the back door of the house. He hoped he would be able to keep the disgust from showing on his face when he met Trent at dinner.

Edwina's heart beat a little faster when a knock sounded at the door between her and John's room.

"Am I interrupting?" asked John, standing in the doorway.

"No, I was deciding what to wear at dinner tonight," she replied, motioning her maid from the room.

"You'll look lovely in anything you choose," he said, stepping into the room and closing the door behind him.

Edwina could not believe he was flattering her so after all the days of forced courtesy that lay between them.

"I wanted to thank you for changing the seating arrangement. I wouldn't have blamed you if you had packed your trunks and returned to London," he confessed.

"I would never do that, no matter what the situation. I know what I owe our guests," she replied stiffly.

John went to her side and lightly touched her arm. "There, I'm doing it again. I only meant I am clumsy in how I express myself. I can see how you would think what you did."

"I . . ."

"No, let me finish," he insisted. "You must believe that I married you for love and love alone. Your money and your family name had nothing to do with it. I would have loved you no matter what your standing. I want this argument out of the way and for us to be the way we were when we first married."

John could argue politics with fervor, but he was not—and had never been—an eloquent man when it came to expressions of love. But Edwina had lived with him long enough to know when he was sincere. The misery of their misunderstanding was plainly written on his face, and it filled his voice.

"I believe you," she said, reaching up to touch his cheek. He clasped her hand and placed a kiss in her palm.

"I want you to know I'm not here merely because you placed Galen next to Fiona again. I intended to seek you out today no matter what."

"It doesn't matter."

"Yes, it does. I'm a stubborn fool, and I should never have meddled in your plans, but Galen was so miserable with Melissa . . ."

"I started it by moving Fiona," admitted Edwina. "But she was so insistent that I could do nothing else."

"Surely she would have understood if you had refused."

"She was entirely set upon getting away from Galen and threatened to leave if I did not change her seating."

"Why, that is blackmail!" said John indignantly. "You should have let her go. I did not think her such a false friend."

"She isn't. She's been going pell-mell lately," explained Edwina. "Then Galen insulted her—or offered a comment that she took as an insult—and she would not tolerate him any longer."

"Pell-mell?" echoed John in a bewildered tone. "She has been at a house party where nothing is required of her except that she relax and enjoy herself. And I cannot conceive that Galen would purposely insult any lady."

Edwina realized she had said too much. How could she explain the situation without giving away her secret? "I believe he was unaware he was offending her."

"What did he say?" demanded John. "I'll take him to task for it."

"No, don't make any more of it," she pleaded. "They seem to have gotten along very well last night at dinner. I'm certain it's already forgotten."

"Normally, I wouldn't inquire any further, but this involves my friend also, and I insist upon knowing what he said."

They had just patched up their differences, and Edwina did not want to end up separated from him again. Perhaps if she told him what had caused the trouble between Galen and Fiona, that would be the end of it.

"He insulted the port sauce," she replied faintly.

"He did what?" asked John, leaning closer.

"He said that the port sauce was too strong, that it overpowered the roast."

"And that put her in such a taking she had to be moved from his side?" John asked, bewildered at the insignificance of the remark.

Edwina was getting in deeper with every word she uttered. "Fiona is overly sensitive when it comes to food."

"I should say so. I was ready to blame Galen for this whole thing but—port sauce—what a thing to fly up in the boughs about."

Edwina could not entirely desert her friend. She understood Fiona's reaction. It was her recipe, and if the remark was unjustly deserved—as Fiona felt it was—then Edwina would have been insulted, too, had she been in Fiona's place. Perhaps it was time for everything to come out in the open. Then there would be no more deception between them.

Edwina took a deep breath. Despite her decision, it was difficult to actually say the words. "It was her port sauce. That is why she was so upset."

"Hers? How could it be hers? How could port sauce be anyone's, except for maybe being ours since it was on our table?"

"By hers, I mean that it was her recipe. And she had spent time in the kitchen seeing it was prepared properly."

"What the devil is Fiona doing in our kitchen—particularly when we are in the midst of a house party and when we have a more than adequate cook?"

Edwina realized there was no way out. She must confess all in order for John to understand. "That is the root of the problem. We do not have an adequate cook. I mean, we do now, but at the time Fiona agreed to my plan, we had no cook at all."

John appeared bewildered at Edwina's less than clear explanation. "For God's sake, Edwina! Tell me what it is you have to say and do it quickly and plainly," he demanded.

"All right," she said, "I'll do my best. Our cook quit the day before the house party began, and I was left with the arrival of a dozen people who dined at the best tables in England. I was terrified. I knew I would be embarrassed beyond reason, and I was afraid it would interfere with your political aspirations."

"Politicians worry about food for their minds, not their stomachs," John interjected pompously

"Oh, pshaw! Politicians are men, and I have never yet met a man who doesn't want good food on his plate."

"We're getting away from the subject of this conversation," he said, ignoring her claim about mens' dining habits. "What does the cook quitting have to do with Fiona and port sauce?"

"I couldn't find another cook at such short notice," explained Edwina. "So I asked Fiona if she would oversee the kitchen for me."

"You what!"

"It's a secret and you must keep it so, but Fiona is an excellent cook. She inherited it from her grandmother. Her parents have kept it quiet, but Fiona could rival any chef in England if she chose to do so."

"Fiona has been cooking our meals?"

"Well, not every dish," said Edwina. "At first, she had to do some demonstrations, but now—for the most part—the staff can follow her instructions well enough that she does not need to even be present except for the most complicated dishes."

"And how did you manage to pull off this scheme without everyone finding out about it?"

Edwina went on to explain to John how Fiona got up early and slipped in and out of the kitchen during the day in order to achieve the excellent meals they were all enjoying.

"I can't believe you would deceive me so," said John when she had finished.

"My deception—small as it was—was for your benefit," said Edwina, her spirit beginning to rebel at his indignation.

"You should have told me," he stubbornly contended.

"And what good would that have done? Would you have

galloped off to London to bring back a chef? Would you have donned an apron and rushed to the kitchen to take up the slack?"

"Don't be foolish."

"Well, what would you have done? I know very well. You would have looked at me and asked what I was going to do about it. Now, because I solved our problem the only way I knew how, you're angry."

"It was not the thing to do," he insisted.

"Why not? Our house party is a success in large part because of the memorable dishes we are serving. It will be talked about in London. No one will refuse your invitation. Isn't that what you wanted? You can lure all your political acquaintances here and discuss politics night and day, stopping only for meals and a little fresh air."

"But we won't have Fiona to cook for us, will we?" he snapped, angry at her comments about his political friends.

"I will seek a new chef as soon as the house party is over," replied Edwina defensively.

"And how long will you keep him? As I recall, you went on about the new chef you hired before we left London, and how long did he stay? Not even until the first guest stepped over the threshold."

"It wasn't my fault," cried out Edwina.

"It doesn't matter," said John wearily. "You have been dishonest with me in order to cover your own insufficiencies. It's no wonder Fiona was upset with Galen. I must apologize to them both as soon as possible."

"You will do no such thing!" said Edwina. "Do what you like with Galen, but Fiona is my friend, and I will not have you meddle in our friendship. We will settle this on our own without your heavy-handed interference."

"I had no idea you felt this way about me," said John, concealing the hurt her words had caused. "You are right, of course. I will settle things with Galen and leave you to deal with Fiona."

"Must you tell him about Fiona's cooking? Her parents are extremely concerned about keeping it quiet."

"I will say as little as possible," he promised. Without another word, he turned and marched stiffly from the room.

So much for a reconciliation, thought Edwina, throwing herself across her bed and burying her face in the pillow in order to muffle the sobs she was unable to contain.

"Why are we hiding behind the hedge again?" complained Fiona. "I thought secret meetings were a thing of the past with you."

"This is the last one, I promise," replied Adam. A boyish grin appeared on his face. "I wanted to tell you Catherine and I are betrothed."

"Adam, how wonderful," said Fiona, tiptoeing up to kiss him on the cheek. "I am so happy that today was a success for you."

"What a touching scene," said a voice from behind them, causing Fiona to jerk around, a flush rising to her face.

Galen had left the stable and was making his way toward the house when he saw Fiona slip behind the massive wall of hedge again. Curious as to whether she and Trent would be foolish enough to meet there again, he followed, arriving just in time to hear Fiona congratulate Trent on a successful day.

"You should not slip up on a person," protested Fiona as she clutched Adam's arm in order to regain her balance, making her appear even more guilty in Galen's eyes.

"You should not be doing anything that would require it," shot back Galen.

"We were having a private conversation," replied Fiona, stung by his criticism.

"What Lady Fiona and I do should be of no interest to you," added Adam.

"Ah, but it is when it concerns your successful day."

"You heard that?" asked Adam, a streak of red burning across the edge of his cheekbones.

"You left me no choice since I was on the other side of the hedge," said Galen.

"You could have walked away," challenged Fiona.

"Not when the subject is race fixing," said Galen.

"Race fixing!" exclaimed Fiona and Adam in unison.

"What the devil's going on?" demanded John as he rounded the corner of the hedge. "If this is meant to be a private conversation, you're far off the mark. I heard you as soon as I stepped out the door."

"We should keep our voices down," suggested Galen.

"I should be screaming to high heavens," said Fiona. "For I am hidden behind a hedge with a madman."

Edwina had followed John from the house. Their argument had gone on long enough. It was time to put paid to the misunderstandings between them. If they could not be overcome, then she would leave without him at the end of the house party. She watched as he hesitated outside the door, then walked to the tall, thick hedge that bordered the drive and disappeared around it. Lifting the ruffled hem of her green afternoon dress, she followed him, determination apparent in her every step. She heard only Fiona's last remark, but that was enough.

"Are you calling John a madman?" she asked, appearing from the other side of the hedge as if by magic.

"Dammit, Edwina! You shouldn't slip up on us so," complained John.

"I did no such thing. You were all arguing so loudly it's a wonder the whole household isn't here by now."

"It looks as if most of us are," said Duncan, strolling

casually around the corner of the hedge to join the group. "I couldn't avoid the temptation," he explained, a curious smile on his face.

Galen's patience was at an end. "Devil a bit! This is none of your business," he snarled.

"It very well may be. I won't know until you tell me," drawled Duncan.

"Go ahead, tell us all," demanded Adam. "All I've heard so far is some gibberish about race fixing."

Galen's expression was stern, frozen in a mask of disgust. "If you wish the world to know, why should I care? As you well know, there has been a string of race fixing at the different courses this year. The Prince has charged me with the responsibility of finding the culprit," he announced bluntly.

"And you think I'm involved?" asked Adam, his voice a squeak of surprise.

"Everything points that way. Unless you're able to explain some of your actions these past few days, you're my prime suspect."

"I owe you no explanation," said Adam, anger beginning to grow in him. "And I have done nothing to warrant this insult."

"Then you can discuss it with the Prince Regent after I give him my accounting of events."

"Are you certain of your accusations?" asked John.

"Yes, are you? I can't imagine Adam doing anything of the sort," added Edwina.

"Of course, he couldn't," said Fiona protectively.

Galen was beginning to feel as if he were the one at fault. "I cannot prove it beyond a shadow of a doubt, but there is enough circumstantial evidence that it appears he is guilty. I'll leave it up to Prinny to make the final decision."

"Why do you think Trent is your man?" asked Duncan,

flipping open the top of his snuff box and reaching in to take a pinch.

"Yes, tell us," agreed John. "We might feel better about the situation if we are convinced Adam is guilty."

"But I am not!" objected Adam. "You cannot lay this in my dish!"

"You will have your chance," said Duncan, sniffing his personal blend of snuff. "Allow Lord Burke to explain his view."

Galen did not like to be told what to do by the likes of Duncan, but he could see popular opinion was going against him.

"You have been at all the courses where the race fixing occurred."

"So has every man here," said Adam.

"But every man here doesn't have a groom who uses sponges to apply saddle oil," replied Galen.

"What the devil does that have to do with anything?" asked Adam, looking completely baffled.

For the first time since his rage had overtaken him earlier in the day, Galen felt a twinge of doubt. To be certain, his proof was weak, but it was more than he had on anyone else in the party, and he wanted this over and done with so he could get on with his life. Not an honorable thought, to be sure, but a reasonable one.

"I remained at the races today while Merton's Pride was being examined. It took them some time, but they discovered what had happened to the horse."

"What was it?" asked John.

"A sponge had been stuffed up his nostril so he couldn't breathe."

Gasps of horror from the women and muffled curses from the men greeted Galen's revelation.

"And you think because my groom uses a sponge to clean and oil my saddle that I am responsible?" asked Adam.

"You told me yourself that he had run short of them, that you had to get additional ones from one of the ladies. I overheard your discussion with Lady Fiona at this very spot yesterday when she passed an object to you."

"You were listening to our private conversation?" asked Fiona, unable to disguise her astonishment.

"Your voices were easily discernible."

"But you need not have listened," she charged.

"I chose to once I learned the subject."

"How could you know what we were talking about? I don't think we even mentioned it."

"It wasn't necessary. You were angry that you had begun helping Trent, but you said your feelings had overcome your good sense."

"It had . . ." began Fiona.

"If I remember correctly, you warned him of the damage he could do, and then Trent begged you to help him one final time. You made him promise he would quit afterward, and he agreed. He mentioned that if he were wealthy, he would not need to resort to such a thing. Then you gave him what he wanted, warning him that if he were caught the consequences could be disastrous. After hearing his protestations of remorse, you assured him your feelings for him hadn't changed."

"Good God man! Where is your decency?" cried Adam. "A gentleman would have walked away."

"In any other situation I might have, but I am under orders from the Prince."

"Surely he didn't tell you to listen to private conversations!" said an indignant Fiona.

"I am to do whatever it takes to find the guilty party," Galen replied stiffly.

"This still isn't proof positive," pointed out Duncan.

"It's enough to take to the Prince and tell him my observations in the matter. After that, it's up to him. Trent's groom was at the track today. It would have been very easy for him to insert the sponge without anyone being the wiser. That would have left Trent free and clear of any wrongdoing. I know he passed sponges along to his groom. Perhaps that isn't concrete evidence, but it's strong enough."

"But I never gave him instructions to stuff a sponge up a horse's nostril," blustered Adam

"And I did not pass a sponge along to him," said Fiona.

"You would deny it of course," said Galen to both of them.

"It's the truth," replied Fiona, her violet eyes appearing enormous in her pale face.

"And I believe I may be able to prove it," said Duncan.

All eyes turned toward the darkly handsome man.

"If you have something to add, then do it, man," said John.

"How long has your groom been working for you, Trent?" Duncan asked.

A look of relieved comprehension appeared on Adam's face. "Only for a fortnight or so," he answered.

"There you have it," Duncan said, turning to Galen. "How long has the race fixing been going on?"

"Since spring," Galen admitted reluctantly.

"And who employed your groom before you took him on?" asked Duncan.

"Why, you did," said Adam.

"Are you going to accuse me of race fixing also?" Duncan asked of Galen.

"The thought had crossed my mind before Trent made his mistake," admitted Galen, beginning to wish he had never started this discussion with an audience in attendance.

"Your proof would probably be stronger against me. The man was with me for most of the year; but I assure you, I did not provide him with sponges to use on race horses."

"Nor did I," said Fiona.

"Why not put this behind us for the moment," suggested John. "Galen, you can take time to reconsider your conclusions. If everyone will keep this conversation to themselves, we can go on with the house party without anyone being the wiser."

"Why couldn't the groom be responsible for the race fixing without involving anyone else?" asked Edwina, much to John's displeasure. However, he dared not complain since their relationship was barely holding together as it was.

"Because he couldn't profit by it," Galen pointed out. "The idea of fixing a race is to take advantage of the odds. It would be highly suspicious if a groom wagered a large sum of money."

John looked at Galen. "Why don't we move this conversation into the house before anyone else happens upon us? I'll send for the groom and you can question him in private."

Galen nodded in agreement, wishing more than ever he had not let emotion control his decision to confront Trent in such a public place

Six

Contrary to John's suggestion, Edwina had accompanied the party into the library. She had declared that Fiona was her friend and she would not desert her no matter what he said.

"I can't believe you would think me guilty on such flimsy evidence," grumbled Adam once they were all seated in the library.

"You were engaging in secret meetings with Lady Fiona," Galen pointed out.

"You were watching us?" asked Fiona.

"I was watching everyone."

"You never meant a word you said to me, did you? The praise for the juniper berries and the quail floating off the table—it was all just to gain my trust."

"No, I swear it wasn't. I meant every word," replied Galen while the rest of the party looked on as if they were speaking in some sort of secret code.

Fortunately, at that moment, the door opened. The groom stood at the threshold, cap in hand.

"Come in," invited John. "There are a few questions Lord Burke would like to ask of you."

"I ain't done nothin' wrong," objected the groom, stepping into the room.

"What about the sponge you stuffed up the nostril of Merton's Pride today?" asked Galen abruptly.

The groom turned pale beneath his sun-browned skin. "I did no such thing," he objected.

"I didn't expect you to confess," replied Galen. "But there's too much against you to get away with it." Galen did not have nearly enough evidence to convict the groom but he wasn't about to let the man know it.

"Tell us what happened," said John, "and I'll do what I can to help you. We know you couldn't do it by yourself. You had to have help from a gentleman in order to turn a profit. We know who it is. He won't get away with it."

The groom looked around the room. "Then why ain't he here?" he demanded brusquely.

Adam and Fiona looked triumphant. Edwina gave John the look that wives have been giving their husbands for centuries. Duncan retained his usual bored expression while Galen felt his face grow warm.

"What do you mean?" he asked.

"Lord Sanborn. Why ain't he here? I ain't takin' the blame alone."

"Sanborn is the man who put you up to this?" asked Galen.

"As sure as I'm standin' here. He told me what to do, and I did it."

Duncan's voice dropped into the silence like a stone in water. "Perhaps we should ask Lord Sanborn to join us."

John cleared his throat before he spoke. "I believe that would be a good idea." He walked to the door and spoke a few words to the footman in the hall. It wasn't long before Lord Sanborn stepped into the room.

"What's all this about?" he asked, looking about the room and quickly surmising this wasn't a social gathering.

"It's about race fixing, and your part in it," said Galen.

"I don't know what you're talking about," protested Sanborn.

"Your man here says differently," replied Duncan.

"He isn't my man. He works for Trent."

"He does now, but he worked for you before he came to me," said Duncan.

Galen did nothing to reveal Duncan's statement was news to him. "And we believe you began your scheme at that time."

"Then to keep anyone from becoming suspicious," continued Duncan, "you asked me to take him off your hands."

"I couldn't afford him," said Sanborn. "I didn't want him to end up on the street."

"Oh, I think it was more than that," said Galen. "The two of you needed to be separated for a time, yet he needed to be with someone who attended the races frequently."

"And who better than me," said Duncan. "Everyone knows I attend every event I can."

"You're insane," snarled Sanborn. His usual timidity completely disappeared beneath an explosion of anger. "Tell them, Chifney. Tell them we have no arrangement between us."

"Chifney!" exclaimed Galen. "Don't tell me your father was a jockey."

"And a good one he was," the man admitted with a bit of pride. "Rode for the Prince Regent until he was falsely accused of losing a race on purpose. Then he never raced again."

Galen looked first to Duncan, who said, "I knew him as Charles Grayson." Then to Adam, who added, "As did I."

"Grayson's my mum's name," confessed the groom. "No one would hire me when they learned my name was Chifney. But his lordship was interested enough." Chifney darted a bitter glance toward the man standing nearby.

Galen transferred his gaze to Sanborn. "I'll ask Prinny to go lighter on you if you confess," said Galen.

"As if I care what that fat peacock does," snarled Sanborn. "All right, I did it. I deserved it. My father was ruined when the Prince's horse lost that race. I met Chifney a year or so ago. He was working as a groom because no one would trust him as a jockey. We decided to get our revenge. Everything went well. Then a few people began commenting on my ability to be on the winning side every time a horse had problems at the racecourse. I decided to lie low for a time. I thought if Chifney went to work for someone else, no one would connect us. When Duncan decided to let him go, we were lucky Trent took him on. He would be much easier to fool than Duncan."

Adam looked ready to object to Sanford's remark until Fiona pinched his arm.

"What are you going to do?" Sanford asked.

"Nothing to Chifney," replied Galen. "He can't continue the scheme without someone to help him, but I don't think he'll find it easy to secure a position in England's racing circles after this."

"And me?"

"I'll leave that to the Prince Regent. But if you're as smart as you seem to think you are, you'll check on the ships leaving port as soon as possible."

Sanborn stood a moment, considering his possibilities; then he turned and swiftly left the room.

"Hey, you ain't leaving me!" yelled Chifney, hurrying out of the room after Sanborn.

"Well, that's the end of that," said Duncan, strolling toward the open door. "Time to dress for dinner."

The party dispersed quickly, darting all manner of looks toward Galen, some accusatory, others sympathetic. But it was Fiona's that struck him hardest. It was filled with contempt.

The dinner party was subdued that evening. The journey to the racecourse and the upset of the injured horse had combined to cast a pall over the group that sat down at the table. Sanborn's absence was explained by an urgent recall to London, which was accepted without question.

The excellence of the meal seemed to raise the party's spirits, and when Edwina announced that a special treat would be served in the drawing room after the men re-joined the ladies, a murmur of anticipation rose from the assembly.

As soon as the men entered the drawing room, Edwina nodded to the butler. A short time later, footmen with trays bearing delicate, gold-rimmed glasses entered the room.

"This is a dessert from Lady Fiona's collection of recipes," said Edwina, determined to give her friend some credit for the success of the house party. "It's called *Mon Ami* and I think it is appropriate, for each of you is indeed *my friend.*"

A murmur of appreciation rose when the glasses were passed around. There was a ring of small green leaves arranged around the gold rim of the glass. Inside that were rings of crystallized violets covering the entire top of the rich, creamy pudding that filled the glass. The ladies exclaimed that it was too pretty to eat, while the gentlemen wondered whether they could actually force themselves to eat violets.

Galen stared at the crystallized violets, and his appetite for the glorious confection disappeared. They reminded him too much of Fiona's eyes. He had been so caught up in revealing the culprit in the race-fixing scheme that he had put his growing feelings for Fiona second. He had attempted to reject them by blaming her in helping Trent, but he had been wrong about them both.

By the pointed manner in which she had ignored him all evening, it was obvious she was still furious with him. Placing the *Mon Ami* on the nearest table, Galen searched the room for Fiona. Spying her talking to John and Edwina, he made his way to them.

"Would you care to walk in the garden, my lady?"

"No, thank you, my lord," Fiona replied coldly. A dim garden filled with the scent of flowers was the last place she wished to be with Lord Burke.

"Oh, let's do," trilled Edwina.

John and Edwina must have made up their differences, thought Fiona, for Edwina hung on his arm and smiled up at him like a bride.

"Join us," said John. "It would seem rude if the host and hostess left their guests and went into the garden alone."

Edwina giggled at his remark, which made Fiona all the more grumpy. Everyone seemed to be having a wonderful time except for her.

"Oh, all right," she agreed grudgingly.

Lord Burke held out his arm, leaving her no choice but to take it—although she did so as if touching a poisonous snake. As soon as they stepped into the garden, John and Edwina disappeared into the gathering twilight, causing Fiona to regret her hasty decision.

Despite all the thought he had given it, Galen still had not determined how to approach Fiona. However, he could not miss this final opportunity to let his feelings be known. "My lady, I know your opinion of me cannot be good at this time," he began, ignoring her unladylike sound of disgust. "Would you accept my apology for all I've said and done to cause you injury."

"Of course, I will," she answered too quickly.

"May I trust the sincerity of your acceptance?" he asked, hoping he would not offend her further.

"Of course you may, my lord. It's all over and done with. The real culprit has been found out, and Adam and I have been cleared of any guilt. When we leave here tomorrow, we need never see one another again. And if we do so at a social gathering, I'm certain we can manage to avoid one another."

"I do not want to avoid you," said Galen, exerting great self-control to keep from taking her in his arms.

"I should think you would be as eager to be rid of me as I am of you."

"You can't tell me our kiss meant nothing to you?" he demanded.

"It was only a kiss," she replied airily.

"It was more and you know it," Galen argued.

"Are you accusing me of prevaricating again?" Fiona asked.

"I am not heedlessly accusing you. I am making a statement I can prove," he said, taking her in his arms and kissing her with more gentleness than Fiona thought possible.

One kiss became another, and another, until Fiona thought she would melt at his feet like rich, sweet chocolate. All reasonable thought had vanished. She could only feel his strong arms around her, his lips first pressed to hers, then against the pulse that beat rapidly under the delicate skin of her throat.

"The *Mon Ami* you served this evening," he finally whispered in her ear, his voice husky.

It took a moment for Fiona to understand what he was talking about. Her precious recipes were completely erased from her mind. She needed no more sustenance than his kisses.

"Mmmmh," she replied.

"Would you change its name to *Mon Amor,* my love?" he whispered in her ear.

"Of course," she agreed in a dazed voice.

"And serve it at our wedding breakfast," he added.

"What!" she exclaimed, jerking away from him. "You are all about in the head if you think a few kisses mean we will be having a wedding."

"But they were magnificent kisses. You must admit that," he said, pulling her back into his arms and proving it to her all over again.

"They were adequate," she conceded breathlessly a few

moments later, "but nothing I can't live without or get from someone else."

"No one else can love you the way I do," Galen said, still holding her tight and placing a trail of kisses along her jawline until he found her lips once again.

"There is too much between us," she protested.

"We can put it right. Consider my explanations and you'll see everything was an honest mistake on my part. I'll never forgive myself for it, but I won't lose you because of it."

"It is only my recipes that attract you," she charged, grasping at any complaint to keep her heart hardened against him.

"It's nothing of the sort," he protested, afraid she was slipping out of his grasp and determined not to let her go.

Fiona heard the stubbornness in his voice. He did sound sincere, but that often did not mean anything to an experienced gentleman. "I cannot see that we would suit. We do not have the right ingredients for marrying," she explained. "Don't you understand?"

Galen could see no use in arguing when he could be putting this time to better use. "Of course, I do, my love," he agreed, pulling her back into his arms.

"You said it yourself not so many days ago," Fiona continued, wondering why he had agreed so easily. "It's a matter of taste, and ours are just not compatible."

"I'm certain you're right, my darling, but surely it will do no harm for me to sample your sweetness just a little longer."

"But you do agree, don't you?" murmured Fiona.

"Whatever you say, my sweet," replied Galen, as their lips met again.

Below is the recipe previously called *Mon Ami.* Renamed at the request of Galen, Lord Burke, and served upon the event of his marriage to Lady Fiona Atterly.

MON AMOR
(Modern version)

This lovely dessert can be served in champagne flutes for a wedding breakfast. The top can be made to resemble a nosegay with a ring of angelica leaves around the rim followed by smaller and smaller concentric circles of crystallized flowers and a marshmallow in the center carved into the shape of a magnolia and surrounded by a few more angelica leaves.

1 pt (2 1/2 C) thick cream
4 oz (1 C) cottage cheese
2 oz (1 1/4 C) sugar
4 Tbsp honey
1/8 Tsp saffron
1 oz (2 Tbsp) butter, softened
4 egg yolks
crystallized or fresh violets

Boil the cream and set it aside. Beat the cottage cheese and mix it with the cream, sugar, honey, and saffron. Blend well. Beat in the softened butter, in small pieces, and the egg yolks. Pour into a saucepan and cook over low heat, stirring until thickened. Do not boil. Pour into a custard bowl and chill. Decorate with fresh or crystallized violets. Serves 4-6

(Mon amy: To mak mon amy, tak and boile cows creme and when it is bolid set it asid and let it kele then take cow cruddes and press out the whey, then bray them in a mortair and cast them in a potte to the creme and boile all togedure put therto to sugur hony and may butter colur it up with saffron and in the settynge down put in yolk of eggs, well bett and do away the streyne and let the potage be standing and then put it in dyshes and plant ther in floures of violettes and serve it.

Andrew Boorde, 1542. Taken from the book *Seven Centuries of English Cooking: A Collection of Recipes* by Maxime de la Falaise.

HUSSAR'S KISSES

by
Joy Reed

One

"And so we thought it would only be right to give some sort of fete or celebration to welcome the boys back. Just to show them how glad we are to see them home, you know, and how much we appreciate what they did over on the Continent."

The speaker of these words, Jenny Jacobs, paused and regarded her listeners hopefully. She was a small, fair-haired girl with blue eyes and a serious manner. Her companion Maria Banks—a handsome, dark-haired young lady who had been busy admiring her own lilac-colored kid gloves—looked up to add her own support to Jenny's words.

"Indeed, we were sure the two of you would wish to help. Especially you, Camilla. You and Larry used to be quite close, as I recall. Of course you have heard that he won his captainship? I mean to insist that he wear his uniform to the ball, even if he *has* sold out."

The girl to whom these words were directed, Camilla Leslie, made no reply. Maria went on, a slightly malicious note creeping into her voice.

"I am surprised Larry has not been to call upon you yet. He has not, has he? I made sure you would have mentioned it if he had. But of course he must be very busy just now with affairs at home. Old Mr. Westmoreland's gout is very troublesome, I have heard, and so the burden of running the property falls on Larry."

A faint flush rose to Camilla's cheeks. When she spoke, however, her voice was gentle and controlled. "No, Larry has not called," she said. "I am sure it is as you say, Maria, and he is very busy with affairs at home."

"It stands to reason that he would be," agreed the fourth girl in the parlor. This was Agnes Ludlow, a pretty redhead, who was seated beside Camilla on the sofa. With a warm smile toward her friend, she added, "And perhaps he has not heard that Camilla is home yet. It might be that he thinks she is still in London with her aunt."

"No, for I took care to inform him that she was not," said Maria, speaking with some asperity. "So if he has not called on Camilla, it must be for some other reason. But I suppose she doesn't care if a mere captain in the Hussars calls on her anyway. She has her grand London beaux to console her."

These words made Camilla flush again, but Agnes merely shook her head in a half-reproving, half-indulgent way. "Don't be catty, Maria," she said. "You know you'd give your eyeteeth to have had a Season in London like Camilla. Anyway, we're getting off the subject. You and Jenny called to find out if Camilla and I would help with a ball to be given to welcome back our young men who served in Wellington's army. It sounds a fine notion to me, and I would be very happy to help. What do you think, Camilla?"

"Yes, to be sure," agreed Camilla at once. "I am glad to see the village giving some recognition to the returning soldiers. I suppose you mean to hold the party in the Assembly Rooms?"

"Of course," said Maria. "Where else would we hold it? It's not as though we all had ballrooms in our homes, like your grand London friends."

She spoke disagreeably, but Agnes advised her once again not to be catty and turned to Jenny. "Of course

Camilla and I would be happy to help with the preparations. What exactly did you wish us to do?"

"I thought perhaps you might help with the refreshments. Everything else is pretty well provided for. Our kitchenmaid's brother plays the fiddle, so with old Mr. Bass from the inn and Tom Clark from over in Hunsford to help out, that ought to take care of the music."

"Jenny and I will do the decorations, of course," put in Maria. "As we are the ones who had the idea of giving the ball, it is only right we should have the most important work."

"You know it's all important work, Maria," said Jenny with a deprecating look toward Camilla and Agnes. "I'm sure refreshments are as important as decorations. You needn't worry about bringing plates and cups and silverware, you know," she told them. "Mrs. Knapp at the Great House has very kindly promised to send over anything of that kind that we need. And Mrs. Bass is going to provide the punch—and Maria's mama said she would make tea. But if you could just make up some little sandwiches or cakes or biscuits for us to serve along with the tea and punch, that would be lovely."

"Yes, I could make sandwiches," agreed Agnes at once. "And Camilla can make those same kind of little biscuits that she made for the picnic last summer, can't you, Millie? You know, the jam-filled ones I thought were so good."

"Those *were* quite good," agreed Maria with a condescending air. "I daresay those would do well enough, Camilla, though I always think cakes are more genteel myself. However, Jenny and I will trust you to provide all that is necessary. Just see that whatever you make is sent over to the Assembly Rooms on the afternoon of the ball."

"We would appreciate it so much," said Jenny, with a warmth that did much to dilute the offense of her companion's words. "And I am sure Larry and the other young men will appreciate it, too. And since we are selling tickets by subscription, we hope to raise enough money to help poor Will Hutchins. You know he lost an arm and a leg at Waterloo, and it's going to be terribly difficult for him to support his family from now on."

"He was only a common soldier," said Maria with a dismissive sniff. "It's not as though he was a gentleman like Larry and Oliver Atwood and the other boys who went into the army as officers. I'm just glad none of *them* were wounded in the war. It would have been too horrible if one of them came home missing an arm or an eye or something like that." She shuddered delicately.

Camilla looked at her with disgust, but said nothing until Maria and Jenny had left the parlor. When the door finally closed behind them, she vented her spleen to Agnes.

"I do believe that Maria Banks must be the most cold-hearted, pretentious creature that ever lived. Did you hear the way she dismissed poor Will Hutchins's injuries by saying he was 'only a common soldier?' "

"Yes, that was too bad of her," agreed Agnes. "I'm afraid Maria is rather thoughtless sometimes. But even though she spoke so slightingly of Will, she *is* giving this ball to help him. That must be counted in her favor, you know."

"I don't believe Maria's doing it to help Will at all," retorted Camilla. "She is only doing it because she likes ordering people about and because she wants the glory of welcoming Larry and the other officers home." She gave a vengeful poke at the embroidery she had been working on when the visitors were announced. "What annoys me most is that she is not really giving the ball at all. By her own account, she is merely farming out the work of it among half the village!"

"Well, it's a good cause, after all," said Agnes leniently. "I don't mind helping."

"I don't mind helping either. It's the principle of the thing I object to. In my book, it's shabby behavior to invite people to a ball and expect them to bring their own refreshments. They did not do so at any of the balls I attended in London, I assure you!"

Agnes gave her friend a thoughtful look. "Yes, but you know this is not London, Millie," she said. "I daresay we don't do things in Farlington as people do there, but that is only to be expected in a village this small. If you mean to hold us to the London standard for everything, we shall fall out at once."

"I don't hold anybody to any standard," said Camilla in exasperation. "And let me tell you, Agnes, that if you intend to behave like Maria and start talking about my grand London friends, I shall leave the room!"

Agnes laughed. "No, I shan't do that! She made herself very obnoxious, didn't she? And it is all jealousy, for if she had been the one to have a Season in London, you know she would have been boasting about it forever."

"I trust I have not done that," said Camilla with a half smile.

Agnes smiled, too, and reached out to pat her arm. "No, you have not, Millie. I did not mean to imply just now that you have been boastful in any way. On the contrary, you have been terribly closemouthed about the whole experience. Why, we would none of us have even known a baronet was courting you if Maria's mother had not heard about it from her cousin who lives in London."

Camilla winced. The subject of the baronet in London was a sore point with her. Certainly she had never expected to attract such a suitor. And it was unlikely that she would have done so under ordinary circumstances, for since her father's death a few years ago, she and her mother had been obliged to exist on a very modest income. There was enough to dress them both decently, maintain a small house and garden, and pay the salaries of an outside man and a couple of maidservants, but their means certainly would not have stretched to cover a Season in London complete with court presentation, a coming-out ball, and vouchers to Almack's.

The fairy godmother who had made all this possible was Camilla's aunt Dorothy. Like Mrs. Leslie, Aunt Dorothy was a widow, but she had been left very much more comfortably circumstanced than her younger sister. She kept a house in London and another in Brighton, and she had no less than three carriages to carry her from one city to the other. A member of the Upper Ten Thousand, she attended all the *ton* parties, and her letters to Camilla and her mother were full of gay references to the great personages with whom she daily socialized.

From the time Camilla was a baby, Aunt Dorothy had always been the source of lavish and delightful gifts. She had given Camilla a pony when she was a child and, later, when she was a young lady, a string of real pearls. There had been numerous smaller gifts as well: new bonnets, a fur-lined cloak, a volume of Lord Byron's verse signed by the poet himself. But the most overwhelming gift of all had come on Camilla's nineteenth birthday, when Aunt Dorothy had announced that she meant to bring her niece to London and give her a Season.

Camilla had accordingly gone to London, where she had been almost overwhelmed by the reception given her. Aunt Dorothy had not only paid for all her dresses, ornaments, and entertainments, but she had also indicated that she meant to settle a part of her considerable fortune on her niece as a marriage portion.

Given that Camilla was a girl of even moderate attractions, this would have ensured her receiving a fair share of masculine attention. But Camilla's attractions were much more than moderate. Of medium height, beautifully proportioned, with golden hair, regular features, and a pair of large dark eyes, she could endure comparison with any girl making her bows that Season. Her success was immediate and decided, and before the Season was out, she found herself receiving offers of marriage from not one but two eligible gentlemen.

One of these gentlemen Camilla had refused without a qualm. He was a young man of charming manners but expensive and somewhat dissipated habits. Camilla was fairly certain that his proposal had more to do with her aunt's fortune than any sincere or lasting affection for herself. But her other suitor, Sir Eustace Grosfield, was a horse of a different color.

There was no need for Sir Eustace to seek a wife with money. He possessed a comfortable fortune of his own, derived from the several properties that had descended to him along with his title. He was also witty, well mannered, and good-looking enough to make him an object of desire among most of the ladies of London. Indeed, there had been countless matrimonial snares set for him by marriage-minded maidens and their mamas over the ten years or so that had passed since his first entering London Society. But it was not until he had met Camilla that he had shown any willingness to relinquish the bachelorhood that seemed to suit him so well.

Camilla, for her part, had liked Sir Eustace better than any of the other gentlemen she had met in London. He was an entertaining companion, a gallant escort, and—when at last he had made up his mind to court Camilla in earnest—a most ardent and eloquent suitor. Aunt Dorothy liked him, too, and she frequently told Camilla what a triumph she had achieved in attaching Sir Eustace.

"You could not do better for a husband, my dear," she told Camilla over and over. "I have known Eustace these ten years, and I do not know of a better-tempered man. He's a handsome creature, too, though when you're my age you'll realize that a good temper's a deal more important in a husband than good looks—aye, and a deal harder to find, too! But Eustace has both, and a title and fortune to boot. I don't think you could do better, my dear, not if I was to sponsor you for a dozen Seasons."

Camilla was quite sure her aunt was right. Yet when the day finally came on which Sir Eustace made her a formal offer of his heart and hand, she found herself curiously diffident.

It was not that she disliked Sir Eustace in any way. On the contrary, she liked everything about him. He was well bred, good to look at, and unfailingly kind and considerate. He could give her a life not merely of ease but of luxury. And he seemed to genuinely care for her, too, which was perhaps even more to the point. It was most inconvenient, therefore, that try as she might, Camilla could not seem to summon up an answering affection for Sir Eustace.

She had certainly tried. She had told over all his good qualities like a nun telling over her rosary. Every time she danced with him at Almack's or went riding with him in the Park, she reminded herself that such activities might be a regular part of her life if she were to marry him. But it was of no use. Her heart simply would not comply with her wishes. It was as resistant to loving Sir Eustace as a child might be resistant to contracting mumps or chicken pox, and for exactly the same reason. Having previously been infected with the disease in question, her heart now seemed incapable of sustaining a second attack.

And it was Larry Westmoreland, now Captain Westmoreland of one of His Majesty's celebrated Hussar regiments, who had been responsible for this unfortunate immunity.

Camilla had known Larry since they were both children. They had never been playmates per se, for Larry was several years older than she, and this circumstance along with his sex had tended to militate against his having many dealings with a mere "little girl." Nonetheless, Camilla had always liked Larry better than the other village boys. If he teased her, it was always in a good-natured way, and once he had rescued her favorite doll from the depredations of an elder and larger boy. The picture of Larry bruised, bloody nosed, but triumphant withal, plucking the doll from the bully's grasp and returning it to her with a smile had seemed to Camilla for many years the very essence of masculine chivalry.

Looking back, Camilla tended to think that her love for Larry had dated from this incident. At any rate, it had given her a partiality for him that had lasted all through her childhood. And some years later, when Larry had begun to demonstrate the same partiality toward her, it had taken very little effort on his part to finish the work that had begun so long ago.

Although Larry had never made Camilla a formal declaration of love, he had demonstrated his feelings for her in almost every other way. He had given her countless posies and other trifling gifts, squired her to all the local entertainments, and spent hours in her mother's little parlor, talking and laughing and playing at loo or anagrams or any other game Camilla's fancy might suggest. So charming had he been that even Camilla's mother, who was shy in all company and especially in masculine company, declared him "a very pleasant young man."

To Camilla, Larry was all that a man ought to be, and the lover she had dreamed of ever since she was old enough to indulge in dreams of love and lovers. She could still remember vividly the occasion on which he had first kissed her. They had been walking together on the village green and had come upon a party of farming folk gathered about the ancient tree that was locally known as the Marriage Oak. "It must be a wedding party," Camilla had exclaimed with interest. "Look, Larry. They're going to dance around the Oak! I haven't seen that done in years and years."

"Nor I," said Larry, watching with interest as a rosy, laughing girl, decked in the finery of a country bride, made three ceremonious circuits of the Oak on the arm of her rustic bridegroom. "It's amazing how these old customs survive. My grandmother used to speak of the villagers dancing around the Oak in her day, so it's obviously been an established custom for at least sixty or seventy years. And to judge by the looks of some of the carvings on the Oak, it's at least a hundred years older than that."

Camilla nodded. Another of the customs pertaining to the Oak was that courting couples should inscribe their initials somewhere on its bark. This had been going on for so many years that the whole trunk of the Oak was scarred with carved initials—some new and fresh, some so old that they seemed merely part of the pattern of its bark. As soon as the marriage party moved off, Larry and Camilla had gone forward to inspect the great tree with its mass of carvings. Larry had shaken his head over one carving retailing in graphic detail the charms of the writer's mistress. "I don't think that's much of a tribute to one's lady love," he said. "Classic and restrained—that's the style one ought to strive for. Something on the order of this." Taking out his penknife, he had slowly and meticulously inscribed his and Camilla's initials on a branch just over his head.

Camilla had watched, uncertain whether she was merely witnessing a demonstration of carving or something more. "There," said Larry at last, having carved a flourish beneath his and Camilla's initials and encircled them with a heart. "What do you think of that?"

"It's lovely," Camilla had managed to say. "The nicest carving on the whole tree."

Larry had looked at her thoughtfully as he put away his penknife. He had blue eyes, waving light brown hair, and a smile that made his already handsome face more attractive than Camilla thought either fair or necessary. He gave her one of these smiles now.

"Then it's worthy of the lady who inspired it," he said

and bent to kiss her on the lips. Right there in broad daylight he had kissed her—there on the village green! Camilla could only be thankful in retrospect that Mrs. Banks or Miss Maynard or one of the other village gossips had not been by to see it. But there had been no one to see it—no one but the sparrows in the branches above them, and they were the most discreet of witnesses. Thus it had come about that the recollection of that kiss and the ceremony that had preceded it were things Camilla had cherished in her memory ever since.

That had not been the only time Larry had kissed her. He had done so once again, on the day he had departed to take up his commission in the Army. On that occasion, however, the kiss had been much less satisfactory.

For one thing, it had been a hurried business, snatched in the moments during which his baggage was being loaded into the coach. Camilla's mood had already been overwrought at the notion of his leaving, and the sight of him in his brand-new Hussar uniform—so gallant, so handsome, and yet so frighteningly vulnerable—made the tears flow in spite of her most determined efforts. Larry had shaken his head and wiped her tears away with an air that strove to be jocular in spite of his own obvious emotion.

"Don't cry, Millie. You'll see. I'll come home safe and sound and none the worse for it all. Why, I intend to live to a ripe old age so I may be around to torment you when you're an old, old lady." In a more serious voice, he added, "I don't *want* to leave, Millie. But this is something I must do—something any man of spirit would feel he had to do, I should think. I hope you understand?"

Camilla had not understood, but she had nodded. Larry had kissed her then, but it was a hasty kiss that held none of the tender ceremony of the kiss he had given her beneath the Oak.

Camilla had waited to see if he would say anything more. In her heart she was hoping he might say something about love, perhaps even something about marriage. It was not such an unreasonable thing to hope for, she considered, given all that had previously passed between them. For a couple to carve their initials on the Oak was considered nearly as binding as an engagement, among the lower class of villagers at least. She and Larry might not be of that class, but surely his action had signified something more than a mere flirtatious gesture! It had meant more than that to Camilla, at any rate, and she felt she could better bear to part with Larry if there was a formal understanding between them.

Of course she was not so unreasonable as to expect Larry to set a definite date on which their understanding would be translated into marriage. That could hardly be, seeing that neither of them knew what the duration of the war might be. But surely, surely, he would not be so cruel as to leave her without saying any word at all! Yet in the end, that was what he had done. A kiss, a smile, a wave of his hand, and he was gone, while Camilla was left to nurse a sad and disappointed heart.

Camilla could remember that day as though it were yesterday, though in fact it had been several years ago. She could also remember the slow process by which hope had gradually left her. For the first few weeks, she had tried to bolster up her hopes, telling herself that Larry would surely write to her. In his letters he would not be constrained by a waiting coach and might put in all the things he had neglected to say at their last meeting. But as months went by and no letters came, she had been forced at last to abandon hope entirely.

She had received frequent bulletins of his doings, to be sure. Old Mr. Westmoreland, Larry's father, would occasionally stop her on the street to tell her that Larry had asked after her or that he had sent her his compliments. But since Mr. Westmoreland was a notably polite and punctilious old gentleman, Camilla could never be sure whether these messages were real or only what Mr. Westmoreland felt was owed her in light of her and Larry's long friendship. And when finally she *had* received a personal token from Larry, in the shape of a French officer's sword captured in some battle, Camilla had convinced herself it was of no more significance than the string of glass beads he had once won her at a local fair.

The sword, coincidentally, had arrived on the same day that Camilla had received her aunt's invitation to spend the Season in London. It had seemed almost an omen to Camilla. Perhaps it was time to put aside the dreams of the past—time to relinquish once and for all the hopes she had been cherishing since Larry's departure. At the very least, a Season in London must serve to divert her thoughts, which had been too much inclined to dwell sadly on Larry's desertion. So Camilla had gone to London, but even amid the gaieties of the Season she had not been able to escape the memory of Larry. And so, when the fateful day came on which Sir Eustace had asked her to become his wife, Camilla had equivocated.

"I don't think I can, Stacy," she had said, raising unhappy eyes to his face. "I wish I could say yes. I have tried to think we might deal together, but I am afraid it would not do. Please believe that I am very sorry, Stacy. I know how much honor you do me in asking me to be your wife, but the truth is, I am not quite sure of my own feelings."

It was clear from Sir Eustace's face that this speech had come as an unpleasant shock to him. But his habitual urbanity soon reasserted itself. Taking Camilla's hand in his, he had smiled down at her with a reassuring air.

"My dear, you need not apologize," he said. "I quite see that you would not like to commit yourself when you are unsure of your feelings. But you know, Camilla, I do not insist on having an answer today. If you would like time to consider my proposal, you may have it—as much time as you want. Indeed, if there is the slightest chance you might change your mind, I would be willing to wait indefinitely."

Camilla could not think it right to accept such a generous offer as this, but she agreed to consider Sir Eustace's proposal a little longer before definitely refusing it. Accordingly, she had considered it all the remaining weeks of the Season, as she went about from party to party and was dined and feted and indulged by her aunt. But when the time came for her to leave London and return to Farlington, she found she was still of the same mind as before. It was still Larry who possessed her heart, and as long as there remained any possibility of his claiming it, she could not bestow it on any other man.

If she had had certain knowledge, beyond any possible doubt, that Larry did not want her or her heart, it might have been a different story. Then she might have made up her mind to accept Sir Eustace and in time grown quite reconciled to wedding her second choice instead of her first. But of course, she could not explain all this to Sir Eustace. So she had regretfully told him that she was still unable to accept his very obliging offer, and Sir Eustace had accepted her decision with quiet composure. Despite his show of composure, however, Camilla knew she had hurt him. It was this that made her wince whenever his name was mentioned, as Agnes had innocently done just now.

Agnes, unaware of her friend's distress, went rattling cheerfully on. "I am sure if any of the rest of us had a baronet dancing attendance on us, we would have cried the fact to high heaven," she told Camilla. "Have you heard from him since leaving London? Does he mean to come and visit you here in Farlington?"

"Oh, no," said Camilla. She could barely repress a shudder at the thought. But of course, she reminded herself, there was no possibility of such a thing ever coming to pass. Her last interview with Sir Eustace had been so painful that he must undoubtedly be as eager as she to avoid meeting in the future. And though Camilla did not admit it to herself, she had another, less noble, reason for not wishing Sir Eustace to come to Farlington. Thus far he had only seen her in London, amid the trappings of wealth and luxury her aunt had provided her. To have him see her in the much more modest surroundings in which she and her mother lived did not suit her at all.

"I do not expect that Sir Eustace will pursue our acquaintance now I have left London," she told Agnes firmly. "And there is no reason why he should. We were merely friends, after all."

Agnes looked incredulous. "That's not what I've heard," she said. "Mrs. Banks said her cousin wrote that Sir Eustace was quite nutty upon you and that they expected him to propose to you any day! But there, I do not mean to tease you, Millie," she added, seeing Camilla's look of distress. "I must say, however, that I am a little sorry to hear that Sir Eustace is *not* coming here. It would have been quite the most exciting thing to happen in Farlington since Tom Tidmarsh's cow had that calf with five legs."

"I doubt it," said Camilla dryly. "You know Sir Eustace has only the ordinary number of legs, Agnes. He is by no means so exceptional as a five-legged calf!"

Agnes laughed heartily at this and agreed that two-legged baronets were perhaps not so rare as five-legged calves. She was then obliged to fold up her needlework and gather together her other belongings, in response to a message from her mother desiring her to return home immediately. As Camilla bade her farewell, she hoped fervently that the subject of Sir Eustace's infatuation with herself was now permanently shelved along with that of five-legged calves and similar freaks of nature.

Two

In the days that followed, there was but one subject of discussion among the young ladies of Farlington. That subject, of course, was the Returning Soldiers' Benefit Ball. Camilla, who had perhaps more reason to feel deeply on the subject than most of her peers, was for that reason the less inclined to talk about it. But her reticence went unnoticed amid the general clamor. Everyone was eager to discuss her hair, her dress, and her jewelry for the occasion, and there were endless debates on the subject of proper ballroom etiquette. In particular there was debate—and even a certain amount of polite contention—on the subject of whom would be the fortunate lady to lead off the dancing.

"Seeing that it was Jenny and I who had the idea of giving the ball in the first place, I think it should be one of us who leads off," stated Maria Banks during one of these discussions. "After all, it's not as though Mrs. Knapp from the Great House is likely to be present or anyone else who could reasonably demand precedence. So Jenny and I have decided between us that I shall lead—and though I dislike to put myself forward in any way, I do feel I'm the properest person on this occasion. I'm having the loveliest dress made up. Pink crepe, with a tunic and train."

Camilla, who had heard both tunics and trains decried as being out of date in the Metropolis more than six months before, merely smiled in a noncommittal way. Inwardly, however, she was resolved to show Maria and the others exactly what a proper ball dress ought to be. This resolution was strengthened by Maria's next speech.

"Larry was telling me he was looking forward to the ball very much. He came to wait upon us, you know, just the day before yesterday. Of course Papa called upon *him* as soon as ever we heard he was home from the war—but we did not look to have the call returned so promptly. Mama, of course, will have it that Larry had some personal motive in being so punctual. She quite made me blush with her innuendos, I promise you."

Camilla thought this extremely unlikely. There was triumph in Maria's looks, and a measure of spite, but no vestige of maidenly confusion. Maria went on, the spite in her manner becoming more pronounced as she addressed Camilla. "I wonder that Larry has not been to call upon *you* yet, Camilla. Of course, your mama is widowed, so you have no one to present your compliments at Westmoreland House as my papa did. But even so, Larry has had long enough to make the rounds of his old friends in Farlington. I do not remember his being so backward in the old days."

This speech, naturally, did nothing to make Camilla feel more charitably disposed toward Maria. But though she was able to discount most of the other girl's words as spite, there was just enough truth in them to plant a thorn or two in Camilla's flesh.

Larry had been home for several weeks now, and it was obvious that he had found it possible to make at least a few social calls during that time. That he had not seen fit to call upon Camilla and her mother could only mean that he was in no hurry to renew his acquaintance with them. This idea pained Camilla, but it also roused in her a spirit of defiance. She would show everyone in Farlington that Larry's defection had not hurt her in the least. She would attire herself in her very best London style and attend the ball with her head held high. And she would look so gorgeous that Larry would regret having slighted her for a young lady who didn't know any better than to wear a ball dress with a tunic and train!

This resolution was strong in Camilla's mind when she awoke the morning of the ball. She was obliged to rise rather early that day, for she had the work of baking biscuits as well as the task of making her toilette to attend to.

As Camilla hastily tied a cap over her unbrushed hair and threw an apron over a well-worn muslin dress, she sighed a little at the necessity that lay before her. In her aunt's house, she would merely have had to give the order to the cook, and then she herself might have lain abed late as befitted a lady who was attending a ball that evening. But her mother's cookmaid was elderly and uncertain of temper, and Camilla knew that, if presented with a request for six dozen biscuits, Martha would likely either refuse outright or develop one of the mysterious illnesses that afflicted her whenever she was asked to do something outside her usual round of duties.

"Still, it's very vexing," Camilla told herself, as she went downstairs to the kitchen. "They manage these things much better in London. And I could be living there now if I chose, with a handsome husband who loved me and would take pleasure in providing me with every luxury. What a fool I am." Camilla meditated on this theme with some regret as she made up the fire in the oven and began to assemble the ingredients for her biscuit making.

Martha, the cookmaid, had absented herself from the kitchen as soon as Camilla had appeared there, saying with a sniff that she wanted no part of such goings-on. Camilla was just as glad to dispense with her presence. Soon she was engrossed in sifting flour, chopping nuts, beating eggs, and the other work involved in making biscuits. The time passed quickly. She was just removing the first pan of finished biscuits from the oven when Joan, the cottage's other female servant, thrust her head around the kitchen door.

"You've a caller, Miss Leslie," she announced in a stentorian voice. Addressing some person or persons over her shoulder, she added, "Yes, sir. She's right here, sir, in the kitchen. Just step this way, sir, if you will, but mind your step. The floor's a bit uneven."

Camilla, who had been wholly engrossed in her work, turned around in consternation. Beneath her consternation, however, lurked an exasperated satisfaction. It was obvious from Joan's words that the caller must be a gentleman, and in Camilla's mind there was only one gentleman who mattered. It was typical, of course, that Larry should have called at a time when she was employed with such a menial and messy task; it was even more typical that Joan should have brought him into the kitchen instead of putting him properly in the parlor, where Camilla might have joined him once she had tidied herself. But Camilla was prepared to overlook these minor irritants in the joy of beholding her lover once more. When she looked toward the door, however, it was not Larry she beheld, but rather the trim and elegant figure of Sir Eustace Grosfield.

"Oh!" said Camilla blankly.

"I do hope I'm not intruding," said Sir Eustace in a deprecating voice. It was clear he was taken aback to find Camilla in her present situation. But his manners were equal to the occasion. With a tentative smile, he left his position near the doorway and came toward her across the kitchen. "The girl said you were here, but she did not tell me how you were employed. You make a most charming domestic picture, upon my word."

"Thank you," said Camilla, trying to smile back at him. Inwardly, however, she was conscious only of chagrin. Here she was, receiving a visit from one of the first gentlemen of London Society, and he had discovered her clad in cap and apron, flour streaked and disheveled and employed in the menial task of baking biscuits! She could hardly have presented a greater contrast from the way she had appeared to him in London. But there was no help for it now. Summoning another smile to her lips, Camilla said, "I am surprised to see you here, Stacy. How comes it about that you are visiting Farlington? I had thought you meant to stay on your Lancashire estate all this summer."

"Yes, I meant to," said Sir Eustace. He gave Camilla another deprecatory smile. "I meant to, and I really did my best to do so. But I found I could not stay away from you any more than the needle of a compass can help pointing to the north."

"I see," said Camilla. There seemed nothing else to say. Sir Eustace went on, his voice betraying a hint of constraint.

"I am staying at the village inn, so you need not fear my presence here will discommode you, Camilla. Nor need you fear I mean to vex you long with my presence. I only mean to stay a day or two, and then I shall be on my way back to Lancashire." In a more natural voice, he added, "I passed by your Assembly Rooms on the way over here. There seemed to be a great deal of bustle going on—people coming and going and decorations being put up. It looks as though you're getting ready for some kind of fete."

"Yes, we are having a ball tonight for our returning soldiers," said Camilla. "That's why I am baking these biscuits." She indicated the rows of finished biscuits lying on the kitchen table.

"Ah, yes," said Sir Eustace, regarding the biscuits with interest. "They look quite delectable, upon my word."

"They aren't done yet," said Camilla. "I must fill their centers with jam first, you see." She was glad to turn the conversation back to the comparatively safe subject of biscuit making. Mortified as she had been to be discovered at such a menial task, she now felt she could embrace it with enthusiasm if only it would keep Sir Eustace from broaching the more dangerous subjects of love and marriage.

Sir Eustace watched as she took up a spoon and put a bit of strawberry jam into the center of the nearest biscuit. "Ah," he said with comprehension. "Hussar's Kisses!"

"What?" exclaimed Camilla, nearly dropping the spoon.

"Hussar's Kisses," repeated Sir Eustace, picking up the biscuit and surveying it with satisfaction. "That's what my mother used to call biscuits of this sort."

"Well, we just call them jam-filled biscuits," said Camilla. She had a hard time keeping her voice steady. The subject of Hussars was inextricably linked with Larry in her mind, as was the subject of kissing. And even now that she knew Sir Eustace's comment had no reference to Larry, she could not help a faint flush from rising to her cheeks.

Sir Eustace, fortunately, was too busy sampling the biscuit he had taken to notice her heightened color. "Would you like another?" she asked, offering him a second biscuit.

"No, thank you, although that one was certainly delicious." Sir Eustace paused, then went on in a rush. "I will tell you what I would like, Camilla. I would like very much to attend your village assembly tonight—with you and your mother, if possible. Would it be asking too much to join your party this evening?"

Camilla, who had not anticipated such a request, gazed at him openmouthed. Sir Eustace went on quickly. "You say nothing. But you know you need not fear to speak your mind to me, Camilla. I would not wish to intrude myself where I am not wanted."

Camilla thought rapidly. It would be both inconvenient and embarrassing to have Sir Eustace present if Larry meant to approach her that evening about resuming their interrupted relationship. But Camilla was forced to admit that he had shown no signs of wishing to do so up till now. And if he chose to snub her that evening and devote himself instead to Maria Banks (as seemed only too likely), then it would be some comfort to have an alternate cavalier on hand.

Sir Eustace, moreover, was a cavalier who must add greatly to her consequence. Thanks to the gossiping tongues of Maria and her mother, all of Farlington knew that Camilla had been courted in London by a handsome baronet. To appear on the arm of that same baronet would be a most effectual way to show them all that she cared nothing for Larry's defection.

"I do not see any reason why you may not come, Stacy," said Camilla slowly. "It is a subscription ball, so anyone who is willing to buy a ticket is free to attend. We are raising money for one of our local young men who was wounded at Waterloo."

"Well, in that case it's clearly my patriotic duty to attend," said Sir Eustace with a satisfied smile. "I would be delighted to support such a good cause. I only hope the committee will forgive me if I attend in somewhat informal attire. Not anticipating a ball, I neglected to pack full evening dress."

Camilla assured him that balls in Farlington allowed of more latitude in dress than in London. Sir Eustace expressed relief at this, thanked Camilla, and took a ceremonious leave of her, promising to be on hand that evening to escort her and her mother to the ball.

Camilla's mother, however, reacted with alarm when informed of this new arrangement. "Oh, no," she said, shaking her head violently. "I don't think I would feel comfortable, Millie dear, attending the party with a young man I do not know."

Camilla gave an impatient sigh. "Sir Eustace is not an ogre, Mother," she said testily. "He is a very respectable gentleman with an excellent reputation in London. Your own sister introduced us, and she had nothing but good to say about him. Besides, Sir Eustace is not so young as all that. I am sure he must be at least thirty."

"But he is a stranger to me, Millie. You know I am always so stupid around strangers. If it were Larry, now, whom we have known so long—"

"It so happens that Larry did not offer to lend us his escort this evening," said Camilla more testily still. "So I found myself obliged to accept Sir Eustace in his stead. And I have no doubt you will find him quite as pleasant as Larry when you come to know him."

"I have no doubt I will, dear, once I have known him as long as I have Larry. But tonight he is a stranger to me—and you know how I am about strangers." Mrs. Leslie looked apologetically at her daughter. "Would you think it very bad of me if I stayed home tonight instead of accompanying you and Sir Eustace to the party?"

Camilla hesitated. In London, it was not uncommon for a lady to attend a party with a gentleman as her sole escort. Here in Farlington, however, such an act would have a more particular appearance. Did she really wish to give the impression that she and Sir Eustace were engaged or on the verge of becoming engaged? Camilla thought again of Maria's words and of the way Larry had been avoiding her since returning home. Her chin went up. "Of course I would not think it bad, Mama, if you really prefer to stay home tonight," she said. "But if it is merely Sir Eustace's company you object to, perhaps it would be better if I told him we would rather he not join our party."

This rudeness Mrs. Leslie would not hear of, however. She said that she was sure Sir Eustace was a charming gentleman in whose company Camilla would be perfectly safe and that she was really glad for an excuse not to go into company that evening. Camilla, feeling that this was probably the truth, accepted her mother's excuses and went upstairs to begin getting ready for the ball.

This work took a considerable time, though by no means

so long as it would have taken in London. Camilla bathed and washed her hair, buffed her nails, brushed a discreet dusting of powder across her nose, and touched her lips cautiously with the carmine salve she had purchased in London but had not dared wear since returning home. Then she set about the business of dressing. A chemise with real lace trimming and a pair of silk stockings of miraculous fineness came first; then came the ball dress itself, a froth of white gauze and satin embellished with a ruching of lace and bunches of rosebuds. The dress was cut low both in front and behind, with another cluster of rosebuds set in the deep "V" of its decolletage.

It took time for Camilla to single-handedly array herself in this costume. Still more time was required to add the long gloves, satin slippers, and string of pearls that were its proper accompaniments. Her hair she arranged as well as she could without the assistance of a maid, and in the end she was quite pleased with the result. A cluster of rosebuds matching those on her dress encircled her head, with the mass of her hair left to fall in soft curls on either side of her face. Camilla nodded with satisfaction at her reflection; then she took up her best evening cloak and went downstairs to await Sir Eustace's arrival.

He arrived at the appointed hour, and in spite of the fact that he was wearing trousers instead of the more formal satin knee breeches, Camilla thought he looked as handsome and urbane as she had ever seen him. Once again she regretted that she could not love him. She liked him, admired him, and esteemed him, but there was no rush of emotion such as she had used to feel when she looked at Larry. Then it occurred to her that after all these years, she might not feel any rush of emotion at the sight of Larry either. Perhaps that was a thing one outgrew with age. Camilla hoped it might be so. In that case, she need have no qualms about accepting Sir Eustace's suit. If she were capable of feeling passion for no man, then there could be no objection to her marrying in its absence.

Sir Eustace, fortunately unaware of his inamorata's thoughts, was doing his best to make himself agreeable to her mother. "I had not thought it possible for your daughter to look lovelier than she did in London," he told Mrs. Leslie. "But I see I have done her an injustice. She is even more blooming here than amid the fleshpots of the Metropolis."

Mrs. Leslie, who had been regarding Sir Eustace with the same alarm she would have accorded a rhinoceros in her parlor, merely smiled nervously and took the first opportunity to flee the room. "Mama will not be attending the ball tonight," explained Carmilla. "She had planned to originally, but after you left this afternoon she found that she was—well, not feeling quite the thing. I hope you do not mind if there are two instead of three in our party, Stacy?"

Sir Eustace said gallantly that he did not mind at all. He was perhaps not sorry to be spared the company of a third in his party, particularly a third so difficult to converse with.

He waited while Camilla went to bid her mother goodbye. "I'm ready now," she announced on her return. "We may as well go over to the Assembly Rooms, Stacy. The first dance begins at eight."

"What about your biscuits?" asked Sir Eustace as he assisted her with her cloak. "Do we need to carry them over with us?"

"No, I had Joan take them over earlier this evening," said Camilla. She had no wish to be encumbered with a basket of biscuits when making her grand entrance. As she went out to the carriage with Sir Eustace, she reflected with satisfaction that her entrance ought to be all she could desire. She would show Larry and the others that she was managing perfectly well without him!

Three

As Camilla entered the Assembly Rooms on Sir Eustace's arm, she found her heart beating uncomfortably fast.

The Rooms were brilliantly lit and, thanks to Maria and Jenny's efforts, lavishly decorated in honor of the returning veterans. A banner reading, "Welcome," hung over the doors to the ballroom, and Camilla could glimpse banks of flowers and potted plants ranged along the walls. But it was the occupants of the room rather than its decorations on which her attention was primarily focused.

The first person to meet her eyes was Maria Banks, garbed in the pink crepe dress she had described earlier. In spite of the outmoded tunic and train, Camilla was obliged to admit that Maria looked quite handsome in this dress. Her dark hair had been twisted into a Roman knot, also rather outmoded as of that date, but nonetheless becoming. Maria was laughing and flirting with Oliver Atwood, one of the returning veterans. Camilla noted that Oliver looked a good deal leaner and browner than when she had last seen him, but his usual gay and insouciant manner seemed to have survived the war intact. She then transferred her attention to the next group of guests.

This was a mixed party of ladies and gentlemen. Among them were Jenny Jacobs and Agnes Ludlow. Both girls looked very pretty, Jenny in lavender mulled muslin and

Agnes in a eau-de-nil sarcenet that set off her green eyes and copper-colored curls.

Agnes caught sight of Camilla and her partner at the same moment Camilla saw her. Her eyes widened, and she gazed at Sir Eustace with a mixture of curiosity and admiration. Blushing slightly, Camilla nodded to Agnes and then to Jenny, who was also looking with interest at Sir Eustace. But she resolutely refused to notice the unmistakable "Come here!" signals the other girls were telegraphing toward her. Before being cornered by Jenny and Agnes, she wished to ascertain the presence of one other person in the room. And an instant later, she found herself literally face-to-face with him.

She would have known Larry anywhere, even had he not been wearing the distinctive uniform of the Hussars. Like Oliver, he was both leaner and browner than when she had seen him last, and there were lines on his face she did not recall seeing there before. But the hair still curled as crisply over his sunburned brow, and his eyes were as vividly blue as ever. Looking into those eyes, Camilla felt a contraction in the pit of her stomach. She knew then, with absolute certainty, that time had done nothing to cure her of her feelings for Larry. On the contrary, it seemed only to have made those feelings more acute.

It was impossible to tell if Larry was experiencing the same sensations. His face was quite blank as he regarded Camilla. She gazed back at him, her lips a little parted. She had entirely forgotten the presence of Sir Eustace beside her, and it was a shock when he suddenly addressed her in a voice of concern.

"Is something amiss, Camilla?"

Camilla blinked and shook her head, as though seeking to clear her vision. "No, nothing," she said. She went on gazing at Larry. He, too, had been startled by Sir Eustace's words. His eyes flickered to the baronet's face, then returned to Camilla again. At last he gave her a brief, unsmiling nod and turned deliberately away.

Camilla's shock could have been no greater if he had slapped her. This was a rejection equally clear and impossible of misinterpretation. Camilla felt herself trembling. She heard Sir Eustace's voice as if from a great distance away. "My dear, is something amiss?" he asked again with real concern. "You look quite pale. Do you feel unwell?"

"I do feel unwell," said Camilla and so fully did her voice support her words that Sir Eustace lost no time in helping her to the nearest bench. He then, despite her protests, insisted on fetching her a glass of punch from the refreshment room.

"Thank you, Stacy," said Camilla, smiling wanly as she took the glass of punch from him. "You are very kind. I'm sorry I was such a ninny back there. I will be quite well in a minute."

"Are you sure?" said Sir Eustace, surveying her with doubt. Camilla nodded and took a sip of punch. She already felt stronger, although the shock of Larry's rejection was still as painful as a fresh wound. It was clear now beyond any question that the hope she had been cherishing all these years had been cherished in vain. She had nothing left to her now but her pride. And that being the case, Camilla was more determined than ever to show the world—her world—that she was unaffected by this final blow to her hopes. In spite of Sir Eustace's protests, she insisted on leaving the bench and joining the group of guests that included Agnes and Jenny.

"Girls, there is someone I would like to introduce to you," she said, smiling and laying her hand on Sir Eustace's arm as she spoke. "This is Sir Eustace Grosfield. Stacy, these are my friends Miss Jacobs and Miss Ludlow. Miss Ludlow, in particular, has been eager to meet you." Carmilla threw Agnes a mischievous look.

"Indeed I have," said Agnes, laughing as she curtsied

to Sir Eustace. "You must know I have never met a baronet before, Sir Eustace. Camilla has assured me that you are like other men to look at, but I could not be content until I had seen for myself." And disregarding all Camilla's protests, she went on to retail their conversation about the five-legged calf.

Sir Eustace, however, laughed heartily at Agnes's story. "No, I cannot hope to compare with such a curiosity as a five-legged calf," he said with a shake of his head. "But even so, I shall endeavor not to be a drag on the evening's festivities. Perhaps you would do me the honor of dancing with me later on, Miss Ludlow? And you, too, Miss Jacobs. I will do my best to show you that my two legs are serviceable—even if unremarkable in their number!"

Jenny assented readily to this proposal, and Agnes was not slow to do the same. "But if I am to dance with you, it will have to be later in the evening," she warned Sir Eustace. "I am already engaged for the first and second dances. Still, I suppose that will pose no inconvenience to you, as you probably mean to dance those dances with Camilla anyway."

Sir Eustace looked at Carmilla. Camilla nodded and tried to smile. "Yes, of course," she said. "I would be very pleased to dance the first two dances with you, Stacy."

"In that case you must lead off, Camilla," said Jenny, in a matter-of-fact voice. "I'll go tell Maria." And she excused herself to go speak to her friend.

Camilla watched as Jenny approached Maria, who with a self-important air had just taken her place at the top of the floor opposite her partner, Oliver Atwood. The two girls spoke for a moment in a low voice, too low for Camilla to hear, but there was no mistaking the look of surprise and chagrin that overspread Maria's face. She glanced at Camilla and Sir Eustace, shrugged her shoulders, and relinquished her place with a pettish air. Carmilla could not help feeling a certain triumph as she took her place across from Sir Eustace at the top of the floor.

Alas, her triumph was short-lived. A moment later she observed Larry taking a place lower down in the set with a pretty fair girl whom Camilla recognized as Sylvia Atwood, Oliver Atwood's younger sister. Camilla told herself it was natural that Larry should choose to partner the sister of one of his brother officers in the first dance. It was a meaningless gallantry such as he might have bestowed on a cousin or any other female relation. But Sylvia looked so pretty in her gown of pale blue taffeta, and so smiling and gay as she went through the figures of the dance, that the wormwood of jealousy entered into Camilla's soul and made her unable to enjoy the triumph that was hers.

It was a very great triumph, as her friends all found occasion to tell her. "Oh, Camilla, your baronet is perfectly charming," whispered Agnes, during a moment when they were standing together on the ladies' side of the room. "I am already half in love with him, and I've known him only half an hour! And I am in love with your dress, too. It's the loveliest thing I've ever seen, and you look absolutely ravishing in it. My, didn't you take the wind out of Maria Banks's sails tonight! Showing up with a baronet on your arm, in a dress that made hers look like something out of the poor barrel! She looked positively no-how, I assure you."

Camilla tried to smile, but in truth her mood was very low. The triumph of making Maria Banks look no-how no longer seemed so satisfying as it would have a day or two previously. When the second dance was over, she was glad to surrender Sir Eustace to Agnes and retire to one of the benches along the side of the ballroom with the dowagers and chaperons.

Here she was not allowed to remain, however, First one young man and then another presented himself to Camilla with shy invitations to stand up with them. Camilla, who had known most of these beaux since childhood, could not find it in her heart to reject them now, but the pleasure of dancing every dance—which in earlier years would have been enough to make the evening a success to her—felt more like a penance tonight.

In due time she passed into the hands of Oliver Atwood. Camilla, rousing herself to a semblance of gaiety, complimented him on his handsome appearance in his uniform.

"Every fellow looks handsome in a red coat, Miss Leslie," he said with a grin. "I swear I was never half so popular with the ladies before I joined the Army. I've wondered sometimes if these uniforms weren't designed more for their appeal to the fair sex than for any effect they might have on enemy soldiers."

"Indeed," said Camilla, smiling. "That is certainly a novel theory, and I would give a good deal to see it tested, Lieutenant Atwood. Or should I say Mr. Atwood? I believe someone told me you had already resigned your commission."

"Aye, so I have. I only wore the uniform tonight because Jenny and Maria wanted me to. And of course because it gives me such an advantage with the ladies." Oliver gave Camilla a roguish look, his dark eyes full of merriment. "You know Larry's wearing his uniform tonight for the same reason, even though he sold out a week before I did. And if he makes any move to lord it over the rest of us, just because he was lucky enough to win his captaincy through the merest fluke, I shall take leave to inform everyone what a sham he is."

These words were spoken loudly enough to gain the attention of their subject. Larry, who was standing a little way off, turned to regard Oliver with an air of assumed hauteur. "What's that? I thought I heard my name mentioned. But I see it was the merest rattle."

Oliver made a threatening lunge toward him, which Larry parried with a skillful blow. "I warn you, Larry, you call me a rattle at your own peril," threatened Oliver. "If you make me look foolish in front of Miss Leslie, I shall have to call you out."

Larry's eyes went to Camilla, and the laughter died out of them. "Ah, yes, Miss Leslie," he said. He gave her a formal bow. "It has been a long time since I have had the pleasure of seeing you, Miss Leslie. I hope I find you well."

"Very well, Captain Westmoreland, thank you," said Camilla, curtsying stiffly.

Oliver observed these proceedings with an incredulous smile. "Damme if you ain't both as formal as if you was meeting in a bishop's parlor! What's the matter with you, Larry? I don't recall your being so shy with Miss Leslie in the old days." He threw Camilla a mischievous look. "But if you're such a slowtop that you don't care for the company of the prettiest girl in Farlington, I'll be happy enough to stand in for you."

It seemed to Camilla as though Larry were slow to respond to these words. But at last a rueful smile spread over his face. "I have no doubt you would, Atwood," he said. "But I suppose I cannot let you have it all your own way. Miss Leslie, would you care to dance this next dance with me?"

"I would be happy to, Captain Westmoreland," said Camilla. She had hard work to conceal the turmoil in her breast.

Larry took her by the arm and led her onto the floor. He did not speak as he took his place opposite her in the line. Camilla was silent, too. To stand up with Larry for a country dance, just as she had done so many times in years past, brought back memories both poignant and painful. For some minutes she had all she could do to keep from bursting into tears.

When at last she felt she was master of herself, she ventured to look again at Larry. He was regarding her with a searching expression. Camilla flashed him a bright, insincere smile.

"It's been an age since we last danced together, hasn't it?" she said lightly. "How long has it been exactly—two or three years."

It had been exactly two years and three months, as Camilla knew very well. Larry did not respond directly to her question, however. Instead, he said, "It seems as though I have been away from Farlington much longer than that. There were times when I was bivouacking in Spain when I felt as though I'd never had any other life. All this seemed like a dream, something I'd imagined or read about a long time ago." He looked about the ballroom with a musing expression.

"It must have been a relief to get home and find it all just the same as you remembered," ventured Camilla.

"Well, almost the same. There have been *some* changes." Larry looked directly at Camilla. "You, for instance. You have changed a great deal, Miss Leslie."

"I?" repeated Camilla, the color rising in her face. "I think you are mistaken, Captain Westmoreland. I assure you that I have not changed at all."

She spoke with an emphasis verging on aggression. It had seemed almost from Larry's words as though he were reproaching her. Yet it was he who had chosen to break off their relationship, after all. She was certainly not going to stand for such behavior without making some kind of counterattack.

There was an answering hint of aggression in Larry's voice as he responded to her statement. "Nevertheless, I find that you have changed, Miss Leslie. Indeed, I don't think I should have known you if I had met you in the street." He gave her a long look that seemed to take in every detail of her appearance. "You've changed," he repeated, and it was clear from his voice that he thought the change was not an improvement.

Camilla felt anger rising within her. It was bad enough that Larry should reject her. Now here he was insulting her, too! She gave a hard laugh. "No doubt I am not so provincial as I used to be," she said. "I have had the advantage of a stay in London since you left Farlington, so perhaps it is natural that my tastes should have changed. I can only be thankful that the change is so indubitably for the better."

Larry smiled rather grimly. "But you know that, too, must be a matter of taste, Miss Leslie. And for my part, I must confess that I preferred you as you were."

This speech made Camilla so angry that she could not trust herself to reply to it. Larry, too, said no more, and they finished out the dance in silence.

"Thank you, Captain Westmoreland, for a delightful dance," said Camilla, as he led her back to her seat. She did not bother to keep the sarcasm out of her voice.

Larry's voice was equally sarcastic as he bowed over her hand. "No, I thank *you*, Miss Leslie. I cannot tell you what a pleasure it has been renewing our acquaintance."

And with these words, he set off across the ballroom, as though resolved to put as much distance between him and Camilla as possible.

Four

As Camilla reseated herself on the bench, she told herself that it was a good thing Larry had been so deliberately infuriating.

If he had chosen to be kind and conciliatory, for instance, she might have been tempted to regret that he no longer cared for her. She might even have disgraced herself by bursting into tears. As it was, she was so angry that she was more than ever determined not to behave in a way that he might interpret as a compliment to himself.

It clearly behooved her to show him that his words just now had not affected her in the least. Feverishly Camilla looked about the ballroom. Her eyes met those of Sir Eustace, who was just coming off the floor with Agnes. She gave him a smile—a much warmer smile than she was in the habit of bestowing on him. Sir Eustace looked surprised; he even turned to look over his shoulder, as if to make sure that Camilla was not smiling at some third person behind him. But having ascertained that the smile was indeed for him, he warmly returned it and came over to where Camilla sat.

"I need not ask if you are feeling better. Your color is much stronger than it was earlier," he said, regarding her with approval.

Agnes, who had accompanied Sir Eustace to where Camilla was sitting, surveyed her friend critically. "Indeed, you look quite flushed, Millie. Your cheeks are as pink as Maria's dress!"

Camilla had no doubt this was so. She still felt hot with anger and indignation over Larry's rude behavior. But she summoned up a laugh. "Yes, it is dreadfully warm in here. If only we could open a window! But I know from experience that there would be an immediate outcry from the chaperons' benches if we attempted anything so imprudent. Mrs. Banks, for one, is convinced that fresh air is quite fatal in a ballroom."

Agnes nodded. "I suppose all we can do is endure it," she said. "A glass or two of Mrs. Bass's punch might help—and I'm getting a little hungry, too. I think I shall go get some of those biscuits you made, Millie, before the boys eat them all."

"They are certainly delicious," agreed Sir Eustace. He cast a smile at Camilla. "You must know that I had the privilege of being present during their manufacture, Miss Ludlow. I told Miss Leslie that those are the sort of biscuits my mother used to call Hussar's Kisses."

"Indeed," Agnes said and gave Camilla a long look. Camilla was sure Sir Eustace's remark had started the same train of thought in her friend's mind that it had in her own. Surely enough, Agnes's next remark, though unwelcome, was not unexpected. "I saw you dancing with Larry," she said. "I suppose this is the first time you have spoken to him since he returned to Farlington, Millie?"

"Yes," said Camilla shortly.

Sir Eustace looked at her, then at Agnes. "Who is Larry?" he asked. "You know I am a stranger at this gathering. Thus far I have made the acquaintance of only a handful of people."

Fortunately for Camilla, Agnes took it upon herself to answer this question. "Larry is one of the returning soldiers whom we are feting tonight," she told Sir Eustace. "He's really Captain Westmoreland—that tall gentleman over there in the Hussar uniform." She pointed to where Larry stood on the far side of the ballroom.

Sir Eustace turned to look in the direction Agnes had pointed. Camilla could not resist the urge to look, too. She saw Larry deep in conversation with Maria Banks—a rather particular conversation to judge by the flirtatious smile on Maria's face. Camilla's scorn grew deeper. Larry had never had any use for Maria in the old days, but it looked as though he was finding her congenial company now. She turned away abruptly. "I am getting hungry, too, Agnes," she said. "Let us go to the refreshment room."

But Sir Eustace, with a gallantry as gratifying as it was misguided, saw that Camilla had no opportunity to escape the ballroom. "No, no, you two girls stay here," he said with a smile. "It will be my pleasure to fetch you both refreshments. Do sit down and stay where you are. I'll be back in no time at all."

"Why, thank you, Sir Eustace. That is very kind of you," said Agnes, seating herself beside Camilla. She watched with admiration as Sir Eustace made his way through the crowd toward the refreshment room. "Indeed, Millie, if Sir Eustace did not already belong to you, I'd be tempted to try for him myself," she told Camilla in a low voice. "I never met a man I liked better on first acquaintance."

Camilla hardly heard her. She was too busy watching Maria Banks flirt with Larry.

Agnes went on, her voice thoughtful. "And he is very handsome, too. He isn't so tall as Larry, of course, but then I am short myself, so I don't care for that. I just adore dark men with nice manners."

This Camilla did hear. She reflected morosely that it was just her luck to prefer fair men with bad manners. Once more her eyes turned to Larry. He was still talking to Maria, and the sight of Maria smiling up at him was like salt in Camilla's wounds. Agnes, meanwhile, was rattling on. "I must say, Millie, that I envy you tremendously. How I wish I had a rich aunt to give me a Season in London! But of course, I could never look half so handsome as you, even if I had all your advantages. I don't wonder Sir Eustace is nutty about you."

"Don't be silly, Agnes," said Camilla in a weary voice. "Sir Eustace is too dignified to be nutty about anyone. And I am sure you are quite as handsome as I am." Out of the corner of her eye she saw Sir Eustace reenter the ballroom from the refreshment room. She watched him as he made his way through the crowd, moving carefully on account of his burden of food and drink.

It was true that he was very handsome and well mannered. And though Camilla might deny it to Agnes, it was also true that he seemed to be nutty about her. Why else would he have made the journey all the way from Lancashire to Farlington? And now that she had eliminated Larry from the lists once and for all, why should she not accept this alternative suitor who was in some respects a much more desirable match?

To be sure, she did not love him. "But I *like* him," Camilla argued to herself. "If I married him, I have no doubt I would come to love him in time. My relatives are in favor of the match—at least, Aunt Dorothy is, and I am sure Mama would be, too, once she came to know him better. And once I was well married, I would be able to help Mama financially so that she could afford a bigger house and better servants and a great many little luxuries that she can't afford right now."

Although Camilla did not admit it to herself, there was another consideration that weighed even more heavily than these in her calculations. Marrying Sir Eustace would get her out of Farlington—a thing that was no small object with her just then. She felt her chances of being happy with Sir Eustace—or even without him—would be considerably enhanced if she did not have to risk seeing Larry on a day-to-day basis.

"I'll do it," resolved Camilla, and she forthwith set herself to encourage Sir Eustace.

Her first step was to bestow a second dazzling smile on him as he handed her a plate of sandwiches, cakes, and sweet biscuits. "Thank you, Stacy," she said. "Agnes and I are much obliged to you. We shall have to put our heads together and see how best we can repay you for your chivalry."

Sir Eustace turned a surprised look on her. "Indeed, it would be a poor chivalry that expected compensation," he said pleasantly. "To please you is all the payment I expect, Camilla."

"But there must be *some* boon we can bestow upon you." Camilla fluttered her lashes, as she had seen coquettes do in London. "And Agnes and I are both too honorable to leave our debts unpaid, are we not, Agnes?"

"To be sure," said Agnes. Like Sir Eustace, she had been taken aback by Camilla's sudden attack of flirtatiousness, but her nature was too loyal to disavow anything her friend might say. "Indeed, Sir Eustace, we should be glad to repay your kindness any way we could," she said heartily. "Is there some lady you wish to dance with whom we could introduce you to?"

Sir Eustace shook his head, a smile lurking at the corners of his mouth. "No, for I have already danced with the two handsomest ladies in the room," he said. "Anything else must be anticlimactic after that. Of course, if etiquette did not forbid it, I should enjoy dancing with you both again." He looked at them a bit doubtfully. "But I daresay you do not care to dance more than twice with the same partner?"

Camilla laughed recklessly. "Oh, we do not care for that, do we, Agnes? For myself, Stacy, I should be glad to dance with you again."

She knew she was doing a daring thing. It was considered fast to dance with the same partner more than twice in Farlington, just as it was in London. But Sir Eustace did not know that. Agnes did, however, and she gave Camilla a startled look.

"Millie, are you sure?" she said in an undertone. "You know Miss Maynard and Mrs. Banks will be scandalized if you dance a third time with Sir Eustace."

"Miss Maynard and Mrs. Banks are scandalized if one ties one's bonnet the wrong way," said Camilla with a toss of her head. In her heart she knew that what Agnes said was true. But what did it matter? She would soon be leaving Farlington once she had accepted Sir Eustace's proposal of marriage. And before she left, she had a strong desire to show Farlington society—and one member of it in particular—that she cared nothing for its conventions.

Meditating with satisfaction on this theme, Camilla had a further inspiration. If one were to be hanged for a lamb, might one not just as well be hanged for a sheep? She looked up at Sir Eustace, who was preparing to escort her onto the floor. "Stacy, I wonder if these fiddlers know a waltz," she said. "I am growing tired of these everlasting country dances, aren't you?"

Sir Eustace looked at her in astonishment. "But you do not waltz, do you, Camilla?" he said. "I have never seen you do so before."

"No, but that is only because my aunt did not wish it. You know she is friends with some of the patronesses at Almack's, and they are very stuffy about such things. I don't know why, for lots of people waltz nowadays. I understand it is often done at private assemblies."

Sir Eustace acquiesced to this statement rather doubtfully. "I have seen the waltz performed, of course," he said. "And on occasion I have even performed it myself. But you know this is a public ball, Camilla, not a private assembly. And if you have never waltzed in company before—"

"Oh, that's nothing," Camilla assured him. "The other girls in London were wild for waltzing, and we used to practice the steps often in private. I'm sure I can perform it perfectly well. Will you not waltz with me, Stacy?" She gave Sir Eustace a beseeching look.

He hesitated, then acceded with a reluctant smile. "Yes, if you are sure we will not cause a scandal. Your mother has entrusted me with your care this evening, you know, and I would not wish to betray her trust in any way."

This speech gave Camilla a faint twinge of conscience. She knew her mother would indeed hold Sir Eustace responsible if scandal resulted from this evening's performance. But she assured herself that nothing so serious could come of a single waltz. A little gossip, a little criticism from such prudes as Mrs. Banks and Miss Maynard—and with luck a certain amount of heart burning for Larry when he saw her twirling about the floor in the arms of another man—that was the utmost that could result from so minor an act. Of course it was possible that Larry might be indifferent even to such strong provocation as the sight of her waltzing with Sir Eustace, but Camilla felt that if there were any chance at all that he would be piqued, it was worth a try.

Sir Eustace had gone to speak to the fiddlers about playing a waltz. Having made sure he was beyond earshot, Agnes addressed Camilla in an urgent whisper. "Millie, have you lost your mind?" she hissed. "Don't you know what Mrs. Banks and Miss Maynard will say if they see you waltz with Sir Eustace?"

"I neither know nor care what Mrs. Banks and Miss Maynard may say," replied Camilla, with an air of feigned indifference. "I'm tired of dancing country dances, and I don't see any reason why I shouldn't waltz if I want to. Everybody waltzes nowadays except provincials and dowdies."

"That may be," said Agnes. "But in that case I must be classed as a provincial and a dowdy myself. You must know

I've never waltzed before, Millie. In fact, I don't even know the steps."

"Oh, Agnes, I wasn't talking about you," said Camilla with compunction. She hesitated a moment, then went on in an impetuous rush. "The fact is that I am thoroughly tired of living my life by the rules of people like Mrs. Banks and Miss Maynard. They act as though we're all still living in Queen Anne's reign, for heaven's sake! It's high time somebody dragged them into the nineteenth century."

A reluctant giggle escaped Agnes. "Well, your waltzing with Sir Eustace ought to do it," she said. "I must confess, I quite look forward to seeing their faces when you take the floor with him. Why, if only I knew how to waltz myself, I believe I'd join you!"

"I'll teach you in time for the next assembly," Camilla promised, then went out to take her place with Sir Eustace on the floor.

There was a good deal of confusion among the other couples on the floor when the fiddlers struck up a waltz. Some tried to dance to the music as if it were merely another country dance; others took a few steps, faltered, and subsided into confusion. Camilla, as she was piloted deftly about the floor by Sir Eustace, observed a good many people standing about with puzzled looks on their faces. Then they caught sight of her and Sir Eustace, and their expressions changed to amusement, enlightenment, and—in a few cases—shocked disapproval.

"A waltz! It's a waltz!" The words ran around the room, gathering volume with each repetition. A group of guests crowded to the edge of the dance floor to observe this new dancing phenomenon. Thus far the waltz had only reached Farlington in the form of rumors. Camilla saw Mrs. Banks standing at the forefront of the crowd, her eyes avid and her lips pursed into an expression both pleased and scandalized. Then Camilla caught sight of Larry and promptly forgot all else.

Larry, too, was standing at the forefront of the crowd. His arms were folded across his chest, and he stood quietly, watching her and Sir Eustace. But when his eyes met Camilla's, she encountered a blaze of emotion so raw and powerful that she faltered in midstep and would have stumbled if Sir Eustace had not moved swiftly to cover her faux pas.

After that, Camilla was careful to keep her eyes averted from Larry's face. She told herself that she ought to feel triumphant at the success of her stratagem. It was obvious from Larry's expression that, even if he no longer cared for her, he was not indifferent to the sight of her waltzing with another man. But instead of feeling triumphant, she merely felt a little sick.

She had reason to feel even worse a moment later. Her first warning was laughter and a scattering of applause from the crowd. Carmilla, looking round to see what was happening, saw that a second couple had joined her and Sir Eustace on the floor. Sylvia Atwood, pink and protesting but looking pleased nonetheless, was being piloted about the floor by a red-coated figure, whom Camilla recognized with a shock to be Larry. It was obvious that Sylvia was not an experienced waltzer, but Larry clearly was, and his assurance was soon communicated to his partner. Before long Sylvia was circling the floor as confidently as if she had been waltzing for years.

Camilla felt as though she had been most effectually hoist with her own petard. The sight of Sylvia in Larry's arms was more painful than anything she had yet endured that evening. She averted her face and thus missed seeing Oliver Atwood sweep Maria Banks onto the floor, a sight rendered even more piquant by the look of shock and consternation on Mrs. Banks's face. But Carmilla was in no mood to appreciate this turn of events or even to notice that Maria, once her initial confusion was past, seemed remarkably familiar with the steps of the waltz. For the rest of the dance, Camilla kept her eyes cast down and dumbly endured.

Five

The waltz, in due time, swept to its triumphant end. The waltzing couples coming off the floor were greeted by a round of applause and murmurs of acclaim from their fellow guests.

There were a few who did not acclaim the new dance, to be sure. Miss Maynard turned up her nose and remarked that manners had been a great deal nicer when *she* was a girl.

"I would have been ashamed to disport myself in such a style," she informed anyone who would listen. "To allow a gentleman to practically embrace one—and on the dance floor, too!" But she found little sympathy for her viewpoint. Even her usual ally, Mrs. Banks, had deserted her.

It is probable that Mrs. Banks's views would have been somewhat different if her daughter had not elected to join the waltzers on the dance floor. But since Maria had so elected, her mother was obliged to abandon her usual critical attitude and embrace the new dance with at least a semblance of enthusiasm.

"Well, that was very pretty, my dear," she told her daughter, as Maria came smiling off the floor arm in arm with Oliver Atwood. "To be sure, it is a good deal different from the way we used to dance when I was a girl! But then every generation has its own fashions, as I have often observed. And for my part, I see nothing to dislike in this new dance. I daresay we shall see it performed everywhere within a twelvemonth."

Under normal conditions, Camilla would have been much amused by Mrs. Banks's change of attitude. But on this occasion, she was too weighed by misery to find amusement in anything. When Agnes pressed her arm and whispered, "Well done, Millie! I never would have believed it, but it looks as though you and Sir Eustace have carried the day. This is certainly your night to triumph," Camilla could only give her a wan smile and reflect how woefully one could be misjudged by one's fellow creatures.

Although she tried to keep from looking in Larry's direction, she could not help stealing a glance at him now and then. There was a pain in her heart that no triumph on the dance floor could assuage. It was intolerable to be at outs with him this way. Even if she were to leave Farlington, she would rather it not be with the memory of ill feeling between them. If only she could talk to him again that evening, perhaps they might patch things up—not to the extent of being lovers again, of course, but at least so they might part on amicable terms. With all her heart Camilla hoped such a reconciliation might be possible. Her feelings might therefore be imagined when, a few minutes later, she saw him take leave of Sylvia and Oliver Atwood and exit the ballroom without a backward glance.

As far as Camilla was concerned, this was the final straw. The evening was ruined, her happiness irretrievably destroyed, and her only wish was for the ball to be over so she might go home and mourn her lost hopes and dreams.

Once again she had almost forgotten about Sir Eustace. It was only when he addressed her, a moment later, that she recalled his presence beside her.

"We carried that off pretty well, did we not? I must say, however, that I was glad when your soldier friends joined us on the floor. For the first minute or two, I could not help feeling rather conspicuous."

Camilla looked at him and was stricken once more with compunction. In London, Sir Eustace was a man who prided himself on the perfection of his deportment. He was not one who rejoiced in defying the conventions of polite behavior, and she had frequently heard him speak disparagingly of those who sought notoriety through such a means. Yet he had good-naturedly complied with her wish to waltz this evening—and as a result had come perilously close to landing them both in a scrape.

But of course she had intended to make it up to Sir Eustace, Camilla reminded herself. In fact, she intended to make it up to him still. There was no reason why she should not bestow her hand and heart upon him now, for it was a certainty that no one else wanted them. She could make Sir Eustace happy, and perhaps that would make her happy, too. The fact that she could currently feel only black foreboding at the prospect was merely nerves, of course.

"You are very good, Stacy," she said in a voice that was slightly unsteady. "It was too bad of me to use you like that. Indeed, I do not deserve your friendship."

Sir Eustace smiled and patted her arm. "Oh, you must not think of it anymore, Camilla. 'All's well that ends well,' you know—and it appears we shall not suffer for tonight's performance. Ah, there is your friend Miss Ludlow." He gave a smiling nod toward Agnes, who was seated some little distance away. "Shall we go over and join her?"

"No, I would rather be alone at present, Stacy," said Camilla. "In fact—do you think perhaps we might step outside the rooms for a moment? There is something I wished to say to you in private."

She had more difficulty than ever in keeping her voice steady. Sir Eustace looked at her with surprise. "Yes, of course," he said after a moment. "As a matter of fact, I was wishing for an opportunity to speak to you in private, too, Camilla. If you think no one would take it amiss, I should be very glad to step outside with you for a moment."

Camilla nodded, concealing her impatience. Here she was, about to take the final and irrevocable step that would tie her to Sir Eustace forever, and he could do nothing but harp on the subject of conventions! But that was merely concern for her and her reputation, she reminded herself. She ought to be grateful to Sir Eustace, not irritated with him. She cast a sideways glance at his profile as he led her out of the ballroom and into the cool of the summer evening. How could she not love him, seeing how good he was to her? But when she examined her heart, she found it as obdurately opposed to loving him as ever. Indeed, when she tried to prod it into the requisite emotion, she was a little frightened by the fierce rush of anger and resentment that arose instead.

"Never mind," Camilla told herself hastily. "I will learn to love him in time, I'm sure. I am simply nervous right now. It will be better once I have accepted him and it's all settled."

The Assembly Rooms were situated next to Farlington's Town Hall. They were indeed contiguous to it, both buildings sharing a common roof and opening onto the village green. It was here, along one of the paths that traversed the green, that Sir Eustace led Camilla.

Camilla found her state of nerves did not diminish in the open air. She tried to calm herself by concentrating on the act of walking. With great precision she placed one foot in front of the other, stepping with exaggerated care so as not to soil the white satin of her slippers. But here, too, her nerves began to affect her. She found herself deeply disturbed when her foot slipped on a patch of gravel and came in contact with the grass.

"It doesn't matter," she told herself. "It doesn't matter in the least. The grass is not at all damp." But so shaken was she by her petty failure that she found herself close to tears.

She was concentrating so hard on her feet that she did not realize where Sir Eustace was leading her. It was not until he let out an exclamation of wonder that she looked up. "What an enormous tree!" he said. "It looks as though it had been here since the Conquest."

Camilla, raising her eyes from the path, saw they were standing beneath the Marriage Oak. Her heart gave a tremendous jolt. The branches of the great tree were so thick that they shut out the light of the moon overhead, but the glow from the windows of the nearby Assembly Rooms gave enough illumination to see the mass of carving that adorned its trunk. Sir Eustace stepped closer to touch the carving. "What is this?" he asked. "Some kind of rustic posting board?"

His voice sounded amused. "It's nothing," said Camilla. She found herself resenting the amusement in Sir Eustace's voice. The subject of the Oak was a sensitive one with her, certainly too sensitive to be discussed now when her nerves were already on edge. She tried to lead Sir Eustace away from the Oak, but he lingered, looking up at the carvings.

"Some of this looks very old," he said. "Is there a local significance to these inscriptions?"

"Yes, but it's all superstition," said Camilla impatiently. "Cannot we come away from here, Stacy? I want to talk to you."

Sir Eustace, who had been smiling at a quaint rendering of a woman's face, immediately sobered. "Yes, of course," he said. But instead of leading Camilla away from the Oak, he merely took her hands in his and began to speak in a serious and somewhat uneven voice.

"I suppose you know why I am here," he said. "Of course, that is a foolish statement. You must know why I am here, Camilla. And before we say anything on that subject, allow me to say first how grateful I am for the reception you have accorded me this evening. It was very good of you not to take offense at my showing up at your door with no warning and no invitation. And then to allow me to accompany you to this party tonight—it was more than I would have dared hope for. I have had a very enjoyable evening, and I shall remember it with pleasure no matter how things turn out between us."

Camilla merely nodded. She found the solemnity of Sir Eustace's manner oppressive. Now that she had made up her mind to accept him, she wished to get the matter over with quickly without letting herself think too much about it. His insistence on drawing things out rather grated upon her, as did the fatalistic nature of his final remark. *I shall remember this evening with pleasure no matter how things turn out between us.* It was obvious from these words that he expected her to refuse his proposal once again. Although Camilla would have resented an attitude of presumption on Sir Eustace's part, she found herself resenting this other attitude quite as warmly.

Sir Eustace, meanwhile, had continued speaking. "I know you refused my suit before, when I proposed to you in London," he said, looking down at her. "And I know that on the last occasion we spoke, your refusal was in the nature of a final one. Believe me, I have tried to accept it as such, Camilla. I have done my utmost to put all thought of a marriage between us out of my head. But if you will forgive me for saying so, I could not help feeling that during our last interview, there was a hint of—shall we say, ambiguity in your manner? And as long as any hope remained to me, I could not bring myself to abandon the matter entirely."

"I see," said Camilla. Sir Eustace looked down at her anxiously, her hands still grasped in his.

"I hope you do see, Camilla. I cannot tell you how long I have wrestled with this decision. At one moment, I would tell myself I ought to give up hoping once and for all, while the next I would decide it behooved me as a man to make another effort. As you can see, I decided on the latter course." He smiled as he spoke, but his eyes still held a hint of anxiety. "I assure you it will be a final effort, Camilla. I don't mean to harass you at intervals for the rest of your life. But cannot you see that if I am to get on with my own life, I must be certain, absolutely certain, that I have done everything I can to win you?"

Camilla could only nod once again. There was a curious constriction in her throat. Sir Eustace went on, holding her hands now in a grasp that was almost painful. "You must know how I feel about you, Camilla. In my eyes, you are all that is beautiful and desirable in a woman. I would think myself less of a man if I were to allow you to slip from my grasp without making every effort to retain you. At the same time, however, I am greedy enough to want all of you, Camilla—your heart as well as your lovely self. Do you—can you—is it possible you have come to feel differently since we last spoke? Can you possibly care for me as I care for you?"

This was the moment Camilla had been waiting for. All she had to do was say, "Yes," and the matter was settled. But as she looked into Sir Eustace's anxious eyes, she found herself unable to speak that obliging monosyllable.

She could not doubt that Sir Eustace loved her. The gaze that was fixed upon her was almost agonized in its intensity, and the hands that held her own trembled with emotion. It was odd to see a man normally so calm and self-contained betray such anxiety. In that moment Camilla knew and recognized her power—and knew also that she could never use it in the selfish way she had contemplated.

For it would be selfish to marry Sir Eustace when she felt nothing stronger than esteem for him. She would be using her personal charms for material gain, exactly as if she were a lightskirt selling herself to a prospective patron. And it was a question whether her intentions were not more immoral than the lightskirts'. Those ladies, when making their transactions, were at least comparatively honest about what they were willing to give. She could only gain Sir Eustace as a husband by giving him assurance that she loved him—and the fact was that she did not love him.

Even if she somehow came to love him later on, their relationship would be based on a lie. It stood to reason that a deceit of that magnitude must have effects on their conjugal happiness both long term and deleterious. And it remained to be proved whether she ever *could* come to love Sir Eustace. Looking back on the evening's events, Camilla realized that her attempts to make herself love him had not only failed in their object, but had threatened to destroy what tender feeling she did have for him.

Overcome with this realization, Camilla opened her mouth. "Oh, Stacy, I'm sorry," she said. She found she could say nothing more, for her voice was choked with tears. Those few words were enough, however. Sir Eustace smiled crookedly and patted her hand.

"Don't cry, my dear. If you can't, you can't, and that's all there is to it." With a slight catch in his voice, he added, "I'd be lying if I said I was glad you answered me as you did—but it's no more than what I expected, Camilla. At any rate, I'm glad you did me the honor of answering honestly."

"Oh, Stacy, I am not honest," said Camilla, with a burst of fresh tears. "I have used you abominably."

Sir Eustace looked surprised. "No, how could you? It was I who came here uninvited, after all. If I find myself rejected for my pains, it's no more than I deserved." He gave Camilla another crooked smile. "But this finishes it, I promise you. You needn't fear I'll come badgering you again. I'll go back to Lancashire and endeavor to bear my disappointment like a man."

Camilla nodded and managed a watery smile in return. "I hope you shall be very happy, Stacy," she said. "You deserve to be, that's certain—much happier than I could ever make you."

Sir Eustace grasped her hand warmly. "Ah, we differ there! For myself, I should wish—but there, I shan't say any more about it. All this has been painful enough for you already. And what I wish, even more than happiness for myself, Camilla, is to see you happy."

Camilla reflected dismally that this seemed a most unlikely prospect, given her current circumstances. Sir Eustace patted her hand. "I believe all this has affected you even more than me! Cheer up, my dear. I knew my hope was a forlorn one when I came here." In a more cheerful voice, he added, "I hope we can continue to be friends, even if we can be nothing more. It is as your friend, at any rate, that I will endeavor to comport myself for the rest of the evening. Do you think you are ready to go back to the party?"

Camilla thought of returning to the ballroom with the signs of tears fresh on her face, of trying to dance and smile and pretend nothing untoward had happened while enduring the scrutiny of such critics as Mrs. Banks and Miss Maynard. Her whole soul shrank from such an ordeal. "No, Stacy, I would rather not go in just now," she said with a shake of her head. "Indeed, I am not sure I care to go back to the party at all."

"Then I will take you home," said Sir Eustace at once. But Camilla shook her head once more.

"You are very kind, but that is not necessary, Stacy. I think it would be better if you just left me here for the time being and went back to the party by yourself. If you want to go back, that is." Camilla looked up at him earnestly. "If you would rather forgo the rest of the ball and start back to Lancashire tonight, you need not fear I would be offended. It's a lovely clear night, and my home is only a step away. I can easily walk from here, once I am recovered a little from—from all that has happened."

Sir Eustace looked shocked. "But I cannot simply go off and leave you here, Camilla," he protested. "I brought you to this party, and it's my duty to see you get home safely."

Camilla gave a shaky laugh. "This is not London, Stacy! I can be trusted to get home safely on my own, I assure you. As I said, it's only a step."

Sir Eustace looked unconvinced. "Still, I cannot think it right to abandon you, Camilla," he said. "People will think it very odd if I return to the party without you. Certainly your friend Miss Ludlow will think it strange. You must know I promised her earlier that we would drop her by her own house when we were ready to leave tonight. I thought you would not mind, as she has no carriage of her own and it is hardly out of our way."

"Of course I do not mind. Take Agnes home by all means, but let me be," said Camilla with a touch of impatience. "You know that, if you do not want to appear without me at the party, you may simply have one of the servants call Agnes and so arrange matters in that way." She smiled apologetically. "I'm sorry, Stacy, but I really would rather be alone right now. If you will humor me in this, I would be very grateful."

Sir Eustace finally acceded to Camilla's wish and went off to have his carriage called. Camilla stood beneath the Oak, watching as his figure disappeared into the night.

Six

After Sir Eustace had disappeared from view, Camilla sighed and put a hand to her forehead. She felt tired and overwrought, but the flow of tears seemed for the moment to have subsided. Camilla found comfort in this circumstance. She knew that when she got home she would find her mother sitting up for her, and if there were signs of tears on her face, her mother would want to know what had caused them. It had been bad enough to simply endure the evening's events; to have to describe them over again to her mother was a torment Camilla earnestly wished to avoid.

Sighing again, she slumped wearily against the trunk of the Oak. But she straightened again the next moment, remembering that the delicate fabric of her dress would not bear such treatment. She might feel at the moment as though she never wanted to attend a ball or wear a ball dress again, but such a mood would pass, she supposed. And it would be foolish to ruin her best dress simply because of a passing mood.

Laying a hand on the Oak's trunk, Camilla looked up at its mighty branches. Somewhere, on one of those branches, were her and Larry's initials. The thought of Larry brought back the old pain to her heart, but she was curious to see if the carving was still there. She began to search amid the mass of other initials for the heart enclosing the letters C.L. and L.W. She could not find it, however, and after a few minutes she concluded that it had either worn off with time or—more likely—been effaced by some later artist.

"How appropriate," she said aloud with a disillusioned laugh. "Of course it would not have endured all these years. I am a fool to have expected that it would."

"Look a little higher up," suggested a voice just above her head.

Camilla gasped and took a hasty step backward. Then she realized that the voice had emanated not from the Oak itself, but from some person concealed in its branches. Reproaching herself for her momentary idiocy and feeling a good deal annoyed at the unknown speaker (who, she reasoned, must have overheard her interview with Sir Eustace), Camilla stepped forward again, peering up into the dark mass of foliage above her.

"Who's there?" she demanded. "Who is it?"

For answer, there was a rustling of leaves and a scraping of bark. Presently a pair of long legs clad in Hessians and white pantaloons made their appearance, followed by a befrogged scarlet jacket. With a sensation of disbelief, Camilla watched as Larry's familiar face came into view. Edging out onto the lowermost branch, he hung suspended by his arms for a moment, then dropped lightly to his feet, landing only a few feet from where Camilla was standing.

For a moment, he and Camilla stood regarding each other in silence. It was she who spoke first. "Captain Westmoreland, I see," she said. "Are you not a little old to be climbing trees?"

She made her voice deliberately scornful. Larry colored slightly, but gave no other sign that her gibe had discomposed him. "No doubt I am a bit old for tree climbing," he said calmly. "But I cannot be sorry that my old skill has not deserted me. It has stood me in good stead tonight, at all events."

"I don't doubt it," flung back Camilla. "It has enabled you to spy on me with a great deal of ease and comfort!"

Larry shook his head vehemently. "No, that part was purely accidental, I assure you. I had no intention of spying on you when I came out here tonight."

"But spy on me you did, nevertheless," said Camilla with heat. "Seeing what has been the result, I can hardly be expected to believe that the act was unintentional."

"Nevertheless, I do ask you to believe it," said Larry. "The fact is that I was here long before you and your—your gentleman friend came out."

"Oh, yes?" said Camilla skeptically. "And what, pray tell, were you doing out here all by yourself in the dark?"

Larry looked self-conscious. "I was—er—merely getting a breath of fresh air," he said, avoiding Camilla's eye. "I felt I needed it after that waltz, you know. When it was over, I felt all at once that I had—er—had enough of dancing, and I decided to come out here to cool off."

"And?" prompted Camilla, as he paused.

Larry drew a deep breath. "And while I was out here, I heard you and—and your friend approaching. Fearing my presence on the scene might be inopportune, I sought refuge in the only place of concealment that presented itself. How was I to know you would choose to hold your conversation here beneath the Oak?"

Camilla bit her lip. "I suppose you could not know," she admitted grudgingly. "I must say, however, that I think you might have declared your presence sooner, once you saw we did mean to converse there."

"So I might, of course. But you know your conversation proved to be rather—er—personal in tone. Once you had begun, I judged it would be even more embarrassing if I interrupted things to make my presence known." Larry looked into Camilla's downcast face. "If I judged wrongly,

Camilla, then I am very sorry," he said gently. "It was all an unfortunate accident. Can we not leave it at that?"

Camilla shook her head. Once more she felt the tears starting in her eyes. Larry studied her closely. "You are crying," he said.

"No, I'm not," Camilla said childishly and averted her face.

Larry laid his hand on her cheek, however, and gently but firmly turned her face toward the light again. "You're crying," he said positively. In a somewhat altered voice, he added, "I suppose it is natural that you should be upset with me, Camilla, considering the circumstances. But you know I did not mean to overhear your conversation."

"I am not upset with you," said Camilla, sniffing and blinking her eyes in an effort to hold back the tears. "I quite understand how it came about that you heard what you did, Larry. You need not apologize anymore."

"But you *are* upset," said Larry, making the words a statement and not a question. Camilla merely nodded. At the moment, she could not trust herself to speak.

Larry hesitated a moment, then went on with an air of studied casualness. "The gentleman who was out here with you—Sir Eustace, was it not? I thought I heard his name mentioned as such."

Again Camilla nodded. "I was agreeably surprised in him," continued Larry. "I had heard of him before, you understand, but I never met him until tonight. He seems a good sort of fellow."

"He is," said Camilla dolefully. "Much too good for me." Abandoning all pretense at self-restraint, she buried her face in her hands.

"No, indeed," said Larry strongly. He came over and laid a hand on Camilla's shoulder. "Oh, Millie, you must know I could not help overhearing a good deal of what was said between you and Sir Eustace. And I thought—I thought you behaved superbly."

Camilla merely sniffed. Larry gave her his handkerchief, and she took it, applying it to her eyes. After a minute Larry went on, his voice holding a note of contrition.

"Indeed, I owe you an apology, Millie. As I said, I had heard of Sir Eustace before—that he was courting you, I mean. And when I saw him with you tonight, I thought—well, I thought you were bound to accept him. And that's why I spoke as I did when we were dancing together. But it was wrong of me, even if you *had* meant to accept Sir Eustace. You were, of course, quite free to marry whomever you liked. It was only that, for a moment, I let jealousy get the better of me."

Camilla looked at him in surprise. "You knew Sir Eustace was courting me?" she said. "How could you know that, Larry?"

It was Larry's turn to look surprised. "Why, any number of people have mentioned it to me. I heard it spoken of even when I was still with my regiment. My colonel had relations who were members of the *ton*, you see, and I heard it from him first that you were in London and being courted by Sir Eustace. And after I returned here, I heard it from Maria Banks. She spoke as though your engagement was a certainty."

"And you believed her?" said Camilla, in a voice of scorn. "You were not used to take your news from Maria Banks in the old days, Larry!"

Larry flushed. "Perhaps I ought not to have done so. Indeed, I don't think I would have, if it hadn't been merely a confirmation of what I had heard before. But you must see that it all looked pretty conclusive, Millie. After hearing it from so many people, what could I do but believe it?"

"You might have waited till you heard it from me," said Camilla, angrily wiping her eyes with the handkerchief. "Why did you not come and ask me, Larry? I would have told you the truth. Sir Eustace has certainly been courting me, and he has asked me to marry him two or three times before tonight, but I have always refused him." Sniffing again, she looked directly at Larry. "I waited and waited for you to call on me, Larry. I had thought you must at least pay me that courtesy, especially since I had heard from Maria and some of the other girls that you had called on them. But you never came. And then when you behaved so rudely to me tonight while we were dancing, I thought—well, never mind what I thought. But I do feel badly about the way I treated Stacy." She gave another doleful sniff.

Larry's expression was a curious mixture of laughter and contrition. "What a fool I have been," he said.

"Yes," agreed Camilla. Her voice was stern, as was the look she flung in Larry's direction, but he did not seem to mind. Coming a step closer, he laid his hands on Camilla's shoulders.

"Millie, I've wanted to call on you ever since I came home," he said. "The plain fact is that I was too much of a coward. I was afraid, you see, that you would merely confirm what I had already heard from Maria and the others. And I knew it would be too much for me to hear you loved someone else."

Camilla was silent, looking up at him. Larry went on, his expression sober now and his eyes fixed steadily on hers. "You must know I've loved you ever since you were a little girl, Camilla. There was never anyone else for me but you. The hardest thing I ever did was go off and leave you—"

"Was it so hard?" said Camilla sharply. "I remember the day you left Farlington very clearly, Larry. And I know you never said a word on that occasion about—about caring for me."

She colored as she spoke. Larry looked down at her in astonishment. "No, of course I did not. How could I? I had nothing to offer you—nothing except my feelings, and they weren't much to the point just then. You know I couldn't speak of marriage, or even an engagement, not knowing when I might return—or whether I'd return at all. I might well have come back like poor Will Hutchins, less an arm and a leg. A fine thing it would have been for you to have been tied to me then!"

"Oh, Larry!" said Camilla. She wanted to assure him indignantly that she would have sooner been tied to him, even less an arm and a leg, than be engaged to any other man. But Larry did not wait for her further comment. He continued with his address, still looking down at her steadily.

"And you know you were only seventeen when I went away, Camilla. Hardly more than a child—and you'd seen nothing of the world outside Farlington. It didn't seem fair to ask you to commit yourself to an engagement that might stretch to several years, when at any time you might meet someone you liked better."

"Oh, Larry," said Camilla again. She said it reproachfully this time, and Larry paused, looking down at her.

"I don't mean to imply that you were fickle or faithless in any way, Camilla. But such things do happen, you know. It happened to one of the fellows in my regiment, as a matter of fact. The girl he was engaged to back home wrote and told him she was marrying someone else."

"The wretch!" said Camilla indignantly. "How could she treat him so? When he was fighting for his country, too!"

Larry smiled at this patriotic fervor, but shook his head. "Ah, you mustn't blame her too much, Millie. Life's an uncertain thing at best, and being in the midst of a war doesn't make it any less so. Why should the poor girl have to wait years for an event that might never take place at all? I don't suppose you'll understand, Camilla, but it was actually a comfort to me, when things looked blackest, to reflect that I'd never asked you to pledge yourself to me in any way. Not that that wouldn't have been a comfort, too, mind you. I would have liked beyond anything to have the right to address you as my affianced wife—to write you letters directly, instead of merely sending messages through my father, and all that sort of thing. But it would have been a selfish comfort, bought at the price of my own self-respect. Can you see at all what I mean?"

Camilla swallowed hard and nodded. "Yes, Larry, I see what you mean," she said in a small voice.

She spoke the truth, for not only did she see and understand his viewpoint, she wondered how she could have failed to see it long before now. What she had taken for coldness and indifference had been in truth a self-denial so generous as to border on nobility.

And seeing the nobility of Larry's conduct only made her feel worse about her own. How wrong, how foolish had been her plot to make Larry jealous by means of Sir Eustace's addresses! And how ill it had served her ends, for it had only resulted in pain and misunderstanding for all three of them. She looked into Larry's face and spoke aloud, unconsciously echoing the words he himself had spoken only a short time earlier. "What a fool I have been!"

As if determined to show himself her superior in this matter, too, Larry instantly disclaimed Camilla's statement. "No, indeed, Millie! You have done nothing that was not perfectly natural under the circumstances. But I—I have been worse than a fool. I should have come to you the minute I returned home and asked you openly about Sir Eustace instead of relying on hearsay. And even if you had said you *were* planning to marry him, I ought to have taken up arms and fought to win you away from him until I knew for a certainty there wasn't any hope. But instead I went sulking about like a child denied a sweet."

Larry spoke with self-disgust, but there was a hint of laughter lurking in his eyes as he looked down at Camilla. "If only he had not been a baronet!" he said. "I believe that's what caused most of the mischief. Had he merely been rich and good-looking, I wouldn't have felt so hopeless—but he was rich and good-looking *and* a baronet. And everyone I asked gave him a good character, too, which was even more depressing. And if I had not heard you refuse him with my own ears a few minutes ago, I should still be inclined to think the matter hopeless. But I did hear you." He paused, looking down at Camilla. "And fool though I may be, I cannot help taking comfort in that circumstance."

Camilla preserved a discreet silence. Larry continued to look down at her, his hands still resting on her shoulders. "You don't speak, Millie. I know I've made an awful ass of myself since returning home, but I beg you to believe I have never changed in my feelings toward you. Can you possibly forgive me and let us start all over again, as though these last few weeks had never been?"

Camilla felt a rush of joy rise up within her heart. She wanted to weep, to laugh, to sing, but all she did was nod with a tremulous smile hovering on her lips. That proved to be response enough, however. An answering smile lit up Larry's face.

"Thank God," he said. "Oh, Camilla, I don't know what I would have done if you'd said no. Probably gone and made a bigger fool of myself than I already have done this evening."

"I do not know that you have been such a fool," said Camilla. "Certainly not any more of a fool than I have been. I can forgive you quite easily, Larry, though I am afraid some of the things you said will rankle for a while." She gave him a rueful smile. "You said that I had changed, you know. And though you did not actually come out and say so, it was easy to see you did not think the change was for the better!"

Larry laughed and looked self-conscious. "I daresay I may have given that impression, Millie. But please remember that at that time, I thought you engaged to Sir Eustace.

And a man in the throes of jealousy isn't necessarily the most just or dispassionate critic." He looked down at Camilla in a considering way. "That's not to say that you haven't changed, however. I was speaking the truth about that, Millie—but I didn't go on and say the rest of what I was thinking. The truth is that I thought you beautiful before, but you're even more beautiful now. It took my breath away when I first saw you walk in this evening."

"Oh, Larry," said Camilla softly. Larry went on looking down at her, his expression smiling but abstracted.

"Indeed, that's part of what made me so savage, I suppose," he said. "It made me sick to see you looking so beautiful and know you belonged (as I thought) to someone else. I've been nine different kinds of a fool this evening, and I still can't believe you mean to forgive me for it. But you've said you will, Camilla—and I mean to hold you to your word."

"I hope that you may," said Camilla. "You know I have always prided myself on being a tolerably truthful person, Larry. You will not find me changed in that respect, however much I may have changed in others. Indeed, if you try me, I think you will find I have changed very little indeed."

Larry contemplated her a moment in silence. "Do you mean—" he began, then stopped. Camilla said nothing. Finally he began again, rather haltingly.

"Millie, I know I have made any number of gaffes this evening. Perhaps I made the biggest one years ago, when I went away without telling you how I felt about you. But—" He drew a deep breath. "But if I've learned anything from these past few years, it's the importance of seizing one's opportunities. This seems like a heaven-sent opportunity to me." He pointed to a branch above Camilla's head. "Tell me, Camilla. When you were looking at the Oak a while ago, were you looking for that?"

Camilla looked and saw above her the heart encircling

the letters C.L. and L.W. "Yes," she said. "I wondered if it was still here. And when I could not find it, I thought—"

She stopped. Larry looked at her, a faint smile curving his lips. "You thought it had disappeared—and that its doing so was somehow symbolic of the feeling between us. But see, Camilla, it did not disappear. Here it is, looking as fresh as ever. Or if it is a little faded, I can easily restore it. It may be that I can make it even better than it was before." He took out his penknife and showed it to Camilla, still smiling but with a searching expression in his eyes. "Shall I do it, Millie?"

"Yes, Larry," said Camilla in a low voice.

In silence Larry cut the faded letters, adding an extra flourish beneath them and broadening and elaborating the heart-shaped border. When it was done, he folded the knife and put it away in his pocket. He then very deliberately took Camilla in his arms. Camilla went to him most willingly. For a moment, Larry only held her close, his arms wrapped tightly around her.

"Ah, Millie, now that I've got you I shall never let you go again," he whispered.

"See that you don't," said Camilla, raising her face to his. Larry bent to kiss her then, and if anything could have exorcised the memory of their first kiss beneath the branches of the Oak, it was the kiss that ensued. So thought Camilla, at least, and there was no reason to suppose Larry felt differently. Indeed, he apparently found the experience so satisfactory that he followed it up with two or three additional kisses.

"Oh, Millie, I hope you do not wish for a long engagement," he murmured in her ear. "I have done without you so long that I cannot endure to wait much longer to make you officially mine."

In an inarticulate but entirely comprehensible fashion, Camilla signified that she felt the same. Larry went on, holding her close against him. "And I am in a position to provide for you now. You must know my father's health has been declining in recent years. He recently told me that he means to turn the family property over to me entirely and retire to Bath. He has friends there, you know, and the doctor thinks the waters may do something toward alleviating his ills. So if you marry me, you can have a house of your own without fearing you must share one with my father."

"As if that mattered!" protested Camilla. "I would not mind at all sharing a house with your father. Indeed, I have always liked him extremely."

"And he likes you extremely, too. In fact, he has already given his blessing to our marriage. I did not receive it quite as graciously as I ought, I am afraid, for you know at the time I was not very sanguine on the subject of a marriage between us." Larry's eyes sparkled as he looked down at Camilla. "But it turns out the paternal blessing will be useful after all. Now if only I can cajole your mother into giving us *her* blessing, there will be nothing left to wish for."

Camilla laughed. "There will be no difficulty there, Larry! You won Mama's heart long ago, and she is already your most devoted supporter. She will be delighted to hear we mean to marry, I am sure. If there is any opposition to the idea, I expect it will come from Aunt Dorothy rather than from Mama."

"That is the aunt who took you to London?" said Larry rather jealously. "The one who introduced Sir Eustace to you?"

Camilla nodded. "Yes, he is a friend of hers. But she knew I had refused him when I left London, so it's not as though she is expecting me to marry him now. And I am sure that once she knows you, Larry, she will like you, too."

Larry shook his head doubtfully. "I hope you may be right," he said. He was silent so long after this that Camilla begged to know what was troubling him.